I0628457

IN THE LANGUAGE
OF SCORPIONS

Borgo Press Books by CHARLES ALLEN GRAMLICH

Bitter Steel: Tales and Poems of Epic Fantasy
In the Language of Scorpions: Tales of Horror from the Inner Dark
Midnight in Rosary: Tales of Vampires and Werewolves in Crimson and Black
Swords of Talera (The Talera Cycle, Book One)
Wings Over Talera (The Talera Cycle, Book Two)
Witch of Talera (The Talera Cycle, Book Three)
Write with Fire: Thoughts on the Craft of Writing
Writing in Psychology: A Guidebook (with Y. Du Bois Irvin and Elliott D. Hammer)

IN THE LANGUAGE OF SCORPIONS

TALES OF HORROR FROM THE INNER DARK

CHARLES ALLEN GRAMLICH

Introduction by Sidney Williams

THE BORGO PRESS

MMXII

IN THE LANGUAGE OF SCORPIONS

Copyright © 1989, 1991, 1992, 1994, 1995, 1996, 1998, 1999, 2002, 2003, 2004, 2008, 2009, 2010, 2011, 2012 by Charles Allen Gramlich

FIRST EDITION

Published by Wildside Press LLC

www.wildsidebooks.com

DEDICATION

To Robert Reginald, Editor Extraordinaire

and to

Charles Nuetzel,

Who Introduced Me to Borgo Press

CONTENTS

ACKNOWLEDGMENTS

THESE STORIES AND POEMS WERE previously published as follows, and are reprinted (with minor editing, updating, and textual modifications) by permission of the author:

"Abraded by Light" was first published in *GothicRevue.com*, 2004. Copyright © 2004, 2012 by Charles Allen Gramlich.

"A Choice of Ghosts" was first published at Brutal Dreamer's Website, 2003. Copyright © 2003, 2012 by Charles Allen Gramlich.

"A Curse the Dead Must Bear" was first published in *Return of the Raven*, 2009. Copyright © 2009, 2012 by Charles Allen Gramlich.

"All God's Children Got Guns" was first published in *Detective Mystery Stories*, No. 11, 1999. Copyright © 1999, 2012 by Charles Allen Gramlich.

"Blind" was first published in *GothicRevue.com*, 2004. Copyright © 2004, 2012 by Charles Allen Gramlich.

"Branded" was first published in the *HWA Newsletter*, 2009. Copyright © 2009, 2012 by Charles Allen Gramlich.

"Chimes" was first published in *The Chapbook 1994: Deep South Writer's Conference*. Copyright © 1994, 2012 by Charles Allen Gramlich.

"Cold as Love" was first published in *Penny Dreadful*, 2002. Copyright © 2002, 2012 by Charles Allen Gramlich.

"Crypto" was first published in *Intermix SF/Fantasy Online*, 1995. Copyright © 1995, 2012 by Charles Allen Gramlich.

"Death Turned Away" was first published in *Tales on the Twisted Side*, Vol. 1, 1989. Copyright © 1989, 2012 by Charles Allen Gramlich.

"Do As I Say..." was first published in *Fusing Horizons*, Issue 1, 2003. Copyright © 2003, 2012 by Charles Allen Gramlich.

"Forever" was first published in *Vicious Verses and Reanimated Rhymes*, 2009. Copyright © 2009, 2012 by Charles Allen Gramlich.

"Good Night; Sleep Tight" was first published in *Micro 100*, 2009. Copyright © 2009, 2012 by Charles Allen Gramlich.

"Haunting Place" was first published in *31 Eyes Fantasy* 2003. Copyright © 2003, 2012 by Charles Allen Gramlich.

"I Can Spend You" was first published in *Strange Days*, 1992. Copyright © 1992, 2012 by Charles Allen Gramlich.

"In the Ruins of Memory" was first published in *Just Write*, 1995. Copyright © 1995, 2012 by Charles Allen Gramlich.

"Machine Wash Warm, Tumble Dry" was first published in *Crossroads*, Vol. 1, 1992. Copyright © 1992, 2012 by Charles Allen Gramlich.

"Monster Spray" was first published in *Classic Pulp Fiction Stories*, No. 87, 2002. Copyright © 2002, 2012 by Charles Allen Gramlich.

"Old Bones" was first published in *After Hours*, No. 12, 1991. Copyright © 1991, 2012 by Charles Allen Gramlich.

"Old Dead Woman" was first published in *Star*Line*, 1996. Copyright © 1996, 2012 by Charles Allen Gramlich.

"Once Upon a Time with the Dead" was first published in *Bits of the Dead*, 2008. Copyright © 2008, 2012 by Charles Allen Gramlich.

"Razor White" was first published in *Dark Voices 4: The Pan Book of Horror*, 1992. Copyright © 1992, 2012 by Charles Allen Gramlich.

"The Road to Hell" was first published in *Nox*, No. 7, 1996. Copyright © 1996, 2012 by Charles Allen Gramlich.

"Ruins and Wraiths" was first published in White Cat

Publications, 2011. Copyright © 2011, 2012 by Charles Allen Gramlich.

"Smoked Meat" was first published in *Intermix SF/Fantasy Online*, 1995. Copyright © 1995, 2012 by Charles Allen Gramlich.

"Splatter of Black" was first published in *Dark Terrors*, 1995. Copyright © 1995, 2012 by Charles Allen Gramlich.

"Still Life With Skulls" was first published in *Twisted*, No. 6, 1991. Copyright © 1991, 2012 by Charles Allen Gramlich.

"Your Nightmare or Mine" was first published in *Classic Pulp Fiction Stories*, No. 54, 1999. Copyright © 1999, 2012 by Charles Allen Gramlich.

"Wall of Love" was first published in *Agony in Black*, Volume 3, 1999. Copyright © 1999, 2012 by Charles Allen Gramlich.

"With Eyes Like Fangs" was first published in substantially different form on D. Lynn Frazier's blog: "Writtenwyrdd," August 24, 2010. Copyright © 2010, 2012 by Charles Allen Gramlich.

"Altar," "Floater," "The Gray Man," "Hell Is for Children," "The Little Things," "Outsider," "Roadkill," "Scritch Scritch Scritch," "Spot," and "Twenty-Four Mile Bridge" are all published here for the first time. Copyright © 2012 by Charles Allen Gramlich.

INTRODUCTION

Tales with twists and chills, dark deeds and eerie atmosphere
await you just a few pages ahead. Charles Gramlich offers stories that go in unexpected directions, then take abrupt turns, and
from there they make another left. The only certainty as you
turn the next few pages is that you will encounter tales that will
make you shiver.

Charles Gramlich has written in many genres. Tales in which
men carry swords and tales in which men carry guns. He brings
a powerful sense of storytelling and a gift for language to each,
but the collection you hold features work he's produced in the
horror genre. Charles proves here he is a master of the short tale
of terror as well.

Brace yourself, dear reader. You're about to be strapped to a
chair and fed relentless, unflinching fiction. You'll get no mercy
here, so don't expect any.

Not the kind of treatment you'd expect from a polite professor
of psychology, but Charles is living proof of what I've believed
for a long time: horror writers are some of the nicest people
you're likely to encounter. Dark impulses are dealt with on the
page—saved for the page, in fact—where stygian ideas will
serve the ultimate master and purpose, The Story.

Charles is as supportive of other writers as he is dedicated to
the craft. He's quick to leave a comment of encouragement on a
blog and quick to offer ideas and other support, and I can attest
personally to his hospitality.

We met sometime right after the first fish decided to leave the primal muck and check the weather on the beach. It was at the New Orleans Science Fiction and Fantasy Festival.

My old friend and collaborator Robert Petitt and I were having beers in the hotel bar and talking over a Robert McCammon story. Turned out the guy next to us had read it too. That was Charles, and we've been buddies ever since.

Another year at NOSFF or maybe it was when World Fantasy was in New Orleans, Charles and I got away from the activity for a while, picked up New Orleans poor boy sandwiches and sat in his room full of books at his house for lunch.

It was everything you'd expect a writer's lair to look like. Pulps and classics filled his shelves, and beyond the capacity for the shelves, books of all styles and genres were arranged in neat stacks with an organization that made me envious. Robert E. Howard to be sure—Charles is a major Howard fan and a significant contributor to REHupa—but tales of terror and mystery as well, purchased new or discovered in long, careful searches through New Orleans used bookshops.

I tell you that to note again what a nice guy Charles is, but also to observe that the magic in those books is reflected in the pages ahead. Charles has read voraciously, and just like those tellers of tales who've come before, he's absorbed the old and dreamed new dreams, dark dreams herein, carrying on the legacy of the campfire tales and the early pulps, while infusing new energy and vision.

It's all fresh, new, exciting, sprinkled with the flavor of the things Charles loves and that we all love. It reflects that afore-mentioned devotion to craft, and an endless energy and enthu-siasm for fomenting fear.

So, are we clear? Charles Gramlich: nice guy, voracious reader, great writer. Brace yourself. It's about to get brutal.

Sidney Williams
2010

PREFACE

The stories of *In the Language of Scorpions* span many years and many styles, though in all of them I've tried to explore the dark and the strange. Such emotions and experiences have been a constant in my life, beginning with the frequent nightmares that first struck in childhood and which continue to this day. And then there was that time in the Ozark Mountains, in the brooding forest....

It has become a cliché for writers to say that their art is what keeps them sane. It's exactly the opposite for me. Without writing I would be completely and totally sane, and can you imagine anything more boring? I don't want to look only toward the brightly lit side of the street and ignore the shadows that are also children of the sun. I don't want to spend every working day with no thoughts beyond my job, and every evening sitting on the couch while the idiot box pulses "reality" TV into my brain.

Personally, I'd rather dream, no matter the consequences.

I hope you will dream with me.

Charles A. Gramlich
Abita Springs, Louisiana, 2011

IN THE RUINS
OF MEMORY

Amid the dregs of a human soul
one finds many things,

dolls and dust and empty tin whistles,
wheels off a hundred matchbox cars,
a mother's face and a whisper of silk
that passed away

It is a world of tombs, of coffins,
filled with bones and stones and sins,
rich with places to hide

And all the scars from all the dreams
that have been given up on....

live there

They know how much it hurts
to face one's past,
to be reminded of failures

That's what keeps them fresh,
keeps them so quietly in wait,
till it's time to give you pain

And you'll never see them there,
in the ruins of memory

STILL LIFE WITH SKULLS

There were eyes in the canvas that I had never drawn, desert eyes of bronze, sulfur eyes like cicatrices, and river eyes of green—eyes full of dark wings and teeth. There were round mouths open to the night air, and sanguine tongues whose dance burned with holy words. And in the chiaroscuro wastelands of the unfilled canvas there were ruins whose outlines I could not yet trace. I knew only that they held a bitter rapture and smelled faintly of ashes.

I reached out and lowered a sheeted covering down across that chaos face, knowing that I had not yet captured my piece, thinking that, perhaps, I had captured something else. It seemed suddenly smoky dark when I turned out the light, and the shadows came to gather around my still form as if they were dust and I a statue left long on the shelf.

I sat there for an empty time, listening to the beat of my heart, like hungry baby birds, feeling the breath run out of my mouth and down on the floor as if it were dry ice fog, and waiting for riddles to be answered. No answers formed and after a hollow period filled with early morning silence I went coldly to bed, only to dream of chalk bright skulls with jutting brows and liquid black tongues that tickled at my lips seeking entrance.

The dreams were only harlequin shapes in the clouds when morning came at last. Only their perfume and their laughter remained.

I rose up in that dawn and the sky was like white ashes full of dew-killing heat, like a burnished metal shield on which a fallen warrior is carried home to his pale widow. But the gardens where I walked were cool and shaded, sprinklers drawing rainbows in the quiet air. I had not eaten, for the taste of night still filled my mouth. Nor had I looked closely at my canvas, though the sheet had blown away in the darkness from its sainted and porcelain face. Rather, I let the garden flowers bend their heads to comfort me, their skulls petalled in brittle jewels. Would they shatter at a touch? Should I stroke them and watch them die?

I did not.

Striding along there, the path seemed a desert paved with dunes, the hedges and flower beds a jungle, silent as when stalked by predators. I felt like a god, knowing that should they anger me I could cast among them stillness and lay their bodies to waste.

But again I did not.

For a moment, a stone bench seemed open to me with its silent lion's mouth at either end, as if here two cats mating tail to tail had been quick frozen and their backs sliced away to provide a seat for a god. It hurt me to see those faces turned up in sculpted agony. I touched them in coolness but they did not change, and, of course, I knew that I was no god to set them free. Instead, I passed them by and came in time to the pool where it waited for me gray-faced.

Why was it that Lovecraft, and Poe, and Chambers wrote so frequently of pools, often black and noisome and writhing as if with life? Why does the frowning of pools stir fear? Even this one, clear and bright as it was, held something in it of death. I knew that should I enter it and stand looking down at my legs they would be broken, as a spoon is broken when it is placed in a glass of water.

Yet, there was something else also in this pool, a beauty that I had first seen many days ago, on the day Alisha—my wife—had left me forever. I had stumbled on it by accident as I watched the slow settling drift of a frost-killed leaf from the surface to the depths. Through tears I had seen the colors fade from the autumn-clothed leaf and swirl outward through the water as if they were liquid soluble paints. Faces had formed there, faces of such utter loveliness that they had ripped me to my knees only to watch them fade into gray steel emptiness as they melted together.

For a week I had been trying to capture those water dreams on my canvas, and it sometimes seemed as if some greater artist's hand guided my brush. For I could not always remember what it was that I had drawn.

And sometimes there seemed things there that I had *not* painted.

Still, I had not yet captured the truth of what I had seen. I wept for fear that I had not the skill and each day I came to worship here, praying for guidance.

But Alisha did not come back.

The faces in the pool, too, remained distant, only faintly echoed in the black map of dead leaves and fishes that coated the bottom. I knelt there for long and long, gazing down to stain my memory with the faint lines, to chisel those traces to the inside of my skull. Only when a breeze came up to swamp those patterns in waves as if they were sunken Atlantis did I rise and go back to my work. The garden was alive around me with calling winds, but I did not listen. I filled my ears up with night songs and passed back into the womb of the house.

My painting was in the sun and two new eyes had grown in one corner of the canvas while I was away, one copper bright like the pennied lids of a corpse, the other hot and wet and crimson like a whore's tongue. About them were hints of other lines, apparent contours that commanded me to take up ivory and shadowed paints and trace them. Soon, there took shape in that corner, in what had been blighted lands, a hollow-eyed skull with one fair black rose rising up from a blank socket, so shadowy yet, not at all like the neural fires that coated the inside of my own lids.

I could not quite capture it, though I stared at it and stroked it for hours, not stopping to eat. I could not capture it, and I cursed my weak fingers and the dim medium of paints that tried and failed to mirror reality. Screams lifted up into my mouth and I swallowed them down. Sainted ghosts tried to break from my ears and throat, and, failing that, they drove in fangs that bled white into my brain. I threw down the brushes and pulled at my face where they clung with tiny little clawed feet, and at last I rose to rush about, shouting, stalking this way and that on bowed legs, on broken stilts, spinning with fingers speaking runed words while the world slowed and slowed to the speed of a vulture circling on desert thermals.

Only later did I realize that I had been standing still, and I went from there feverish to my bed. Evening was born in that stillness.

That night my dreams were jagged, of white rocks screaming in crimson fields, of ice in chalices that cooled dark wine, of rocks and bones opened by swords. My memories were wrapped in shrouds and buried in the moist earth while mourners stood around with fangs in their eyes and wept that I was not in pain.

And I dreamt of Alisha, whom I loved, Alisha with silver hair and a goddess's crown. She was lovely, yet her face was distorted as if with agony. She twisted and writhed on a bed of eyes. I kissed her and tasted foulness.

For long I lay among the rainbow dreams while bloody-winged ravens pulled worms from my chest, and only when the moon danced through my window did I wake. When the light touched my canvas a writhing began there, of maggots in open wounds. The wet sheets around me blew away and I went to stand before my work, naked though I did not remember how.

And the twirling winds came crying to me, lifting my hair as they talked their ancient unholy languages. In the waste-land—where all had been empty—a landscape formed, a place of skulls, a Golgotha drawn in pink dawn, filled with empty white crosses. I put my finger to it and felt the paint run over and become a part of my skin until my hand formed the bar of a last crucifix, diamond bright as a ring.

Raging were the teeth there, nipping at my flesh, but they told me by their touch what I must do. So much beauty, so real a face as this could not be captured with mere paints. I took up the canvas and a knife and went to the bathroom. I sat it before me and looked beyond it to the mirror, smiling at the white faces there behind my own.

I did not know that it was dawn until I heard a call. A raven on my shoulder told me that it was Alisha and I gurgled in joy to know that she had come back to me after all. I loved her so. But I did not leave the bathroom yet. In just another moment I would have something to show her. I wanted a finished work and it needed only one more stroke.

But she found me before it was done. I glanced at her and wondered why the birds screamed so loud this morning when for many days there had been none. Alisha's eyes were strangely wide, pupils drawn like caverns, and I turned back to the mirror to see there the beauty that she must see.

How fair was the bone behind pink vessels, how lovely and crimson the wide mouth with its back teeth open to the air and the skin peeled back like that of a grape.

But—one last stroke.

I reached up fingers to my face and felt the cool sucking sound of opening flesh. Now the canvas was finished.

I handed the eye to Alisha but she was too touched by my gesture to take it.

CHIMES

AUTHOR'S NOTE: This version of the "Chimes" is different from the Kindle ebook version published in 2010. I discuss the differences further in the section called "about the stories and poems."

Dena Parker came awake to the sound of wind chimes tinkling. Dozens of them hung on her back porch, just under her bedroom window, and others were scattered beneath the eaves of her house. They were made of river stones and sea shells, of cut glass and polished metal, of thin wires that were like the fragile rib cages of birds. She had collected them over many years and normally she found their music sweet and pleasing. Now she heard the sound as a warning, a warning that the opening winds of Hurricane Carmin were beginning to sweep over New Orleans.

It was only 2 A.M. by her clock but Dena knew she wouldn't sleep anymore tonight. She reached to switch on her reading lamp, and the chimes rang again as the coming of brightness lanced her eyes. The sound was louder now, as the delicate pieces whipped about in the grip of a mounting breeze.

She should have brought them in when she put the plywood over the windows, Dena thought. She'd have to do it now. She was sitting on the edge of the bed with her feet fishing for slippers when she remembered. She *had* brought them in. They were hanging downstairs in her living room, where there was no wind to move them.

Dena's sympathetic nervous system reaction was instantaneous and almost painful as her mouth dried and the skin stitched itself taut over her muscles. She thought about Jeremy, her three-year-old, and before the thought finished she bolted out of bed and down the hall the few short steps to her son's room.

Jeremy was untroubled by the chimes, or by the gathering moan of the storm outside his window. He breathed soft and even with sleep, and his face in the dim, butter-yellow of the night light reminded Dena so much of his father. But she couldn't think of that now. She reached out to shake the tiny frame, then stopped herself. Maybe she shouldn't wake him. Maybe she'd left some chimes outside by mistake, or maybe the gale had found a crack and was exhaling into the house. And if there were someone in the house with them, the last thing Dena needed was to have her little boy clinging to her in fear while she tried to react.

Call somebody, the thought hit her, and she turned and ran back into her bedroom for the phone. The police line was busy—Dena had figured it would be with the hurricane—so she punched the number for the Kellers next door. Morgan was an ex-marine, Marge an artist. They had helped Dena a lot after her husband left. Maybe they could help her again.

Outside, the wind tested itself on the boarded up windows, though Dena knew it would be hours before the main part of the hurricane reached them. The phone started ringing, sounding more distant than the wind, and Dena prayed her friends would answer. A moment later they did, or at least their recorder picked up. Before Dena could tell which, the first assault of rain swept against the roof; the chimes sounded as heavy drops exploded on the shingles; and the phone voice died in a crackle of static. Dena wanted to blame the storm for that static. She wanted to believe the lines had gone down outside the house. But her bedroom light was still on. Why hadn't the electricity gone too?

At that moment, softly, the chimes began to clink together, glass against metal, curled shells against tiny brass beads. A melody wove itself into those sounds, a tune Dena recognized but wished she didn't. Her nervous system iced over as she glanced at the dresser where her music boxes sat. An empty space marked where one piece had been thrown out. She was hearing its song now, though, transformed but recognizable.

Coincidence, Dena told herself. The human mind often added meaning to random collections of sound, like making footsteps out of an old house settling. Her body didn't believe that line of reasoning. It just kept pumping out fear and adrenaline.

Dena bit her lip, then put down the phone and opened the drawer of the bedside table. Inside lay the 9mm Browning automatic she had bought for her husband after he was raped in the house, and before he went away to escape the self-loathing that had filled him afterwards. She thought of the music box again, and wondered if Troy really had thrown it out. The rapist had caught Troy asleep and had knocked him out and tied him up, then waited for her husband to awaken before sodomizing him. The bastard had let the music box play during the assault, and it scared Dena to think that Troy might have taken it with him.

A loaded magazine for the pistol was hidden under an old *TV Guide* in the drawer, and Dena stuck it in the gun and chambered a cartridge. The slide popped loudly as it closed and Dena reached out and switched off the lamp. It was near black in the house with all the windows dressed in plywood, and she didn't want to silhouette herself with light while anyone else could stay invisible in the shadows. Besides, what if the lights went out like the phone and her eyes weren't adjusted to the dark? Anything could come at her then. And she wouldn't know until it had her.

With the gun in her right fist and her left hand feeling along the wall, Dena moved back toward her son's room. She stopped just inside the door there, listening to everything with ears as wide as they would go. They reported nothing but the storm outside, nothing but rain and wind.

Inside, Jeremy slept, curled up with one bandaid-ornamented knee out from under the covers and both hands clutching his stuffed panda. Dena decided against waking him. *God*! She had to make sure no one could hurt him, but she didn't dare run for it through the darkened house with him. And the plywood was nailed over the windows from outside; they couldn't get out that way. She'd have to go downstairs by herself. Dena gripped the pistol tighter, wishing she'd practiced with it more.

She stepped into the hall and every hair follicle on her body came to life as the chimes belled out a jangling, discordant note, as if they had been ripped from the ceiling to adorn the body of someone dancing a berserk chorea. Dena sucked in a mouthful of air and almost yelled. The chimes gonged and clanged. Her finger tightened on the automatic's trigger and she clenched her teeth instead. A gagging sound came from downstairs. Quiet followed.

"Mommy?"

Dena jumped, and turned to see Jeremy sitting up in bed. He was rubbing his eyes and she moved quickly over beside him, putting her arms around him as she lay the small head back on the pillow.

"It's all right, Sweety. Just a noise. Go back to your dreams."

Jeremy's arm found his panda and pulled it to him. "Kay, Mommy," he said. As fast as that he fell asleep again.

Dena turned back to Jeremy's door, peeking around it to study the upstairs hallway. Her eyes were fully dark adapted now but the house stood so black that she couldn't make out her own feet. Her ears could listen, though, and had gotten better at screening out the gale. She found herself able to ignore the outside and focus on what was inside. There was nothing to hear, however, as if all sound had been flushed from the house and the tank had to refill itself. She found herself wishing for a sound, a drip of water in the tub, a clock ticking, just something to let her know the rest of the world wasn't all gone away.

Even more than sound, Dena wanted light. The switch for the stairwell tickled just under her hand, but she wouldn't let herself touch it. If she touched it, she wouldn't be able to stop herself from turning it on. And once she had light she would never be able to stand the dark again, even though the dark would come. Through the agency of the hurricane, or through a more human act, the dark would come. Dena could picture herself screaming when that happened, and it would be better not to have had the light at all.

As she fought her need for light and won, Dena felt the blunting of her adrenaline rush. At least temporarily, her physiology was listening to her brain. She knew someone was in the house now. She knew she had to protect Jeremy. But she could visualize the place better in the dark than her visitor could. And she had a gun. True, she hadn't shot much in the last few years, but she had grown up in hunting country with four older brothers and she understood how to squeeze a trigger and hit what she aimed at. She shut Jeremy's door behind her and padded softly toward the stairs.

Dena's way to the first floor was clear and at the base of the steps she crouched. The front door stood behind her and she could have walked out easily if she'd brought Jeremy down. But she hadn't known the stairs would be safe. To her left opened the garage. Across the other way was the kitchen. In front of her ran the hall that split kitchen and living room off from the den and from her home office beyond. Dena's eyes hurt as she strained to see down that hallway. Even as she stared, a set of chimes rang, as if someone's head had brushed lightly against them.

Now Dena would allow herself light, but not the room-brightening light of the overheads. She needed something to ruin her visitor's night sight and leave hers alone. That meant the heavy duty Maglite in the closet just down the hall. She started snailing her way toward it.

Somewhere ahead of her was a slow drip. *A leak from the rain*, Dena guessed. Her foot found the residue of it just as she reached the closet, and the slick wet spot that had spread across the floor almost felled her. She grabbed the doorknob for support and it creaked under her hand. The chimes rang, soughing as if a faint wind ghosted among them. Dena wanted to run, her imagination telling her that something was coming down the hall toward her in the blackness. Instead, she forced herself to open the closet and reach in for the Maglite, her skin crawling as the sleeves of raincoats and old sweaters brushed against her hands like the shed husks of monstrous insects.

The long, thick handle of the flashlight made a comforting weight when Dena's fingers gathered it in. She didn't turn it on yet, though. Her mind shrieked for a look down the hall but she didn't want to be holding the flash when it lit. That would only shout out her own location. She stepped into the closet and knelt, laying the Maglite on the hall floor. Then she switched it on and quickly stood up amid the clutter. One glimpse down the hallway made her wish she'd left things in the dark. The drip she'd heard didn't come from the rain.

Where the hall intersected the living room there hung a cheap, brass chandelier, and a body in black clothes and black knitted cap dangled from it. Blood dripped from the leg to the floor, but the person had not been killed at that spot. Someone had dragged them across the linoleum, leaving red smears behind. Those swirled patterns started outside the closet and Dena looked down to see her feet stained and sticky with crimson. The sight made her gag and she fought to swallow the acid lifting in her throat. Then it hit her. The killer had hid in this closet too!

Dena stiffened, started to suck in air that seemed too weak to feed her. In the reflected light of the flash she could see shoes sitting next to her reddened feet, and she could imagine them full of legs. She could imagine the empty clothes behind her gradually swelling with human shapes. She could hear breathing, ragged. *You're hyperventilating*, her mind yelled, but the adrenaline was shouting too loud for anything else to be heard. Something brushed her cheek and she whooped in fear as she leaped out of the closet. Her feet slipped in blood and she fell.

The chimes whipped into sound as Dena's fingers scrabbled for the Maglite. They found it, closed around the handle. The closet was empty; she could see that now. But the sliding glass door at the back of the house had just grated open. Dena pushed to her knees, both the gun and the light stabbed down the hall. A gust of hurricane struck her in the face. Shadows spattered before the light, made grotesque by the gale-stirred movements of the dangling corpse. The plywood that had covered the sliding door at the rear of the house was peeled back and the glass was open, letting rain into the living room, letting in wind that sent the chimes into a mad skittering dance.

Dena jumped to her feet and ran across to the back door, trying not to glance at the dead body hanging from her chandelier. The killer must have fled, she figured, and through the left-open doorway the gale came roaring into Dena's living room. She pushed the glass closed and locked it, the chimes falling silent as their wind supply dried up. The house still thrummed in the big wind outside, and Dena could see trees in the yard bending down like old men. She also saw something else, an odd design scrawled on the glass door. It was a heart with a cobra inside it, drawn in shiny lipstick. When she realized what it was she stepped back, her stomach suddenly churning with bile.

The symbol represented a tattoo, the one Troy's rapist had worn on his chest. Troy's attacker had hidden behind a mask and a long blonde wig, and the tattoo had been the only identifying characteristic Dena's husband could remember. Dena had sat in horror as Troy described it to the police sketch artist in a voice that held an emotionless void. And later, she had accidentally surprised her husband while he was drawing the symbol in a cold hand in the notebook where he kept his private thoughts.

"The bastard came back," Dena muttered, staring at the image of the tattoo and lashing herself with words. But who had been in the house with him? A friend? A burglar? And who had killed who? Was it the rapist hanging in the hall? She hoped it was.

A single set of chimes rang.

Dena spun away from the sliding door, flashing her light

over the walls and ceiling. The chimes hung still and stiff as cocoons. And there were no others in the house. Except! When Jeremy was born she had put a set of porcelain teddy bears over his crib, and though the crib was long gone the chimes were still there above the place where he slept. Jeremy wasn't tall enough to reach them.

Dena started to run, heading down the hallway on the fastest route to the stairs. She didn't even glance at the hanging corpse; she was too busy swallowing the terrified shouts her throat wanted to let out. They would only warn the invader that she was coming.

The teddy bear chimes rang again, louder than before, as if someone had picked up Jeremy and brushed him against the wires. And Dena heard her son's voice, murmurous with sleep as he asked a question.

"Mommy?"

Dena was on the stairs, taking them three at a time, making noise now that she couldn't control. She heard Jeremy's bed creak as something was dropped on it, and by that time she was to the doorway of her son's room and stepping inside. The night light had gone dark—the hurricane had finally killed the electricity—but the glow of Dena's flash was enough to still the scene, enough to see her little boy fallen on the bed, screaming of a sudden as he saw his mommy at the door and not in the shadow looming over him.

That shadow moved toward her, its hand gleaming with a knife. Without thinking, Dena pushed the gun out from her body and pulled the trigger twice, aiming for the torso. She saw the figure stagger as it was hit, saw its hand still moving, reaching out. She fired again, the slug punching into the face. As the shape went back and down, the reaching hand closed over the porcelain bears and ripped them shrieking from the ceiling. A knitted cap spun away and long blonde hair poured out to frame a sharp-featured face that shown waxy and bloodless in the Maglite's glow.

A woman!, Dena thought, as she saw the cloud of hair and

the crimson lips. Then her mind translated what her eyes had registered. *No. A mask and wig.*

She looked down at Jeremy. He was staring at the body where it lay pinned to the floor by the stabbing beam of the flashlight, and she stepped forward and scooped him up, tucking his head into her shoulder where he couldn't see anything but her T-shirt. He wasn't crying, but his arms went around Dena's neck so hard that she thought she would choke, in more ways than one. She put her hand to her son's back, holding him tight, and she was crying for him as she started out of the room and out of the house. She wanted him away from here, though she had an idea that it would take more than just walking out the door.

* * * * * * *

Twenty minutes later Dena walked back into her house without Jeremy. It had taken a while to wake Morgan Keller next door, and by the time he had answered the bell both mother and son were soaked by the slanting rain. Keller had brought towels and blankets for Jeremy, and Dena had explained the night's events while she rocked her son back to sleep. As soon as the little boy's eyes closed, the man carried him upstairs to bed. Morgan had asked Dena to stay while he woke his wife, but she had decided against waiting to see Marge. Jeremy trusted the woman. Keller had said he was going to call the police, too, but it might be hours before they could get here and Dena wasn't going to wait to see them either. She had to put faces on the dead.

Down her hall was the chandelier with its cargo of the dead, and Dena went toward it with the Maglite in one hand and the pistol in the other. She wanted to know which of the two corpses belonged to Troy's rapist. This one had been strangled with a set of wind chimes but Dena didn't think it was the rapist. She looked up at a face that had turned all purple from lack of air, and she realized that Marge Keller was not next door with Jeremy. She was here, with her shirt torn away and a lipstick tattoo of a heart and a cobra scrawled between her breasts.

As if to accompany the sudden insane thud of Dena's heart, a music box started to play. The tune was familiar. Dena had already heard it once this night, and many times before when she owned the box from which it tinkled. With fear daggering her spine, she turned to see a figure in the doorway of her house; a light in its hand was strong enough to brighten the whole hall. Morgan Keller stood behind that light, a shotgun leveled at Dena's chest. The music box sat on the floor, its lid open.

"Marge always liked that tune," Keller said, as if reminiscing with an old friend. He started walking forward, kicking the door partially shut behind him. "Troy gave it to her," he continued, stopping a few feet away. "You know...after. I think he couldn't bear having it around. But he didn't wanna throw it out either." He chuckled. "Maybe your husband secretly enjoyed his experience. You think?"

Dena's right hand moved slightly, almost involuntarily, and Keller's voice turned hard as the shotgun lifted. "Drop...the damn...pistol! Or I'll turn you inside out with this thing."

Dena's eyes swallowed the cold gleam of the 12-gauge and she knew the man would enjoy using it. She let the Browning slide from her fingers to clatter on the floor.

"Where's Jeremy you son of a bitch?" she demanded.

"Sleeping." The calm had already returned to Keller's voice. "I gave him a Valium to make sure he won't wake up for a while."

"If you've hurt my son—"

Keller chuckled again. "Don't worry. That was more Marge's line of work. I like my humps a little older."

"You raped Troy?"

"I've got the tattoo. And I have to tell you, it was a hell of a lot of fun watching your husband dying inside while I was right there on top of him. He had been bullshitting himself too long; that was his problem. It's always worse for the ones who lie to themselves. Because they can't lie anymore while I'm there with them."

"You're sick."

"And you're just full of original observations. Way I see it, I did your husband a service. I could tell by the way he looked at me he was a homosexual. God, I hate those scum."

Though not a psychologist, Dena sensed more than a paranoid homophobia behind Keller's words. She might have called it evil if she'd had time to think about it. But right now she had to keep him talking while she figured a way out of this mess. "So why come here tonight?" she asked. "You know Troy's gone."

"Oh, I'm afraid your hubby was a bit smarter than I'd hoped. I think he figured out the mask I wore on the big night was Marge's work. I got a little note yesterday telling me you and Jeremy would be going to your mom's for the hurricane, like you always used to. Hell, I thought you were gone too. Never even looked in your garage for the car."

"My parents are in Vegas."

Keller shrugged. "Too bad. I guess Troy didn't know they'd gone. Anyway, he sent me this note inviting me over. Said he knew what I'd done and it was payback time. He wanted to kill me. Scare me first, then kill me. That's why the chimes and the tattoo on the glass door. He just didn't realize that Marge was my huntin' buddy. That threw him off."

"Troy was in the house tonight?" Dena interrupted, her chest tightening as she realized what Keller was saying.

"Who you think killed Marge? While I played tag with shadows. I never thought he'd be that good, and when you came down it was two against one. Course, I didn't know it was you. Figured he'd hired a professional and it was time for old Morgan to go home."

Keller was grinning widely now, as if he'd just heard the punch line to a dirty joke. "I know you saw him, though. Dressed sort of like I was that first night he and I were together. Mask. Wig. Didn't you tell me you shot somebody like that upstairs?"

Dena had known what Keller was going to say, but actually hearing the words still spiked nails into her soul. She slid to her knees, throat heaving but nothing running out. Keller sat his flashlight on the floor and took a step forward to kiss the 12-gauge to Dena's forehead. The metal was cold. "Guess I'll have to adopt Jeremy," he said. Then the door behind him blew open and wet leaves and rain swirled in on a rushing wind. Chimes rang and Morgan turned halfway around in surprise. Dena hurled herself into his legs.

Keller fell backward, the shotgun discharging, spraying the ceiling with pellets. Chimes shattered, and Dena came to her knees and smashed the Maglite across the man's face with all her might. Glass popped and the bulb winked out, but Keller's flash still burned and its light showed the man's head snap to the side from the blow. She would have thought it was enough to knock him out. It wasn't. The ex-marine lashed out with his left leg, his booted foot crashing into her chest with enough force to knock her loose from her air. She fell back against the wall, throat aching as she tried to draw in just a little of the wind that raced all around her.

Keller started to lift the shotgun and Dena kicked out as hard as she could, knocking the gun from his grasp and sending it spinning against the wall. As he lunged after it Dena's hand found something angular and cold on the linoleum. *The pistol!*

She grabbed the automatic by the butt and swung it around, starting to fire before the barrel even aligned with her target. Two shots walked across the wall; the rest began to hit meat. The 9mm cartridges weren't very powerful, but the gun held fifteen of them, minus the two misses and the three she'd used earlier. The other ten bullets kept snapping and snapping and snapping, and Keller kept jerking and jerking and jerking. He was dead before the last shot took him in the throat.

But Troy might still be alive, Dena thought, as she picked up Keller's flashlight and ran for the stairs.

Behind her as she ran, the house seemed full of the hurricane's boom and roar, full of wild chiming, but Dena ignored it all as she stepped into her son's room and listened for the sound of breathing. She heard none, and Keller's flash lit up a space that was empty of her husband's body. Then the front door slammed downstairs and the house fell still.

Dena turned, listened, the empty gun useless in her fist. She heard movement downstairs, heard a sound like cloth ripping, and a moment later footsteps came up toward the second floor. Dena wasn't surprised when Troy walked into the room. She didn't run into his arms, though.

Her husband had removed the mask and wig, and Dena could see dried blood on his face where one of her shots had creased him. She figured the other two slugs had hit the bulletproof vest Troy was wearing beneath his now opened shirt. Covering the front of that vest was a badly tattered symbol that dripped red mucous. Morgan Keller's tattoo didn't look much like a heart and a cobra anymore.

Dena lifted the flash slightly, light spattering off the knife in Troy's hand and then falling into his eyes. The pupils constricted but the lids didn't blink, and the face behind the eyes was a pale oval etched in white wax. A phrase came to Dena from a college class in abnormal psychology, "flattened affect," no facial expression at all. Her husband was over the edge, long gone into a Freudian landscape from which there would be no easy return.

"Troy.... Troy!"

Dena's voice seemed to hot-wire Troy's emotions and he looked at her with hatred dripping from his lips. "You watched him didn't you?"

"I don't know what you're talking about, Troy. You're hurt. You need a hospital."

"You watched him *use me*! I know you did! Maybe you and him were doing it together yourselves. Is that right?"

"You're talking crazy, Troy." Dena fought the tears that wicked toward her eyes. "You've gotta calm down and let me help you."

"Where's Jeremy?"

The abrupt change of subject startled Dena but she quickly recovered. "That's right. You've gotta think about Jeremy. He needs you."

"Don't play with me, bitch. I want my son. We're going away from here. I won't let him stay another day in this house with you."

Dena felt wetness on her cheeks and realized she had lost the fight against tears. "Stop it, Troy," she shouted. "Can't you see it's over. We've got to—"

"I said *don't play with me!*" Troy's eyes went wild in the light. His shoulder lurched against Jeremy's dresser, tipping it over and spilling toy trains and Little Critter books onto the floor. Then he was coming at her, swinging the knife from side to side. Dena threw the emptied pistol at him, saw it bounce off his chest. She tried to dodge around him but he caught her with one arm and threw her back onto Jeremy's bed. He stabbed at her, missing, and she swung the flashlight at his head only to have it batted from her hand. She watched it flying, saw it hit the wall. The light went dark.

Dena slapped out, fingers curled as she tried to find Troy's face in the pitch black room. Instead, her hand found the knife blade coming down and she screamed as it went through her palm and drove her arm into the mattress.

Troy straddled her chest, pinning her, screaming with her. "Do you know what he did? Do you know? I'll kill you, you son of a bitch. I'll kill you." And Dena knew that Troy wasn't talking to her anymore, wasn't feeling his wife struggling beneath him. He was feeling Morgan Keller raping him again.

Abruptly, the knife was wrenched free of Dena's hand, wringing another scream from an already raw throat. She couldn't see the blade lifting, but she could feel it. And she could feel Troy's legs tense as he readied the knife for another plunge. She bucked the lower half of her body upward, her feet finding precarious purchase on the side of Jeremy's bed. Troy's balance was poor and Dena's desperate lurch threw him off onto his side. She slipped from beneath him and bolted for the door, slamming her shoulder into the frame as she went past. She heard Troy coming after her and knew there would be no reasoning with him now. She could think only of getting away, of getting to Jeremy and protecting him.

The stairs loomed and Dena went down them in a stumbling, sliding lurch, grabbing at the handrail in desperate hope of keeping her balance. Somehow she managed it. Troy didn't. Dena heard him curse and felt his weight as he pitched forward to strike her in the back. She fell, landing on elbows and carpet-burning her cheek. Troy rolled over her, smashing hard against the door, blocking her exit.

Dena's thoughts danced away from the door, tripped over the 12-gauge that Morgan Keller had dropped in the hall. For a moment she shoved the thought aside—Troy was still her husband—but then she felt the knife again as Troy spun around onto his stomach and slashed through the dark with the blade. A line of agony scorched across her ankle and she threw herself backwards. Her scooting hand struck the shotgun, sent it sliding further down the hall. She scrambled for it, tears on her face, her mouth filled with a steady keening. Troy's knife slapped into the linoleum where her foot had been an instant before.

Dena's hands found Morgan Keller, and lying just beneath him was the long length of the shotgun. She grabbed it and spun around, back to the soft wall of Keller's body. She heard Troy coming, sounding huge and alien in the darkened hall. She screamed at him to stop, screamed that she had a gun. Yet she could hear what he was saying, like a litany. "Kill you kill you kill you."

She pulled the trigger into the blackness, felt the slam of recoil and heard the awful chunk-thud of a hit. And then she was just shrieking, just shrieking, feeling the horror like a wind swirling over her. Insanity was a hurricane, full of roaring chimes that rang like hyena laughter. She wanted it, could feel her need for it. How easy it would be to fly away. Only one thought stopped her:

Jeremy.

DEATH TURNED AWAY

Was it midnight yet?
Would it ever be?

The thoughts whispered in his mind as the wind whispers through ruins, and they rattled around in his skull like dried peas in a bowl that had been shaken up. Needing answers to the thoughts, the young man in the bed looked up at the ceiling where the time was reflected in foot high orange numerals from the clock on the dresser. It was 11:29 in the evening. Still early. Too early for the visitor he was expecting at midnight.

To pass the time he glanced out the window. The moon bulked hugely above the horizon, its summer light turned to saffron by the orange curtains his mother had chosen for the room. He hated that color, just as he hated this room, as he hated the bed on which he was lying, and the pajamas in which his mother had dressed him. He thought sometimes he hated his mother but he could not be sure. He was certain, though, that he hated himself, the useless thing that he was. But that would all change, would all be better, if midnight ever came.

He twisted under the bed covers as much as he could, nearly stifling in the night's heat, and finally succeeded in working the sheets down off of his thin body with pained and fumbling fingers. He looked down at his legs. What he would have given to see them strong again. But they were nearly gone.

A glance spared at his arms showed them pale, and thin, and wasted. Soon, they and the legs would be like dried sticks, and he would lie here and only his eyes would move. He would have cursed the disease that chained him down but his curses had long since dried up into dust that clogged his mouth.

If only it were not so hot, he thought. Even the breeze from the window blew superheated, but at least it stirred the air in the room.

He closed his eyes after a while and let his mind drift, trying to escape the room, the heat, his illness. He pictured himself in younger days, skinny dipping in the chill water of Flanagan's lake with Robert and Danny. He remembered the frozen ice-cream bars that dripped and ran in the summer heat and got sticky all over your hands. Yet they were so icy at first that they stuck to your tongue, and it hurt your teeth to bite them. He thought, also, of his grandmother's back porch, always so shadowy and cool, and of the tea she would make for him and Danny whenever they came in tired from playing soldiers.

And, as always when he freed his memories, he thought of Theresa, his mind skittering around her name like a dog that had been beaten too often. He had once sworn never to forgive her for leaving him to suffer the illness alone. He had let the anger and pain build up inside of him and had waited for them to bloom, like black flowers from ashes. That had been long ago. He no longer had the energy to sustain those emotions. He only wished she would come back, and knew she would not.

Footsteps in the hallway snatched him from his thoughts. For a moment he hoped they were Joey's—fourteen and his only friend—but the sound was too light for his brother's feet. Most people would not have been able to hear those soft shuffles at all, but he heard them. There was nothing wrong with his ears. They seemed even better now that the rest of him was dying. Thank goodness for small favors.

He listened as the feathery steps strayed closer. *Go past*, he begged. *Go on past.*

They stopped just outside his door. The old porcelain knob started to turn and the door opened. He glanced at the time. The numerals changed as he watched—11:32—and his mother peeked into the room.

"Are you all right, Frank honey?" she asked. "Need more covers?"

He shook his head but she didn't seem to be watching.

"My goodness," she said, coming closer. "You've gotten your sheet off. Here, let me tuck you in."

"No," he croaked. But his jaws would scarcely move, and his tongue was dry and swollen in his mouth, and nothing came out but a faint expulsion of air.

His mother leaned over him, fluffed his pillow, and pulled the sheet up under his chin. Her breath smelled like mint mouthwash. Her hair looked orange under the curtain-distorted moonlight but he knew that it was gray. Mother was not old but she seemed old. Her eyes hurt him with their wrinkles and she had left her teeth in the bathroom.

Slowly, she walked around the bed, and as she went she snapped the sheets taut and tucked them beneath the mattress. All the way around she went, sealing him in as if sewing him into a shroud. He squirmed, trying to raise his shoulders, but she pushed them down, surprisingly strong against his weakness, and patted him on the cheek.

"There, there now," she said. "It's all right. Mother's here. You mustn't fight you know. It's not good for you to strain yourself."

He was afraid to nod, afraid of what she might read into it. His glance went past her shoulder, seeing the curtains stirred by the night wind. *Don't look at the window*, he whispered to himself. *Don't look. Don't feel the breeze. It's blowing cooler.*

"And my word," she scolded, clapping a hand over her mouth. "You've gotten the window open. Now how on earth did you do that?" She tsk tsked deep in her throat.

He didn't, he couldn't, tell her of the pain, of the struggle to get onto his crutches and over to the window, to fumble with numb hands on the lock so he could open the glass and catch a breath of air that was not stale with age. He couldn't tell her about Joey or she would be angry—Joey, who helped but let him do so much on his own because the boy knew his older brother needed to. He could not tell her though he wanted to. His grunt was loud in the room.

His mother moved to the window and stopped, her faded hand on the glass to close it. She looked back over her shoulder, smiling at him as if to savor what she was doing for her boy, her loving son.

Doing for him, doing to him! The echoes of the thoughts were like the laughter of clowns. He shook his head at her as if to tell her no, and she shut the window and locked it.

"There," she said. "Now you won't catch your death." She went past him, brushing his damp forehead with dry and brittle lips. "Goodnight honey," she crooned. "Goodnight, sleep tight, don't let the bedbugs bite."

She picked up his crutches as she was leaving and took them with her. The door clicked shut just as a sudden cool breeze rattled twigs against the window. Frank closed his eyes tightly and shook his head.

The reflected light of the clock seemed dark against his shuttered lids, more red than orange. It was 11:39 he knew, and had his knowing confirmed by opening his eyes and looking up. The numerals did not change again, even though he watched, and at last he turned away, only to think of heat.

Sweat was running on his face and a bead caught suddenly at the tip of his nose, tickling. He could not raise his hands from their prison beneath the sheet so he shook his head. The droplet clung perversely. He began working his shoulders back and forth to loosen the covers so that he could free his arm. After an eternity he succeeded. One hand came free and reached up, and the bead let loose before he could touch it and ran down his neck like a scuttling spider. Almost, he thought he would cry.

He had lost track of the time and for a moment could not recall where to look. His thoughts were whirling around in his head. His mind seemed hot, hot, and the bed was wet beneath him. He wanted to call out to Joey who slept across the hall— Joey would help him—but he knew that his voice would no longer carry that far. It was failing like the rest of him. Even if he could call out it would only bring his mother back, and the little rituals would start again, the little horrors that she did because she loved him. She must have loved him very much because she spent so much of her time caring for him.

He wondered if she hated him for it.

The clock gave a little buzz that drew his attention and he glanced at it, remembering. The minutes ticked over and raced away, 11:45, 11:46, '47, '48. The color was definitely darker now, almost bloody red, and it seemed to pulse with his heart. He reached with his free hand to pull back the sheets and stopped as a sound bruised his ears.

Down the stairs and to the right was a door leading to the outside. He remembered where it was though it had been months since he had used it. Now there was the tinkle of a hand on the door and the whisper of a breeze coming in. And there were footsteps, shuffling, but they were not those of his mother. Oh yes, he heard those sounds. His hearing was so acute, so exquisite, and he had been waiting so long, so long. He looked at the time. It was 11:51.

Faster, he urged it. *Go faster.* And, as if it had heard him and was giggling to itself, the clock gave a click and the time slipped back—11:50.

He half sobbed before realizing that it really didn't matter anymore. The visitor was already coming up the stairs. He could hear him on the first step. Time could not stop forever and in a few minutes....

He closed his eyes and listened—to footsteps. The first ones were breathlessly light on the old mahogany stairs—the sound of ivory knuckles sliding on the worn railing was much sharper—but they quickly grew louder as they came closer. The visitor was at the landing now and turning. Only fourteen steps to the top and a few more to his room. He knew because he had thought about this many times, and prayed for it.

Now he caught the faint rustle of a cloak against something. Black, yes that cloak would be black like night. And he knew what limbs it swirled over. Ten steps, nine steps to go, eight. He stole one glance at the time—11:54.

You're early, he thought, but there were still a few steps to go.

Then there was only one. The rustle stopped and something hovered in stillness. He could almost picture the slow turn of the head, the movement of thin hands that were so pale, and the shadows of the eyes. Now those eyes were looking toward his room. He held his breath and counted to ten. At eleven the steps moved again, until they stopped outside his door. He listened but heard no breathing.

* * * * * * *

Waiting, like an autumn leaf clinging to a tree waiting to fall, like an old house waiting for its owners to return.

* * * * * * *

He'll come in at 12:00, Frank thought. But now that midnight was almost here time seemed to have stopped dead still.

"Come on," he said. He thought he spoke aloud. He wanted to hear the hand touch the doorknob. He wanted to see the knob twist. It did not. He felt the cloaked figure turn away and glide across the hall to a second room. A spidery hand sounded like rattling dice on that other door and it opened. There was breathing now. It was Joey's.

Frank listened deeply and the fear coiled like worms. "Wrong," he yelled, croaking. "Wrong. Not that room. Not there. I'm here."

The visitor didn't hear, didn't stop, didn't care. Frank struggled awkwardly with the covers but his hand had somehow gotten pinned beneath his body and he could not get it loose. He struggled, and suddenly ceased struggling. The breathing had stopped. There was only a sigh and silence, and, quietly, the tears began to run down Frank's cheeks, washing away the sweat.

In a moment, he heard the hands on his own doorknob but

that did not stop his weeping. The door opened and something came in. It held a broken bundle over one shoulder and carried a curved scythe in its free hand. Its face was hidden by the cowl of a black cloak. The figure moved over to him and stood looking down.

Frank glanced at the time. The numerals ran like blood on the ceiling and they were showing 12:00 midnight. He looked at the shape of his visitor and closed his eyes. "Damn you," he whispered, and then thought of how ludicrous that curse was. He could not help but open his eyes again and look up at Joey's face. The light from the clock flashed off of it, and it was dead.

"It was supposed to be me," he said. "It was supposed to be me."

A bony hand reached out and tucked the sheet back beneath the mattress where Frank's struggles had pulled it free. Then Death turned away, laughing like hell.

MACHINE WASH WARM; TUMBLE DRY

It was around one in the morning when I came downstairs from the apartment with a big load of dirty clothes. I had deliberately waited until late and there was no one in the Laundromat, as you might expect. The six washers and four dryers stood empty, their mouths open to the humid night air as if they were panting from the heat. I didn't much like the imagery called up by that thought, and I especially didn't care for the darkness that pooled in the backs of the dryers, the shadows that moved every time the neon lights flickered. I went and shut the lids on all but two machines, one dryer and one washer.

Some stuff that was already wet went into the dryer, and I threw my jeans and socks into the fifty cent washer and pushed in the tongue to start her. I left out the detergent and smiled when I thought of how much that would piss my mother off if she knew. Course, it had never taken much to piss that woman off.

I had brought down the sports section out of last Sunday's paper and was drinking what was left of a half warm beer that tasted like crap. I tried hard to read but couldn't do it for long. There wasn't much but baseball in the paper anyway and I'd just never been that interested in the game, though I used to sit and watch it with my dad when he was alive. You know, I really miss that old man sometimes.

But it wasn't just the baseball filled newspaper that kept me from reading; it was feeling the darkness down there in the bellies of the laundry's empty machines, coiling itself tighter and tighter, and finally I had to get up and go open the lids again. I felt a little silly opening them when I had just closed them ten minutes before, but I was still glad when it was done. Darkness ought not to be cooped up for long.

My beer was empty by then and I went upstairs for another, and to find something a little more interesting than baseball scores to read. The apartment was quiet for a change. There hadn't been much of that since my mother had moved in with me last year, one week to the day after my dad had died. Boy could that lady nag!

"Wipe your feet. Turn down that stereo. Brush your teeth. Pick up your clothes." As if I weren't twenty-five years old and this wasn't my own apartment. Sometimes I wondered how Dad had put up with it for all those years without killing her. Luckily for him, he had some ear trouble and could always just turn off his hearing aid. My hearing was perfect.

Because of Mother, I had been only too glad to leave New Orleans at eighteen and go out to California to live with Grandma and Grandpa. I'd only come back here when Dad got bad with the cancer. He knew he was dying and wanted me with him. I had intended to go back to L.A. right after the funeral, but one thing led to another and before I knew it my mother was moving in with me and telling me to get a job. Of course, Rhonda wasn't my real mother, just my stepmother. But she had always insisted I call her mom or mother. I called her mother. My mom had died when I was seven and Rhonda had married my dad two years later.

I didn't like to think about Rhonda much so I got myself another beer out of the fridge and then went into the bedroom for a *Playboy* magazine to take downstairs with me. It was the same issue Mother had found in my closet this morning and thrown in the trash. I'd gotten it back out a little later and there wasn't much more than a few tea stains on it. By the time I got back down to the Laundromat both my machines had stopped. I unloaded the washer directly into the dryer, leaving what was already in there for another round. It wouldn't hurt to dry some things more than once.

I sat down then and opened my second beer. It tasted a lot better than the first, and the *Playboy* held my interest better than the newspaper had. I only had to get up once, when the heavy load in the dryer got off balance a bit and the machine started to shake. I opened her up and shoved things around, then started her again with another quarter. Some of the stuff sure seemed to be taking a long time to dry.

I had gotten through most of the magazine before the dryer cut off for the third time. It was almost three o'clock and I was starting to feel sleepy anyway. I went over and took out the clothes and began to stack them in nice, neat little piles on the laundry-room table. It was a few minutes before I noticed that one of my socks was missing.

Shit, but I hate losing socks in the dryer. And it always seems to happen. I was pretty well convinced I wouldn't find the thing when I opened the machine. But there it was. Damn if it hadn't gotten itself lodged in Mother's throat somehow.

ABRADED BY LIGHT

Scorched and poetical,
abraded by light,
I lay in silence,
loud with whiskey
on sands of lost harmonics,
and the dreams in me
are like lepers,
like plague-blackened flowers.
they rise like wolves,
sweeping over the borders
of my thoughts,
dying out in gutters,
empty and void,
wasting out their life,
in blood.

ROADKILL

No moon.

A sky flecked like mica with stars.

My Harley is redlined, the V-Twin burning between my legs. It's always been dangerous riding fast at night. More dangerous now. But since the "Change" I have nothing to lose, no one to care if I lay the machine down.

Then I see her, lying across the blacktop.

Dead, I think.

But she moves when I swerve to avoid her.

I get the bike stopped, u-turned, wince as I see.... Her back is broken.

I hang the bike on its kickstand, the headlight painting her, refracting jewels from her liquid eyes. I rush to her, kneel.

She opens her mouth but makes no sound. How can she be alive? How can she breathe with a chest half crushed? What is she doing so far from the protection of a Safe-Haven? What sick fate sent a vehicle to rendezvous with her at this lonely spot? There are no signs of burnt rubber. Whoever hit her hadn't even slowed down.

I try to force, "It's OK," through my lips. The meaningless words won't come.

Then she looks past me toward highway's edge. I turn, see some shadowy movement. When I turn back she looks like she's sleeping but her chest no longer rises and falls.

My feet follow where her gaze had pointed, and I see why she'd been crossing the road. See what she was returning to. Or running *from*.

Her puppies had been born dead. But in this new world they haven't stayed that way. Their eyes aren't open but their noses work. They smell me, and squirm toward me through their mother's afterbirth, their baby teeth stark and white and gnashing.

I back away, then scream as a sudden flashing agony lances my legs. I fall, roll instinctively away from the source of pain. The mother hound's mouth is flecked with foam and blood. My blood. Her eyes have been reborn as scarlet hells.

I try to get up, find she's torn out my Achilles tendons. Still screaming, I scrabble away along the highway. The hound growls and hitches herself toward me, her front paws slapping at the asphalt. Intestines unravel behind her.

I laugh hysterically as I realize the mother's broken spine will keep her from catching me.

Then I see the puppies. On the road. They can't walk either. But they're crawling faster than I am.

RAZOR WHITE

AUTHOR'S NOTE: The next two stories, "Razor White" and "Splatter of Black," and a later one called "Wall of Love," were written at a time when the horror subgenre known as "Splatterpunk" was in vogue. Splatterpunk was a movement toward very intense, very visceral horror, and as a result these stories are quite a bit more graphic than most of the rest of the tales in this collection. I liked Splatterpunk myself. I enjoy "goring it up," but I thought I'd warn you in case you're squeamish.

SEPTEMBER 9TH; SUNDAY:

He climbed toward wakefulness through scarlet-tinted dreams, rising up to a morning sky that burned pink outside his window, like watermelon flesh. A hundred images cracked and ran as the dream period ended and heavy lids shuttered back over eyes that were yellow-brown scars in an otherwise pale face. The empty pupils dilated suddenly with pleasure as he slid from beneath sticky wet sheets and stood looking down, his body finger-painted red.

One hand slid up over the matted hair of his groin as he eyed the humped shape that remained in the bed, the touching and the looking triggering the sharp sting of an almost painful arousal. His other hand went out to stroke the pearl and silver hilt of the knife that nailed the woman's head to the pillow. The blade was caught among shattered teeth and he tore it loose, spilling a sliver of dried tongue out onto the bed as the weapon came free of the open mouth. His lips dripped shadows as he smiled, as he reached in the candy jar on the bedside table and took out a handful of lolly drops. He chewed them hard, cracking and splintering their sweetness while he quickly relieved tension with his fist.

The twice desecrated sheets served as a nice shroud as he wrapped the body up and carried it down the steps to his basement. There, he selected a straight razor from the collection he kept in an old army surplus locker and used it to remove the dead woman's hair as close to the scalp as possible. The shaved head looked alien beneath the fluorescent lights and he turned away, preferring to remember the long and living blonde mane as it had looked spread out on the sheets while they fucked.

He slipped the cuttings into large Ziploc storage bags and slid them into the locker beneath the trays of razors and other utensils. He then used a hacksaw to take off the woman's hands at the wrists before carrying them over and nailing them to the wall beside the other three pair. The blood that had dripped down from the sawn flesh scrawled abstract images on the white plaster, and he stared for a while at the surreal designs before pulling a tarp down from the ceiling to hide them. He'd often thought it was a pity no one besides himself would ever see those paintings. Sometimes, he even fantasized about bringing one of the women down here and doing it to her while she shrieked at those red-tipped wings. But that was not how he hunted. He liked them all dewy-eyed with love when he laid them waste. He licked it up.

Cutting up the rest of the body was always difficult, though the heavy saws and cleavers that he had bought from a defunct slaughterhouse helped. Still, he was drenched with sweat by the time he had finished hiding the plastic wrapped pieces away beneath the false floor of the cellar. Some scattered throw rugs helped to cover the places where he had taken up the boards, and half a can of Lysol knocked most of the thick blood-scent out of the air. He knew that he was going to have to get more ventilation in here eventually though.

There was a sink in one corner of the basement and he used it to wash up his tools before locking them away in the surplus trunk where they were kept. The soiled linens were left in the sink to soak while he went upstairs to shower, standing long in the heated water until it flushed the sweat and blood from his skin and carried it down the drain. The swirling of the pinkish fluid triggered his memory, and the sex and the killing played over and over in his mind, linked forever by hippocampal threads. He would dream about the way the soft flesh had parted from the bone.

SEPTEMBER 15TH; SATURDAY:

For a week he had the dreams he wanted. They fed him and warmed him, wrapping him up in soft lips and cool tresses, in bone and in blood. Across the years, there had been times when he felt that he could live forever in the world that he created out of the murders. But the pleasure had always faded, worn down and swept away by the stresses of whatever job he held at the time and by his constant need to live well. Sometimes a killing fed him for months, sometimes only for days, but it had never been too long before he felt the need to hunt again. And the intervals between needs had been getting shorter and shorter of late. On Saturday evening, one week after his last kill, he dressed in a suit and tie and put the long knife away into the sheath that he had sewn inside the jacket. Then he left to stalk, humming the tune to *Moon River* under his breath.

It was cool in Boston's Combat Zone but the hookers were out anyway in their silks and leathers. He passed them by for now, knowing that one of them would be an easy mark. He had money for a lure, and if he couldn't find anything better then he might have to use it on a whore. Normally, though, he didn't like to do hookers. They were too harsh, and sometimes too stoned or brain-burned to really know what it was that destroyed them. Some didn't even seem to care. He much preferred a sweeter prey, and they should all be unwary. After all, there had been no talk of killing. And he had only done four...here. Before that? Well, he had spent most of last year wandering through Mexico, until he tired of women with dusky skins. It was pale flesh he craved now.

He turned down a side street, letting himself drift along the edges of the crowd that strolled, and walked, and drank. He bought beers himself occasionally, as camouflage, but he only sipped at them. Even though his mouth was dry, he wanted his head clear. Once, he sensed someone following him and turned to see a tall youth approaching almost casually through the tourists. He slowed to a stop at an untenanted corner and slid a hand inside his coat. He even smiled and licked his lips as the man came by, but the would-be pickpocket read him for what he was and hurried on past, quickly disappearing among the other people on the street.

The corner lamppost made a convenient place to lean as he closed his eyes and imagined what it would have been like, the knife going in beneath the soft pad of the waist and ripping upward. The terror in the thief's face would have been a nice taste of meat, and it would not have mattered that he had killed a man. He had killed them before, when the need had grown too great and there were no females about. Such was not the case here, however. There were enough women for his taste.

He pushed away from the post and walked on. Thoughts of killing the man had put an edge to his hunger, but that would only make the coming feast more pleasant. And on the next street over he saw her. She was not alone at first, though soon her companion had gone. He followed her for three blocks before he was sure she was the one, older, late thirties perhaps, a little overweight. Such were always the best. They were often lonely and wanted so much to find a friend. He could be a friend. His throat constricted as he tried to swallow the laughter that bubbled up at the thought.

He moved in smoothly, a skill built of long practice. Within fifteen minutes he had made her acquaintance. In thirty more he was her friend and had her laughing. Three hours later he slaughtered her in the midst of their sex. This time he did it from behind, driving the thin blade into the spinal cord at the base of the skull while her head was thrown back in ecstasy. She grunted and jerked, and he held her tight, feeling almost as if his cock were inside of her at two places, as if he were fucking her in two places at the same time. Then his own orgasm rippled his spine and he let go of the knife so that her head flopped forward to let the blood run out of her mouth. He withdrew from her body and pushed it away, falling back on the bed and gasping for breath. It was some time before he could sleep.

SEPTEMBER 16TH; SUNDAY AGAIN:

Sunday morning came out of violent dreams that were his to enjoy. He woke from them reluctantly, rising and stretching until his joints snapped and popped. The woman in the bed with him was frozen and rigid, and, as with the others, he took her downstairs to be ruined in the cellar. He whistled while he sharpened his razors, but when he went to remove the hair he stopped, his fingers clenched in the thick mane. For the first time he noticed the black roots and realized that the woman was not a natural blonde.

No wonder she wanted the lights off, he thought.

He slammed her head down on the floor in anger and kicked at the inert body until it rocked like a sack of feed. All his work wasted. *Wasted*! He did not like being fooled. He kicked the body again. Oh, he'd have to cut her up. He'd have to hide her. *The bitch*! But he would put the whole damn pile of her under the ground, right down in the dirt where she belonged. He wouldn't even put her hands on the wall. And then he would show them. Even though the weekend was over and the hunting would be hard, he would show them.

He waited only for the night to come before leaving the house.

The streets were more crowded than he expected and he was pleased at first. It made him think that it was going to be easy, but he found out it wasn't. Most of the women he saw were with someone, and the one or two he made attempts at did not bite. It angered him that his charm was failing. It had never done so before. But maybe the hunger was too apparent in his eyes, or maybe there was something else making them wary.

It was almost like the times when his mother used to go out and scare away the local cats and dogs that came to the garbage pile out back of their house. She only did it so his daddy couldn't play with them. She had never liked daddy's idea of fun, the battery-acid filled eggs and the fish-hooked pieces of meat. She had certainly hated it when her son joined in, at daddy's urging. But daddy had taken momma out at the end. And he could remember himself as a little boy watching the holiness of his father's face during the swinging, and the swinging, and the swinging. He remembered even better the hard candy daddy had given him afterward, the pieces all sweet and sugary, and at the same time all red and sticky. He wanted some of it now, and something else for the electric dampness between his legs.

At last, in desperation, he began to study the prostitutes, and he soon found a blonde one who lounged at the foot of a stairwell in metallic gold shorts and a silken gold shirt tied up around her midriff. She had not been there before, or else his hunt would have been over earlier. Despite his aversion to hookers, this one was too lovely to pass up. Her hair was heavy and thick, hanging pure and pale to the shoulders, and her eyes were green, the exact shade of emerald that he loved. It was almost hard for him to believe that such a beautiful woman could be a street-whore, but the look she gave him when he mentioned money left no doubt. His mouth began to dry up and his teeth started to ache. It was all he could do not to touch himself. He wanted this one badly, and he knew he could have her as he reached for his wallet.

"How about my sister?" the little minx interjected, as she saw the flash of green that filled his palm. She put out a hand to toy with his tie. "The two of us are nearly as cheap as one."

"What sister?" he asked.

The woman gestured to the shadows within the stairwell behind her and a second whore stepped out. She seemed identical to the first, except for being dressed in silver shorts and a silver blouse. They were twins and he had never done twins before. Even though they were hookers, even though they would be easy, the thought of killing them both was almost more than he could handle. His erection was so painful that he could hardly stand up straight, and he only nodded at their encouraging words and passed out his cash. He could scarcely wait until he could get them home and unwrap them from their pretty packages.

It wasn't for nothing that he had rented a house so near the Combat Zone, though, with the girls striding along beside him, it seemed to take forever to cover the few short blocks to his place. He was sweating and shaking with impatience by the time he got his front door unlocked and ushered the two of them into the living room. They wasted no time once they were there.

The whore in gold kissed him hard on the mouth and then slid down his body, pulling open his shirt and licking at the hair and sweat beneath. On her knees, she nuzzled her face into his crotch and tongued open the hard zipper of his pants. A red-nailed hand slid up across the sweep of fabric at his front and unsnapped his trousers. He sprang out at her and she took him into her mouth, hollowing her cheeks as she drew on him.

The second whore slid a tongue into his ear, lapping softly at the delicate whorls; the pink tip probed deeper as she pushed up behind him and ground her mons into his backside, her hands sliding down across his waist to toy with the place where his cock was going in and out through her sister's lips. He twitched and groaned, almost unable to believe the pleasure. But it was all too fast. In another moment he would come, and he had to finish it. He had to finish it now.

His hand slipped beneath his jacket and brought out the knife. His heart thudded with need. But before he could strike, both women stepped back and away, suddenly out of reach. He blinked, then palmed the blade before either whore could see it and tucked it up inside his sleeve. Only then did he realize how cold his cock was outside the woman's mouth, and how much he wanted desperately to be back inside that warmth.

"What's wrong?" he asked. His voice was rough and vibrating, but he hated the almost whining undertone that threaded through his words.

"It's all right. Nothing's the matter," the one in gold said. "We just don't want to finish too fast do we? Besides, I don't think your front curtains are completely voyeur resistant, and I'd like to be where we can do anything we want without worrying about being watched."

He nodded, knowing that he should have been the one to make that comment. "The bedroom is upstairs," he said.

Her lips pouted. "How absolutely ordinary," she said. "Beds are much too conventional. What about...the basement!"

His heart skipped and a dim suspicion bloomed, only to fade as the two sisters slipped the knots on their blouses and shook their breasts free of the tissue-thin silk.

"But it's dirty down there," he said, making a halfhearted attempt to dissuade them.

"We know," the golden one said, arching an eyebrow. "We like it that way."

She walked up close and took him into her palm, milking him as she tugged him forward. "Come on," she breathed. "It'll be fun."

He could do nothing but follow as she led him through the kitchen toward the cellar. Her sister had already opened the door ahead of them and the light was on. They went down the steps together, the three of them side by side. There wasn't a speck of dust on those stairs, nor anywhere in the basement, but neither of the whores made a comment. They were too busy taking off their clothes. He watched them, and, at the same time, watched the room around him. There was no sign of death in the place, no smell except for Lysol. The tarp over the wall completely hid the nailed up hands, and the rugs on the floor lay just right over the loosened boards.

His eyes dilated. *Yes,* he thought to himself. This would be even better than upstairs. He could do it to them here, right on top of the other bodies he had buried. And they would never know. *Unless*— Unless he told them just before taking them out. His smile might have seemed nice to those who didn't know what it meant.

The first whore, the one who had been dressed in gold, mistook his smile and went down on him again. Her sister lifted his left hand and started to lick and suck at the little pads of meat between the fingers. He didn't mind at all. It was the right hand he used to kill.

He palmed the knife just as a tooth nicked his erection. But what was a little pain compared to the pleasure to come. He glanced down, smiling, and she looked up from her knees to meet his eyes. Her face was glowing, the bare skin shining almost translucently beneath the fluorescent lights, just like his father's face when killing and his mother's face when dying. He watched her slide a hand across her breasts and up her throat, across her lips where their two bodies merged. He could see her tongue moving beneath the drawn skin of her cheeks and could hold himself back no longer. Her eyes widened as his come spurted into her mouth. His own eyes closed, for a second, and when they shuttered open again the knife was out where everyone could see it. Only, he didn't use it.

The woman had released him from her lips and was smiling at him, drooling his thick ejaculate as she grinned up at the knife in his hand. She replaced his cock with two of her fingers, with two fingers and then her whole fist. And she was tugging on something; her face suddenly spiderwebbed with cracks. His eyes screamed, and his mouth screamed, and his body screamed, as her hand went down her throat and pulled her face off from the inside.

Behind that face was another, and, when she pulled that one off, another. He saw women that he had killed—the chubby Texas teen, the Mexican Banker's wife—but there were others, too many others that he had never seen, women, and men, and children, and animals, all of them dead. These weren't whores.

They weren't even human. But he had a sudden knowledge of who they were, or, rather, what they were. He knew because they were telling him, because he could watch the images flashing on the inside of his retinas like the fast-forwarded frames of some horrid movie.

They wanted him to know, he realized. They wanted him to understand how they had been following him since his childhood, using him for a stalking horse and then helping themselves to his kills, and those of his father before him. He had thought his daddy killed only animals before killing his mother! He should have known better, and now he did as these things unfolded the story for him. The beatings and the sexual abuse had never been random, as they had seemed at the time. The candy had never been an afterthought. His daddy had been nurturing him along, but it had been these creatures that had filled the bottles with hatred. And now they wanted him to believe that he was finished, used up, a worn-out tool whose charm was fading and whose urges were increasingly hard to control.

He stopped screaming and lifted the knife. He would show them who was used up. He would show them what it took. All he wanted in the world was to drive that blade down through the top of the kneeling thing's skull, but she was faster than he was as she bent her head forward and bit off his cock.

The knife slipped from his right hand, and at the same time the second whore/thing dropped her pretense of humanity and began to feed his left hand and arm into the clashing daggers that suddenly filled her mouth. The new pain was nothing compared to the first, however, and he was still looking down when the kneeling whore spat pieces of him out and opened the cavity of her face to the arterial stream that burst out at his waist. His arm gone, the second creature moved around to snap his spine with her hands, holding him up for a moment to bleed for her sister before dropping him on the floor like a wet bag of groceries.

He was beyond screaming now, and beyond moving. He could no longer even feel the pain. But he could still see. The first whore/thing got up and walked over to the basement wall where she stripped away the tarp that covered his trophies. She plucked out the nails with one finger and tossed a pair of dead hands across to her sister, keeping another pair for herself.

The being that had broken his back knelt down beside him with her pair. She kissed and licked them gently, and when they were completely covered with saliva, and with pearl-like strands of something else that had come up out of her throat, she slipped them on over her own hands as if fitting on gloves. He watched as the dead fingers came to life and started to move, dancing and twisting like a bowl of eels. They jerked and leaped at the end of their new owner's arms, dragging her forward with their strength.

And then they were on his chest. He did scream again, even though he would have sworn that he had nothing left, and the hands crawled up under his skin like dried white razors. His eyes bulged as they tore into a lung and then sliced downward into a kidney, bypassing the heart that thumped alone amid the white heaps of cracked ribs. The first whore had begun ripping up the boards underneath which he had hidden his victims, and the second got up and went to join her, leaving the hands buried inside his body like dead birds. Only, these birds were still moving, and digging swiftly deeper.

The blood that had been streaming out of him in a dozen places began to slow to a trickle, though that probably just meant he was dying. He found that he didn't care anymore. In fact, he welcomed it. He watched one of the whores peeling the skin off of a dead face and patting it into place over the void of her own features. He heard the two of them laughing and giggling over which piece to try on next, and he was grateful when his mind began to empty.

It wasn't so bad, he thought. *Not really. Bleeding to death doesn't take that long.*

But then, he wasn't quite dead yet. And it wasn't quite over either.

One of the creatures stepped on his cock where it lay like

a discarded toy on the floor. He watched as she bent over and picked it up, and he saw a new awareness come into her eyes. He saw her slide the wet piece of meat up the long slope of her thigh and shove it root first into the hole she had been using for a vagina, and he saw the pink flesh seal up around it like the puckering of a wound. A few strokes of a hard-nailed hand and it was erect, harder on the body of a whore than it had ever been on him.

The second hooker came and kicked him over onto his belly, then carefully positioned his head so he could watch as her sister knelt down behind him and pulled off his pants. He knew what they were planning to do, but that didn't mean he had to cooperate. He squeezed his eyes tightly shut as the thing moved up between his legs, and he was thinking about how a broken back would prevent him from feeling anything below the waist. He figured the bitches had finally outsmarted themselves there, and he almost smiled. They had made a mistake that neither he nor his daddy would ever have made. You didn't give the prey a way out of the pain.

At least that was what he figured for a moment, until the creature kneeling by his shoulders used her fingernails to rip off his eyelids and hold his head in place. Then he had to watch. And he found out that he could still feel *some* things, like the searing agony of a whore/thing's come spewing into his rectum, like the scraping of dead hands inside his body shell as they sealed off ruptured arteries and veins to keep him alive.

In the end though, when the thing had done with him and he had been nailed to his trophy wall and had his cheeks stuffed with sweets, his thoughts did not dwell on his pain. They were focused on the squirming movements inside his peritoneum as the dead hands curled up tightly and began to encyst. The whore/things had one more use for him, he realized. When the hands had gone inside his body they had been covered with strands of tiny beads that resembled pearls, but which he now knew to be eggs. And those eggs had just been fertilized.

SPLATTER OF BLACK

The moonlight settled over the December beach like snow birds coming in to roost on an arctic plain. And the midnight world was brush-stroked in white, the white of sand and shells and stones, the white of bones and ghosts. In the midst of that white was a splatter of black, or what could have been red in brighter hours. It reminded Kyle Dupree of a snowflake in negative, and he thought it was incredibly beautiful until he realized what it represented. Then he dropped the cigarette he'd walked out on the beach to smoke, and reached down with his thumb to unsnap the strap that held his Colt Trooper in its holster.

The pop of the hammer strap coming undone was louder than he could have imagined, loud enough to draw attention. A dozen sleek heads lifted from their feast, like orchid petals blooming in time-lapse photography, and the moon washed their faces pale. Down across blood-layered muzzles and hollow cheeks, Kyle watched the slow drip of gore, the power of the vision matched by a medley of growls and coughing grunts, and by a noise like children giggling. But below that night fugue was the sound that truly jelled Kyle's horror, the bubbling rasp of a half-eaten man trying to scream through his own fluid.

At one small level of mind, above the nightmarish shrieking of his brainstem survival mechanisms, Kyle understood that he had just solved the riddle of the Bay St. John disappearances. It was a case he and the rest of the police had been working since late October, when Hurricane Carmin had lightly slapped the Mississippi coast town and more folks than expected had turned up gone. Others had disappeared since.

A disturbing the peace call had brought Kyle to the Bay Yacht Club tonight. After sight of a uniform calmed the two women who'd been arguing, Kyle had taken a moment for a walk and a smoke, lured by the calm acceptance of the night into going further than he intended. Half a mile down the beach he'd stumbled on a scene out of a freak-zoo nightmare. That nightmare had twelve incarnations and there were only six shells in his pistol. He had two autoloaders at his hip, some spares in his belt, but didn't imagine he'd have time to reload. He took a step backward.

Then another.

A glance to the west showed the Yacht Club lights glistening moistly. Marsha would be there. Kyle had hoped to see her tonight, had been glad of being switched unexpectedly to coast patrol. He'd met her here while moonlighting as a security guard to cover his father's gambling debts. She had slept with him on this beach...and done other things. He'd been falling in love with her before the hurricane cut them apart—though she had certainly not been among those who disappeared. Kyle had heard of the places she'd been seen, and of the things she was seen doing. He didn't know whether he hated her for those other men or not, but he knew he couldn't lead these things on the beach back toward her.

As if to punctuate his thoughts, one of the creatures took a step toward him and Kyle drew his Trooper and fired into the ground to frighten it. Most animals didn't like the sound of gunfire, but the pop of a .38 going off didn't faze these things. It only made them spread out away from the body on the ground, good evidence that they knew what guns were for. That meant he'd just wasted a shell.

At the east end of the beach lay an abandoned sawmill of the fifties that had still been sturdy enough to resist Hurricane Carmin. Kyle had played in it as a kid and knew it well. If he couldn't head for the Club he'd have to go for the mill. He turned and ran.

Kyle's explosion of movement took the night creatures by surprise and he added another twenty yard lead to the twenty-five he already had. And he knew how to run. A few college track trophies still hid in his garage, for what he had always rather perversely called the 440 and 880, measured in yards rather than meters. The sawmill was about four hundred yards off, and though Kyle was heavier than he was five years ago he still remembered to tuck his head down and pump his arms perpendicular to his body.

The tightly packed sand gave a decent surface and on an unseasonably warm night he'd left his cumbersome coat in the car. Even the heavy steel frame of the revolver in his right hand didn't upset his balance. Nor did the jingling of his belt gear bother him. He could hear the pursuit beginning behind him and that motivation took care of any nagging details.

Kyle glanced back to see that he was holding his own, though the pack hadn't found its stride yet. Strangely, the creatures didn't seem that adept at running, as if four-legged motion were new to them. Kyle figured they could catch an aging sprinter, though, if they had enough distance. His chest was already starting to feel like a fired-up barbecue inside.

His next backward glance verified his fear. The pack was moving more smoothly now, as if learning how to run at the same time as they hunted. Even their bodies seemed to have altered, becoming leaner and more sharply angled, like animated wind sculptures. And they had closed the gap by ten yards, in almost an instant.

Kyle tucked his head into his chest again, concentrating on wringing the last measure of adrenaline from his body and trying to ignore the growing sound of moving sand behind him. With nearly a hundred yards still to go he could feel his lead peel away, to twenty yards, fifteen, to ten. But the sawmill loomed now. He could see the ramp leading up from the beach and the door beyond with its weathered paint and broken panes of glass. He needed just a few more steps but didn't think he was going to get them.

Then, as his right arm swung back he let it continue behind him and fired the pistol into the pack at his heels. The bullet hit something and punctured a scream, a near human scream, and the distraction slowed the pack for the seconds Kyle needed. He kicked in the last of his strength to vault the railing and slam through the door into the mill. Teeth and bodies grazed his leg as he crashed the heavy oaken panel shut and shoved home the rusted bolt with enough force to tear open his palm. He scarcely noticed the blood.

To his left was the old supervisor's office, above the tool room, and Kyle took the stairs in a few running steps. He was at the top when the remaining glass in the mill's door shattered inward. The door itself came apart next, with the rotten sound of an overripe watermelon splitting on cement. Kyle fired into a roiling mass of shadows but heard only the whine of a ricochet. They would be coming in a moment.

There was no door on the supervisor's office, and nothing to build a barricade, but the heavy block and tackle that had once been used to unload timber trucks hung in front of his face, and holes in the roof let in enough moonlight to show him the narrow I-beam that ran the length of the building. He grabbed the rope from the block and tackle and swung the long way out onto the beam.

A pair of slanted eyes flared red at the railing of the office behind him, and the ivory gleam of incisors shone in the moonlight. Kyle fired twice, spacing his shots, and grunted in satisfaction as the creature was slammed backward by a lead fist. Satisfaction turned to dismay as the thing got up again and leaped from the railing toward the beam where he stood.

It was an impossible jump, but the creature made it, catching both front feet on the narrow strut. Kyle glimpsed a massive hydrocephalic cranium wrapped around a blunt muzzle that was far too full of teeth. Then he fired his last shot point-blank into its face as it started to pull its way up. The .38 Specials that Kyle used had heavy powder and 158-grain leads. They were plenty strong enough to take down a man. But this one bounced off. At less than ten feet it bounced off. Kyle saw it all, with the split-second vision that occurs only at times of great stress. The bullet struck the creature between its staring eyes and the flesh just seemed to flow beneath it and shrug it away. Apparently they adapted to bullets even quicker than they did to running.

The slug's impact did knock the thing back, but didn't knock its paws loose from the I-beam. Even as those paws started to elongate into something that resembled hands, Kyle stepped forward and kicked it in the mouth. This blow snapped its hold, sent it spinning down into the darkness.

Kyle quickly flipped open the revolver and ejected the spent .38s. The brass casings winked in the moonlight as they tumbled down through space. An HKS autoloader hung at Kyle's belt and he slapped it into the pistol, twisting the knob to the right to fill the weapon's hungry maw again. He had the hammer cocked over a loaded chamber before the first empty tinkled on the concrete floor below.

So they piss on .38s, he thought. *Let's see 'em eat a few .357 hollowpoints and get up again.*

Feeling exposed, Kyle turned and began to make his way down the long beam toward the far end of the building, putting one foot straight in front of the other with barely an inch to spare on either side. Where the beam wed itself to the southern wall of the mill he faced around again. Just above him ran a long row of mostly shattered windows that looked out over the night ocean and flooded this end of the building with silver light. Kyle's back might be to the wall, but his hunters had only one way to come at him, down that beam in the full brightness of the moon.

Kyle took his first deep breath in what seemed like hours, but he scarcely had time to exhale before a new assault began. All along he'd been thinking it was animals he was dealing with. Smart maybe. With some pretty strange abilities. But animals nonetheless. That changed when he heard the wrenching sounds of tearing metal from the opposite end of the span on which he stood. Down there in the darkness, down there in the suddenly hard-edged night, something was using tools to rip the I-beam from its moorings.

An undulating wave passed through the steel, like a suspension bridge whipped by earthquake-powered winds, and Kyle felt metal turn to spaghetti under his feet. He leaped for the wall as the beam fell away, his flailing left hand catching a window frame and clutching hard. Slivers of broken glass pierced his palm, wringing a moan from thinned lips, but he hooked the revolver in his other hand over the wooden frame and used it to pull himself up. Howls of disappointment rose from the shadows below him, and then his feet found purchase on the mill wall and a final surge carried him through the window to tumble free in the space beyond.

He dropped only a few feet before his fall was broken by the massive spill of sawdust that had built up over years outside the mill. Hitting at the top, he cartwheeled to the bottom. Only a dozen feet away lay the Gulf of Mexico, and he wanted it. But between him and the water moved shadows that he feared. Within those shadows he saw the wink of red eyes, but they were still looking above him at the window through which he had crashed. To the right lay the deep-well darkness of the sawmill's foundation, undermined by high tides. It looked too much like a grave to suit Kyle, but better a darkness he didn't know than one he knew was deadly. He rolled into it and started to crawl.

Inside of a minute Kyle began to wonder if he'd made a mistake. The seemingly open foundation had closed around him until he was crawling in a narrow tunnel that recalled childhood nightmares of being buried. And he could smell the animals that had dug it, could feel the slime of their passing on the floor beneath and the walls around. It was too late to turn back now, though, and the tunnel too narrow even if he tried. He began to panic.

Kyle always carried a flashlight with his belt gear. He hadn't used it yet because he didn't want to ruin what little night vision he had. But now his panic screamed for brightness. He tried to unhook the flash, then tore it free from its loop and switched it on. The lens was cracked but the bulb still worked, and the coming of light stilled enough of the fear to let the human part of his mind reassert control over his body. The tunnel was as empty as a ruin ahead of him. And he could see where it began to rise and widen.

Something grabbed his boot.

Kyle was thrown over onto his left side as a huge form filled the crawlspace behind him and a set of flensing-knife teeth ripped into the leather protecting his foot. He shoved the pistol toward his attacker and fired twice, bludgeoning his eardrums with noise and filling the burrow with ozone. The shape behind him vented a jackhammer shriek and turned tornado in the tunnel, twirling about itself like some hopped up kitten chasing its tail.

Kyle didn't know if the .357s were too much for the thing's defenses or if he had just gotten lucky and hit a vital spot. He didn't even know if the thing was dead, but at least his boot was free. He used it against the soft soil as he started pushing himself hurriedly away.

A crackling, tearing sound bloomed in his ringing ears, like Styrofoam crumpling in a man's hand. The thing he had shot went limp and seemed to deflate, and something small and whip-thin, a lot of somethings, flashed past him in the tunnel, sliding over his legs and under his buttocks, snaking past his face to kiss his cheek with slime. Their touch was worse than what had grabbed his leg, and he hooted in fear and tried to throw himself backward. The tunnel ended abruptly and he sprawled out into an open space. There was a faint light there. It came from candles set in sconces along the wall.

He was in the engine room beneath the mill. It didn't look abandoned. The old diesel-fed generator, which had rusted badly with years of salt air exposure, was clearly in the process of being refurbished. It had even been turned on recently. Kyle could smell diesel oil and see where someone had worked over a small leak in the fuel tank housing. Beside the tank was a rack containing brand new 12-volt batteries for use in sparking the generator, and various tools were scattered about on the ground, tools that required human type hands.

Behind the generator were the rococo shadows of more equipment, to one side a cement wall strung with what he took to be old sawdust bags. One of those bags seemed to twitch and Kyle turned his flashlight on it. He wished he hadn't. It was one of a dozen bodies that hung along the wall, some partially eaten and some intact. Most were dried out husks with the flesh like string jerky over their bones, but there were a few in better shape, some with skin that looked almost alive. Kyle recognized one of the best preserved ones as Billy Matranga, the Yacht Club cook who had been among the first to disappear.

Billy opened his eyes when the light hit him, though the pupils were rolled so far back in his head that he surely couldn't see anything. The mouth opened too, but it wasn't Billy's will that moved it. Something was pushing his lips apart from the inside. Kyle gagged as a wallet-thick mass of black eel-like shapes slid down the cook's chin and dropped to the floor. A few more individuals forced their way out through the man's nostrils and followed their brethren into the shadows.

Acid saliva filled Kyle's mouth; acid tears burned his eyes. He couldn't tell if it were from anger or fear. He had known Billy, had dipped snuff with him behind the gym in high school and even dated his sister a time or two. The gun was in Kyle's fist and he walked up close and pointed it at Billy's face. The man's drifting pupils rolled down till they were looking right at Kyle, but the policeman saw no intelligence in those holes, no fear of death, no begging for release. His memory supplied a more human expression and he lowered the pistol and stepped away.

The rasp of sliding sand in the entrance tunnel spun Kyle on his heels. His heart shifted into running gear but there was nowhere for his feet to take him. He squatted, both light and revolver thrust out before him. The flashlight beam caught something moving quickly and his finger tightened on the pistol's trigger. But the light was reflecting off human skin instead of leathery black hide, off a human face instead of a muzzle and teeth. He held his fire as Marsha came scooting out of the tunnel on all fours and threw herself into his arms.

"Oh, thank God, Kyle! Thank God! I— One of the girls said— She saw you. I came...to find out. And those things!"

Her body thrummed with tension as he held her close. After a moment, though, he pushed her back to arm's length. Her emerald dress was filthy from bellying through the dirt and her blonde hair was matted and slimed. She was still lovely to him.

"How did you get past them?" he asked.

"I— Well I didn't. I mean...they...seemed to want me here." She closed her eyes for a moment to regain composure. "It was like they were herding me," she added as she looked up again.

"Did you see anything in the tunnel?"

"The tunnel?"

"Yeah, I shot one of them in the tunnel. Did you see it?"

"No, nothing."

"Shit! Shit! Shit!"

"What do they want from us, you think?"

Kyle dropped his hands from the girl's shoulders. "Well I doubt they wanna party with us," he said bitterly. He knew his tone would hurt her, or maybe he hoped it would. He kept seeing her with those porcelain legs open for someone else. He'd like to hurt her at least that much.

Marsha's eyes didn't tear but her gaze lost its lock on his face and turned down to the earth. Kyle saw her shoulders quiver, thought he heard the hiccup/hush of a sob.

"You hate well," she said. Her words were flat, without emotion, like the crack of high-powered rifle being fired. She turned away, moving slowly toward the shadows of the wall.

Kyle could still feel the silk sweetness of Marsha's dress in his hands. He started to call to her, to tell her that he could never hate her. Then he remembered what was hanging on the wall toward which she moved so casually.

"Marsha! Wait!"

Kyle didn't want her to see. But by that time she was at the wall and would have had to see. He switched on his flash, splashing a yellow glow against the shadows, against Marsha. The woman of his dreams was looking over her shoulder at him. Her pupils were wide. She had taken out one of Billy Matranga's eyes and was eating it.

"Sorry, lover." She shrugged. "I'd intended dragging the game out a while longer but that might leave you wired too tight to enjoy what's coming. Besides, there is a certain elegance to utter brutality. Don't you think?" She was laughing openly now, not trying to stifle it as she had when Kyle had mistaken giggles for the sobs he wanted to hear.

All emotions except anger burned suddenly out of Kyle, like a light bulb going dark as its filaments fused. He raised the pistol and cocked the hammer. Marsha froze, cruel laughter fossilized on her lips.

"What the hell are you?" he asked.

The woman's eyes glittered with light; her mouth was a saber curve of shadow. "Power," she answered. Her glance flicked toward Kyle's feet and at the same time the ground erupted beneath him, spewing a shrapnel of sand into the air. His legs were sucked into a pit and razored talons slapped the Colt from his hand. Something meaty and slick enveloped him from behind and he was dragged down onto his back, dark shapes all around him. For the first time he saw the creatures up close.

Like many of his friends, Kyle had collected insects as a kid. One he remembered in particular, a spiky yellow and black caterpillar that had spun a clear, grayish-brown chrysalis around itself. You could see the worm right through the skin of the cocoon, and he had dropped it in the formaldehyde just like that and kept it for years.

These things were like that chrysalis, like a clear and elastic exoskeleton the same color as the sap that comes out of old pine trees in winter. The only difference was that inside each cocoon was a woman. Each was alive and moving, their limbs directing the flow of the chrysalis into whatever shape was needed or desired. Kyle saw muzzles and beaks and half-human faces, suckered tentacles and paws. He saw hands, as they picked him up and slammed him against the generator's fuel tank, as they bound his wrists in front of him with nylon cord. The stench of diesel oil filled his nose as the hole in the tank came unplugged and began to drip into the soil. It ran down under his back to soak his pants.

Marsha's eyes were on him and Kyle looked up to match her stare. She smiled, in the way that pouted her lips up as if to kiss. He watched her run her fingernails across Billy Matranga's stomach and his gorge rose as something beneath the man's skin mimicked the slow swirl of her hand. A moment later a long dark body poked its way out of Billy's belly button and curled around the woman's finger like a wedding band. Kyle fought the urge to vomit. He wouldn't give her that, or anything else if he could help it.

"You asked me what I am," Marsha said, as she turned from the wall to face him. "I can't tell you. I don't know myself yet. But whatever it is I owe to our little friends here." She lifted her hand to show the thin ring of living tissue encircling her finger.

"They came in with the hurricane," she continued. "Who knows where the wind picked them up. At first I thought I'd found the only one. Right here on the beach. We were having a hurricane party and I came outside to escape some geek who was pawing me. You were working, remember? Can you believe, I saw it on the sand and thought it was a piece of driftwood? Picked it up to throw it back. It didn't wanna go.

"It was male. The other one was female. The bigger one. Pregnant. But I didn't know that then. The one I found was just looking for a place to attach itself. I won't tell you where. You'll see soon enough."

Marsha threw back her head and spread her arms, her fingers curved like scorpion stings. Her voice was low, throbbing. It echoed in the small chamber. "I tried to fight it," she said. "At first. But the feeling! The feeling was so immense! Of having all your senses running on nitroglycerine, of having power to do all those things you always wanted to do but couldn't get away with."

She looked back at Kyle and smiled like a predator showing its teeth. "Better than sex," she said.

Kyle saw lips he had kissed filled now with savage glee, a body he had held strained with barely leashed violence. He had to try and break through to her, had to find something left that was human.

"This isn't you, Marsha. You know that. Inside. Somewhere. You have to keep fighting!"

A fingernail of hope scratched lightly across Kyle's neck as Marsha's smile faltered and her eyes seemed to soften. She lowered her arms, tucked them behind her back. "Kyle!" Her voice had filled with hurt. But the sound of pain didn't go with the other sound Kyle heard, the rasp of a zipper sliding open. He leaned forward in confusion. Then hands reached around from behind Marsha to cup her breasts. And Billy Matranga pulled himself loose from the wall and nuzzled up against her.

Marsha grinned at Kyle and tongued her teeth. She turned her head to meet Billy's mouth with hers, her fingers still playing whore against his crotch. Billy groaned at her touch, then drew back from the kiss to gaze at Kyle over Marsha's shoulder, his one eye winking at the joke.

"Afraid it's not gonna happen, my friend," Billy said, his voice like knife blades in a shredder. "Once they're attached they *never* turn loose. 'Cept when you die. And they change you a bit emotionally. Aggression! Fear! Like meat and potatoes to them. Really, they just release what was inside already. You didn't know Marsha was such a vicious hag, did you?"

"Go fuck yourself," Kyle said.

Billy shrugged. "Strange you saying that. I was just going to tell you about what interesting hormones these things have. Their males take to women and their females to men. We get to hatch the babies. I was first. You're the next. But hey, at least we don't have to carry 'em for nine months.

"Of course, you we're going to do a little differently. They're evolving, you see. Learning to mimic the human reproductive system so they can speed up their adaptation to a land environment. That's why Marsha arranged for you to be on coast patrol this evening, and why we staged that little tiff you saw back at the Club. She just thought it would be fitting. 'Apropos,' I believe she said. Since you've had her, it's only right she should have you. After all, turnabout is fair play."

Kyle had no idea what Billy was talking about, but he soon began to catch on as he saw the hem of Marsha's skirt lift and flutter in a tiny breeze. Only, there was no breeze in this place. Then he forgot his resolution not to vomit as a black cylinder the length of a nightstick poked out from under the woman's dress and wrapped itself around her thigh.

Kyle came to his knees as he heaved bile, but in an instant as he looked down hope flared in his chest. He was going to give up smoking for the new year. But this was only December. He had smoked half a cigarette tonight, just before stumbling on Marsha and her friends. There were two more Camels in the pack in his uniform pants pocket, and there should be a cigarette lighter in there as well.

He glanced at Marsha and Billy. The woman had fallen to her hands and knees and the man was leaning forward to insert his penis into her rectum. Black worms, much bigger than any Kyle had seen before, flowed out from the corners of the room to surround the two. Kyle saw necklaces of teeth on their undersides as they bit into flesh, as they stitched themselves into and through the flesh of the lovers and diffused through the skin until they could quilt themselves together.

A caul formed around the doubled body, then wrenched and distorted itself to create horns, sloping jaws, venomed fangs. Marsha's trunk and limbs began to distort themselves as well, to spread out venous streamers as if they were becoming the nervous system of some monstrous crossbreed. Billy seemed to shrink, to be swallowed up even as his penis had been swallowed by Marsha's heat.

No! Kyle thought. These things were not Marsha and Billy.

And he wouldn't be Kyle for much longer if he didn't find a way out of here.

Quivering and twitching in a sympathetic chorea, the other chimeras stood with their eyes locked on Marsha's and Billy's ripening. And in that unobserved moment Kyle scrabbled at his pocket with rope-numbed hands and found...nothing. The lighter was gone, fallen out somewhere along the way. And now Marsha's head was turning to face him, her eyes sparking like railroad flares, her curling mouth dripping an evil smile. "Turnabout is fair play," Billy had said.

The inside of Kyle's head was kaleidoscoping as the woman/man/thing rose up onto spined feet, a dark and living wand whipping madly between its legs. The other creatures had stepped away from Kyle, leaving him for their hybrid Queen. And she was coming at him, teasing him by circling in behind the rack of lead-acid batteries that fed the generator.

Kyle's mind centered. *Batteries. Current.* His wrist-bound hands went out to grasp a pair of insulated wires and drag a heavy battery off the rack onto his knees. The pool of leaking diesel had spread out wide beneath him. The fumes hung thick in the air.

Then the Queen came over the rack at him and he shouted up into her face: "Fair play this, you bitch," as he touched the positive and negative wires together just at the surface of the spilled fuel. He felt current go out along the wires, and a gush of yellow-ugly flame erupted. Kyle's pants caught fire. His attacker recoiled, in startlement at first, and then in fear as the diesel hit critical temperature and fireballed. Kyle was already on his feet by then, on his feet and screaming, and diving head first toward the tunnel that had led him to this slaughtering place.

He hit hard, rolling to douse his burning pants, and out of the corner of his eye he saw Marsha's head swivel toward him, saw her features flicker back to normal as her symbionts fled. He was already in the tunnel but he stopped, turned back. Billy fell from between her legs as he was torn in two by something massive and black that ripped its way out through his pelvis. The fire ate at the thing, sent it writhing toward the shadows. But Kyle's eyes were on the woman. For just a moment, Marsha's face showed a very human fear. Kyle reached his hands toward her, and felt the oxygen suck away from around him as the flames reached the leaking fuel tank and exploded the metal.

Kyle saw Marsha's golden hair turn scarlet with fire as he was smashed backward into the tunnel, his face blistered by a savagely hot wind. The burrow partially collapsed on top of him, smothering the running flickers of red that still chewed at his uniform. He rolled over beneath the dirt and pushed forward into the cool reach of what was left of the tunnel, his closed lids filled with a bright darkness. Behind him in the inferno came the sandpaper shrieks of things that didn't sound remotely human. Kyle's eyes grew wet anyway; one of those things had been the woman he loved.

After a while, Kyle wormed his way out onto the beach and started limping on charred legs toward the sound of distant sirens. The mill burned hugely at his back, scattering smoke and fading screams into the ashes of what would be a cold morning, the first cold morning of a long winter.

A few hundred yards up the beach Kyle saw a faint glint of plastic on the sand. He'd worked the knots loose from his hands with his teeth, and he reached down and picked up his lost lighter. Its flame seemed dim somehow. But it still worked. Maybe he *wouldn't* give up smoking.

A sound made him look up, and on the ground a few feet away squirmed a dark and brutalized shape. A flick of his lighter showed Kyle what was left of the man he'd seen being eaten on this beach at the start of this horror of a night. The face was half gone and the belly had been strip-mined of heart and intestines. But the black eel shapes of the hurricane creatures were hanging all over him and through him, trying to knit him together, trying to animate the dead.

Kyle turned the flame of the lighter as high as it could go and tossed it into the open well of the corpse's throat. He walked on past, not stopping at the sudden blaze of fire that crackled behind him. He did stop when the wind began to rise. It was blowing from out over the ocean. Moving toward the beach.

BLIND

Woke from a scarred sleep,
carrying your bruises
all the way to the bone.

Remembering whisky and hate,
the slide of sick eyes
in mandalas of desire,
sweet acid razors
beneath my tongue...
and yours.

In the heated darkness,
in a sacrament of sweat,
you spilled your need in my face,
wasted my heart and walked away

blind.

RUINS AND WRAITHS

Dawn came red, like a hemorrhaging wound in the eastern sky above a world gone dead. The man who called himself Rayth stepped from the car where he'd slept the night and took a piss in the street. There wasn't a person around to see him. As far as he knew there was no one anywhere on earth. At least not alive.

Three weeks ago Rayth had awakened in the city of St. Louis and found it empty. Oh, the buildings had been there. The cars and buses. But the people? They were simply gone; he knew not where. So far, every new city and town he visited had been the same. Though yesterday, as he'd crossed the Twenty-Four Mile Bridge from Greater New Orleans into a little town called Mandeville, Louisiana, he'd almost run over a dead and stinking body that had been lying out for days and been...fed upon.

Rayth didn't particularly like to remember the body. Nor the strange tracks outlined in dried blood around it. He had a cigarette and a beer for breakfast before climbing back into the sleek black Jag that he'd claimed for his own. He cranked the engine, then stomped the gas pedal and spun the steering wheel in the middle of the road, the tires smoking and shrieking as the machine whipped around in a power slide. He let up on the gas, pumped the brake. The Jaguar rocked to a stop, its nose pointing directly into the new sun. Although he had generally been headed south, any direction was as good as another. He took the road in front of his car, heading out of Mandeville for whatever the east might bring him.

A few hours down the highway, with the warm blue of the Gulf of Mexico gleaming in the distance, Rayth came into a medium-sized town in Mississippi whose name he didn't care to know. A strip mall loomed suddenly to the Jaguar's right, and on the spur of the moment Rayth whipped off into the parking lot and rolled to a stop in front of the beveled glass doors of the main entrance. A sign advertised a music store and it seemed like time for some CDs other than the ones he'd found in the car. At the moment, he wasn't feeling very Tragically Hip.

The Jag's engine fell quiet in the early morning. He got out, then leaned through the open window on the passenger side and took up two pistols from the seat, tucking them into his belt—one in front and one behind. The one in front was a Colt Double Eagle .45, the other a Sig Sauer 9mm, and he felt better for having them even though he'd seen nothing yet that he had to kill.

Barely inside the mall doors, though, Rayth sensed something different about *this* place. It didn't seem dead like everywhere else he'd been in the last few weeks. Maybe it was the smell. *Some kind of faint perfume*, he thought. Or maybe it was some non-random swirl of air that only a living thing will stir. Whatever it was, it made him draw his pistols, thumb back the hammers, and step closer to the nearest wall. And he wondered, if someone *were* alive here, what coincidence had brought him to this same place? Or was it coincidence?

Ahead lay the center of the building, filled with a dry fountain that gleamed beneath sunlight falling through clear windows above it. He used the fountain for cover, circling it on soft feet, then stopped cold as he heard a tearing sound, like cloth being shredded. From a store just a dozen feet away came a dream of movement.

Rayth's eyes narrowed. So he wasn't alone in the world. But who, or what, was here with him? Was it friend? Or enemy? He remembered, all of a sudden, a torn body and bloody tracks that had looked...almost human.

The store had two entrances and he took the one farthest from the source of the movement, slipping quietly over the threshold into the shadows of the place. The grips of the guns felt warm against his palms. He was glad he'd practiced shooting. He hoped he wouldn't have to shoot now.

All around Rayth hung a display of satin and beauty—the store was a Victoria's Secret—and as he stepped from behind a rack of shimmering nightgowns he saw a woman. Young. Tall. She didn't see him. Or hear him.

He watched her.

The woman was dressed in tattered finery, a silken shift of black that outlined her slender form, torn nylons that clasped her legs. And she carried an evil looking silver knife with which she was dissecting pieces of lingerie. She'd already put on the top of a scarlet corset with the sides slashed into bright ribbons.

Rayth let the hammers down on the pistols and she heard the click, spinning to face him, her eyes going wide. His own eyes dilated as he saw her, her body all adrenaline and curves, with pale blue irises and ripened lips. She wore her blonde hair cut very short except for two wings that fell down near the front to brush her cheeks.

The woman lifted her knife, not showing fear. A brittle smirk smeared her mouth. And Rayth smiled and shook his head, lowered the pistols to his sides. In another moment she lowered her own weapon and they stood looking at each other across a distance of a few feet.

"You're not one of them," she said. Her voice was rich and rough at the same time.

"Who are them?" he asked.

"Them! The ones who came after."

It hit him what she meant. After the emptying. After the people were gone.

He started to say as much when a sound from elsewhere in the mall brought both their heads around. The sound combined raucous laughter and the slur of half drunken voices, and four men came striding through the center of the mall with rifles and liquor bottles in their hands.

Rayth moved quickly up beside the woman, and she glanced at him but did not back away. His yellow-brown eyes met her blue ones, and he saw a knowing smile flit across her beautiful mouth. He eased back the hammer on the Sig 9mm and handed it to her. She took it like she knew how to use it.

"The ones who came after," she said again.

And now, as the four strangers caught sight of the two of them in the store and stopped to stare, Rayth saw that they were not *quite* men. The "ones who came after" wore the clothes and faces of human beings, but the clothes did not fit and the faces looked like masks that were not yet finished. The eyes were the worst.

One of the...things whooped drunkenly at sight of the girl. Another stepped forward, as if it were the leader.

"Damn," that one said, in a voice that *almost* perfectly aped the drawl of a good old southern boy. "What a fine lookin' woman."

None of the beings paid any attention to Rayth. That was a mistake. Nor did they seem to notice that his right hand was half hidden behind his back and that a cold smile flickered over his lips.

The leader took another step forward, holding out a bottle of whiskey. "Now, little lady," it said. "You have yourself a drink with us and then we'll all have some fun. Your boyfriend there can even watch."

Though the "mask" that it wore showed the emotions only poorly, the being grinned and winked at Rayth. And Rayth smiled back, a large smile, with his mouth dripping shadows. He shook his head slowly, speaking clearly and quietly:

"It's gonna take more balls than the four of you've got," he said. "If you've got *any*."

The leader stopped smiling, and the woman lifted her pistol and shot it between the legs where a man's testicles would be.

Both the woman's aim and her choice were good. The wounded being double over, screaming in agony, and the other three mimics went for their own weapons, dropping gin and whiskey bottles to crash on the tile floor like soft explosions. Their movements were all too slow.

Rayth slid the .45 from behind his back, punched it forward and shot one being through the throat, the bullet leaving behind the liquid sound of spraying blood. But already the barrel of the Colt had shifted left. Rayth fired again, double-actioning the trigger. A second being went down, knocked flat by the punch of a heavy-grain bullet hammering into its chest. The last creature standing had its rifle nearly into shooting position, its half formed face striving for a snarl as it saw the grin curving Rayth's lips. It had to know it was dead even before the lead slug took out its left eye and half the brain behind it.

From a position on its knees, still screaming in pain, the leader tried to reach for a gun. The woman took a step toward it and emptied the 9mm into its body, petals of scarlet blooming over its stomach, chest, and head. What was left fell forward, thudding face first on the floor.

Rayth watched the faint blue smoke of burnt gunpowder drift in the mall, then glanced at the woman. She was looking at him, no expression on her face. He reached out and took the gun from her hand—she didn't resist—and reloaded it with a fresh clip, chambering a shell before handing it back to her with the hammer down. She grasped it with long fingers.

Rayth hooked his boot under the dead leader's body and flipped the thing over onto its back. Its face came off, hanging down on its shoulder like a clump of half melted candle wax. It wasn't a mask, but some kind of tissue, some pseudo-flesh that had grown over an inner sphere of nearly translucent gelatin.

"They want to be us," the woman said. "I saw a bunch of them. I was at the beach. Wishing I wasn't alone. Thinking maybe I should just walk out into the water and finish what began with everyone else. Then *they* came. They flopped out of the sea like jellyfish on a red tide. But they were big. With no faces. No bodies really. Just lumps. I saw them change. They grew arms and legs. When they started forming heads, I ran, though I knew they'd be coming after me. And I knew they'd be getting more and more like us each day."

"How many do you think there are?"

"A lot, I suspect. I bet they're coming out of every big body of water on Earth. Every ocean. Every river. I think they're here to replace the missing ones. The people. Maybe they're the reason so many went missing in the first place."

"But why? How? And why wasn't...everyone taken?"

She shrugged. "An experiment. An invasion. Maybe it's the Rapture." She looked at him. "You know. When the good folks get taken up to meet Jesus in the sky."

He smiled slightly. "The good folks?"

She didn't look away from him; she didn't blush. "I haven't exactly been an angel," she said.

"I have," he replied.

She shrugged again. "Whatever it was. Maybe it didn't get *everyone* else. If there are two of us, maybe there are more. Like us. Leftovers."

"And what about these things?" Rayth muttered, nodding toward the four corpses, which were slowly disintegrating into wet masses of protoplasm. "If these keep...becoming. Will anyone be able to tell them apart from real people?"

"I don't know," the woman said, but her face gave a different answer.

So they went out of that place.

They found Rayth's Jag and climbed in, and he cranked the engine and the stereo, heading out on the road again. Barely a mile down the way they found the interstate and Rayth let the black machine slip up the on-ramp like a predator hunting. At the top he punched the gas and worked the shift, taking the car into top gear at 120 miles per hour down the center of the freeway.

The woman lit a cigarette and leaned back in the seat, and closed her eyes to listen to the music. After a moment she said one word: "Jill."

He understood what it took in trust for her to give him her name.

And one last time he thought of St. Louis. He thought of waking up on the banks of the Mississippi River. He thought of becoming.

HELL IS FOR CHILDREN

Danny looked up at the sound of his mother's voice, his mouth full of feathers. He spat them out and came quickly to his feet, stopping only long enough to toe dirt and leaves over the dead bird he'd been eating. He wiped his lips on his jacket, careful to leave the blood smear on the inside sleeve where his mother wouldn't see it before he had a chance to clean it off. Then he trotted to meet her, smiling sweetly.

"Yes, mother," he said. "What is it?"

"It's time for supper. Didn't you hear your father call you?"

"No," he said truthfully. "But I'm not really hungry anyway."

He wanted to tell her he had just eaten, but he didn't think she'd approve of raw blackbird. He sniggered at the thought, but quickly blanked his face as he saw his mother frown.

"I don't think it's very funny for a twelve-year-old boy to ignore his father and lie to his mother," she said.

"But I wasn't—" he started to say, then broke off at the shake of his mother's head.

"Just don't say anything else. You'll only get yourself in deeper. Now get on in the house and wash your hands."

"Yes, mom," he said, as he ran on ahead of her.

"And your face too," she called after him. "It needs it."

Danny gave her a backward wave of acknowledgment. His smile he kept to himself.

Danny's father was already seated when the boy came to the table with his hands and face all shiny from a quick scrub. The old man didn't look up and Danny could see his lips moving in silent prayer. He knew there would be a big, black copy of the Bible on his father's lap.

After a moment, Danny began to hope his father wouldn't look up at all, and he winced when it happened anyway. His father's face seemed lit up from the inside, as if phosphor matches burned just under the white skin. Danny knew what that meant. They were going to get a Bible reading before food. And, just like in church every Wednesday and Sunday, the words would drone on and on like the buzzing of a million summer flies. He let out a sigh and his father's mouth tightened. Danny quickly looked down.

His mother came in a moment later and joined them. She sat between them and took their hands, and his father cleared his throat and began to read from the Old Testament. The words ran out like spilling milk, words of sacrifices and burning lambs, of ungrateful children, of crosses and trials. Danny found bits of it interesting, the snatches about red knives and blood, but most of it was just as he expected, a dry, rasping, monotonous string of words and phrases that made about as much sense to him as algebra.

At least beyond the words there was supper, though it was vegetables and Danny didn't care much for it. That was almost all they ever had—vegetables—with maybe a little fish on special days. Danny's father believed it was good for the soul to give up meat. Danny had never seen a soul, but he *had* seen a hamburger. He knew which one he would prefer.

Instead of eating, Danny began to line up armies of peas and push them up the slopes of the mashed potato mountains toward the giant broccoli forests beyond. His mother told him once to quit playing with his food and he stopped. But only for a moment. He had to get his army through the mountains before the spring thaw started.

Then it was too late and an avalanche of gravy swept down the mountain passes and obliterated his troops. One pea not only washed down the hills but bounced completely off his plate and rolled to a stop in front of his father where it sat looking up at the old man like a wrinkled little green eye.

Danny's father picked the offending legume up between his thumb and forefinger and raised it to eye level where he could share his disgust with both the pea and his son.

"Did you hear what your mother said?" he asked gently.

That caught Danny's attention. His father only spoke quietly when he was about to start one of his lectures on being mature and responsible. The boy quickly said he was sorry in hopes of forestalling a scolding. He failed.

"Boy! You've got to learn to do as you're told. An adult doesn't get to do everything he wants in life. He does what he *has* to. Now you're going to eat every one of those vegetables. And then we'll have a second helping. The Good Book says—"

"I know what it says," Danny interrupted.

His father slapped him. "Don't ever cut in on me when I'm telling you something, boy. You're getting way too big a mouth on you."

"John, don't," Danny's mother said to his father.

For that, mother...I'll remember you, Danny whispered to himself.

"Don't interfere, Louise," his father said. "This boy has got to be put on the straight path. He's got to learn his place before the Devil provides a different kind of place for him."

"Now get on your knees," he said to Danny. "We're going to do some praying."

Anger burned in Danny worse than the palm print on his face, and for a second he considered disobeying. But his father's right hand was clenched so tightly into a fist that the knuckles were bled white, and Danny still feared that hand. Slowly, he got out of his chair and knelt, his head just topping the worn oak of the table.

"Repeat the words after me," his father said. "Let us pray for discipline. Let us pray for the courage to do what must be done. Even though it should hurt us."

"Let us pray for discipline," Danny repeated. "Let us pray for the courage to do what must be done. Even though it should hurt us."

And again. And again. And again.

* * * * * * *

Danny's father would not let him leave the house after supper, insisting the boy stay in to help his mother clean the dishes. Then it was homework, though the next day was Saturday, and finally he was sent early to bed. He didn't really mind. They didn't even have a TV anyway. "That vile purveyor of filth," his father called it.

Besides, Danny had no intention of going to sleep once he was in his room. Five minutes after his mother closed the door he was out the window and down the big oak next to the house. He joined his friends behind the unclipped privet hedge at the corner where they always planned their nights.

This evening turned out pretty much as usual. They kicked through the garbage of Deerhaven's few dark alleys and ran a couple of cats up trees. They went all the way down to the dump to chase rats, and they came back by way of White Creek where they could stomp on any frogs too stupid to jump in the water. The killing was the best, but they caught very little and Danny quickly grew bored. He kept arguing that they should try for bigger game.

"Yeah," Joey said. "Like a dog maybe."

"Dogs are...dangerous," Brian stammered.

Danny and the others giggled. Brian wasn't much of a hunter and the rest of them often made fun of him.

"I don't think he even likes the sight of blood," Danny whispered to Joey. But out loud he said: "I was thinking of something bigger than a dog."

"Bigger than a dog!" Joey stated. "What we got around here bigger than a dog? You surely ain't thinking about Old Lady MacDougal's goat, are you?"

Danny only smiled mysteriously and ran off toward home. "I'll tell you what I'm thinking about tomorrow," he hollered over his shoulder.

It was past one in the morning when Danny climbed the trellis to his room. He already had his pants off before he noticed a new shadow in the corner by his bed. Danny recognized the shape of his father and tried to bolt for the window, but the old man got there first and his fingers closed like fangs on Danny's shoulder.

Then they were on the bed and Danny was across his father's knees, his underwear down around his ankles. He hadn't seen the switch in his father's hand but he felt it now as the strokes raised welts across his bare bottom. All the while his father was talking in his scripture voice, saying things about "tribulations" and "sparing the rod." Danny started to cry, but his father only whipped the harder and spoke the louder. When the punishment was finished, Danny felt himself jerked onto his knees beside the bed. His father knelt with him.

"We're going to pray now, son. Pray for your immortal soul so that Satan's mark will be washed from upon it."

He formed Danny's hands into position and held them there while he made the boy repeat the Lord's Prayer through trembling lips. Over and over it they went, until Danny wanted to scream. And still they prayed.

At last the old man got up and let Danny crawl into bed. The boy's eyes, though still red and swollen, had dried, but Danny had to lie on his side because his rear hurt so badly. It took a long time before he began to relax, and during those empty moments, for the first time ever in his life, Danny began to pray openly for himself.

Danny's father had never understood just how much of his religion his son had accepted. But Danny had long been a true believer, if not in interminable prayer, then certainly in the flesh, and the blood, and the sacrifice. In his own way, the boy had been trying to follow the example of the heroes whose stories his father had read to him from the Bible, the tales of priests who hacked out lamb's hearts on stone altars, and of the man—Moses—who called the Angel of Death down on Egypt's children. But now, with the pain still smarting in his bottom, Danny began to believe in prayer as well, or at least to hope in it.

"Let us pray for discipline," he murmured. "Let us pray for the courage to do what must be done. Even though it hurt our enemies."

After a while the praying brought him ease and he slept, only to dream of pleasant things toward morning.

* * * * * * *

Danny woke to find himself grounded, and his father decided that he should stay in his room all day reading the Bible and praying. He did exactly as he was ordered, with fervor, and that night at supper he was a model of humility. His father even voiced his approval, and actually agreed to let the boy go over to his friend Joey's house for half an hour before dark.

Of course, Danny stayed longer.

His father paced up and down the living room while he waited for the boy to come home, alternating between heavy silences and calls on God to help him bear the cross of a wicked son. Finally, Danny's mother asked if she could call the police, but his father would not hear of it.

"We'll handle this God's way," he said.

Just then they heard the noise of the kitchen door opening, and of stealthy footsteps coming in.

"Thank the Lord," Danny's mother said.

"I'll teach that child once and for all," Danny's father added, as he stormed toward the back of the house.

The kitchen was dark as Danny's father stepped in and flipped the light switch. Nothing happened. *A blown fuse*, he thought. Then he heard a furtive scraping all around the room, and one of the cabinet drawers was pulled back and silverware rattled.

"Who's there?" he demanded, as he reached up on the refrigerator to find the flashlight. It slipped away from his hand. "Danny? Is that you?"

"Yes, father. And I've brought some friends with me."

"Well you better send them right home, little boy. We've got some talkin' to do."

His hand found the flashlight a moment later and switched it on. The battery was weak and the beam no stronger than moonlight, but it was enough to show that Danny had indeed brought several of his friends over. They all stood together by the door, Danny at their head with an old feed sack captured in one small fist. The other boys all held something in their hands too, something that glittered. It looked like knives and forks.

"Danny?" The man made his son's name a question.

The boy started forward as if in answer, his friends behind him on shuffling feet.

"Danny! What do you think you're doing?"

"Why, I'm praying, father. But not to *your* God. I found someone better to pray to. Someone else in the Book. He's not nearly as demanding."

The old man took a step backwards, looking down at his son and at the pink tongue that snaked out from between the boy's red lips. He realized suddenly that blood ran from those lips. The boy slipped something out of the bag he was carrying and held it up to the flashlight. Then he pulled the hollowed-out goat's head down over his own to where he could look through the eye- holes he'd poked out with a stick. "Father," Danny said, his voice muffled but full of strange echoes that did not sound... boyish. "For discipline, and for the courage to do what must be done. Even though it should hurt us. Let us prey."

HAUNTING PLACE

One eye.
"Body of Christ."
And a sliver of tongue.
"Body of Christ."
Blood, and silk, and razors
"Body of Christ!"

"BODY OF CHRIST!"

Jessie's fluttering eyes snapped open and he looked up to meet the priest's gaze, and the open disapproval that was sketched there. "Amen," he mumbled, and the slick white host held between the thumb and first finger of the priest's right hand went home between his parted lips. He closed his mouth as the fingers withdrew, tasting faintly the salt of the man's sweat, then turned left past the ranked rows of watching pews and the half dozen or so elderly worshippers who had turned out for Mass on this raw wound of a morning.

He walked on by the pew where he had been praying and continued out the door, feeling the clergyman's glance writing anger on his back the entire way. His shoulders hunched themselves against the weapons in that look, and he muttered words around the thickness in his mouth.

"Give me courage, Lord. Lord, please!"

By then he was out of the vestibule and through the door into the world. A drizzle was falling there, as gray and thin as hospital gruel, and he waited at the top of the steps until his tongue worked the host loose from the dry roof of his mouth and moistened it enough to be swallowed. He was careful not to touch it with his teeth, just as he had been taught in parochial school. Only when the last of the wafer was gone did he turn the collar of his coat up around his face and walk out into the rain.

He headed down the hill from the church, toward the bus station and away from the university where he was enrolled as a sophomore English major. The streets were empty around him, like any university town during Christmas vacation. The rain began to pick up as he neared the station and he sprinted the last fifty yards into the awning shelter that was there to keep away the wet. A mongrel dog waited there as well, shivering in the cold, and Jessie wished he had something to feed it.

"Sorry, dog," he said.

The dog said nothing, only sniffed at the man's pockets and walked away when he found no bite to eat.

Jessie had no stomach for food himself, though his mind desperately wanted something to chew on. There were magazines inside the building but he already had his ticket and didn't want to sit in the station with the few others who had chosen this day to travel. Then his eyes fell on the newspaper dispenser and he dropped in a small tithe in hopes the headlines would feed him. Instead, they gave him filth until he thought he would choke on it and throw it up.

SECRETARY'S DEATH BLAMED ON DRUGS! one read.

ANGEL DUST TRIGGERS MURDERER'S RAGE! another blared.

Below the headlines were wallowing descriptions of the mutilated body, complete with large, black and white photographs of gore covered walls. Jessie turned away, gagging.

"Mary, Mother of God, help me!" he prayed. "Make it not real. Make it not real. Such things should not be *real*!"

The dog knocked over a trash can in a nearby alley; a stray gust of wind spat rain in Jessie's face.

One eye.

The rain.

And a splatter of brown tissue.

The dog.

"Gray matter," they called it.

Though it wasn't gray when it was fresh.

And the bus, the door open.

"Hey buddy, you getting on or what?"

Jessie's fluttering blue eyes snapped open to meet the driver's darker ones, big, and black, and pissed off. "Sorry," he said, as he went up the steps with his ticket held out. The driver only grunted at Jessie's apology and waved him toward the rear.

He went back past the first dozen seats and the empty people sitting in them. For a moment, he saw the seats of the bus superimposed on the pews of the church, and the people were all praying lovingly to something dreadful that had no name anymore. Then he was in his own seat and reaching down into the top of his left boot to bring out the half-pint of Jack Black that nestled there.

He took one quick swallow of the whiskey as the bus started, and nearly choked on it as the driver hit the air brakes and opened the door again with a curse. A boy of fifteen or so stalked up the steps and down the aisle. The youth glanced once at Jessie, snorted through closed lips, then slid into the seat across the aisle and stuck in a set of ear buds. Jessie saw him crank up the volume on the Walkman in his hand, and he could hear, even over the rain that suddenly beat louder on the tin roof of the bus, some black and bloody metal band's shrieking riffs.

Bang the head that just won't bang
My name is Jessie, he thought. *What's yours?*
You should be...
You should be nicer to me.

And she rose up out of the seat in front of him,

eyes like bloody pearls, round mouth opened to scream, opalescent tongue skewered with nails.

"Pray with me," she said, as she spat him out.

He killed her with one long drink, knowing how to handle her by now. He could always drink her under the table.

The boy saw Jessie's whiskey and took the buds down off his ears and let them hang around his neck. The heavy sound of the guitar lay around his throat and Jessie watched to see if it would strangle him. He watched so closely that the boy's voice startled him.

"Hey, man. You wanna share that shit?"

Jessie looked up to meet the boy's eyes, and then leaned toward him, the bottle held out. The youth leaned in to him, and when his fingers were just about to touch the glass, Jessie whispered: "I knew a woman in the hospital once. She liked to put cigarettes out in her pussy."

The boy's hand stopped in mid-air, and his eyes were suddenly dead. "What the fuck's that supposed to mean?"

"Means I should have been nicer," Jessie said. "I could have been nicer. But she wasn't clean. Never bathed."

"You're crazy," the boy muttered.

Jessie came back to himself. His eyes cleared. "Your vocabulary leaves something to be desired," he said.

Hurt more by the near insult than by talk of the woman and the cigarettes, the youth recoiled and spent the next five minutes not looking at Jessie before getting up and moving. Jessie didn't notice. He had his eyes closed and his hands clenched on the bottle, and he was leaning back, and he was praying: "Jesus please. Jesus please. Jesus please. Jesusplease!"

As he prayed he brought the ghosts out from behind his eyes and put them in the bottle, swirled them around and put them in his mouth. He chewed them up like taffy and swallowed them down, at least until the liquor was gone. A little bit of terror began sniffing at him then, but he slept before it could get him. Only later did he dream.

Anyone watching would have seen the slackening of Jessie's facial muscles and the beginnings of rapid eye movement that indicated the onset of dream sleep. They would not have seen what Jessie saw, a woman nailed to a bed by the axe that grew out of her chest like some obscene totem. They would not have seen the intestines that coiled like rope on the floor, abstract paintings scrawled all around them in carmine oils on the white tiles. They would not have seen the pale faces of fear that struggled in his throat, nor the dwellers in the haunting place behind his forehead.

He screamed when he awoke. Out loud.

The other passengers were staring at him, and they kept on staring until he got up and went to the toilet and locked himself in. He stayed there a long time. The bottle was gone and he was alone, and he kept wetting his face so there would be no purchase on his skin for the ghosts. In time the bus came to a stop.

Jessie heard the sounds of people getting up and moving in the aisles, but he waited until all was silence again before leaving the bathroom. There was no town outside the bus windows, only a post office, a gas station and a quick-stop for the freeway traffic that ran nearby, and the restaurant where the rest of the passengers were eating.

Jessie bought a bottle at the quick-stop and then found an empty booth in back of the restaurant away from the other travelers. He ordered a pack of Camels and a cup of coffee, and he laced the black bitterness in the cup with whiskey. The hot smoke and hot drink ached like acid in his mouth as he waited. When the bus started again, he did not get on. This was where he was going, though, he had thought somehow that it was farther.

There were many ways out of the place where he was and Jessie picked one seemingly at random. But he knew his destination. The long road ran like a dust stream to the north, winding upward at a slight grade. Jessie stopped at the top of the rise and looked down into the valley ahead. The sun was setting behind a house surrounded on three sides by pecan groves. He walked down toward it, feeling himself lose every memory except for Christmas a year ago. Unconsciously, his hand strayed to his groin. Her name was Sherry and she would be wearing pink, he thought.

She was.

The night was warm, as was Sherry, and it had been long since he'd had her. His upbringing told him it was wrong; the taste of his past prayers grew bitter with regret. But he and Sherry sweated each other anyway, until the alcohol was almost gone from his system and a headache began creeping in to replace it. For the headache she offered him white dust, PCP.

"For my angel," she said.

Jessie hesitated. His family had always accepted drinking— even Jesus had drunk wine—but good Christian people didn't have anything to do with drugs. He knew he was already committing a sin with Sherry's body, but he thought maybe God would forgive that. He didn't want to make the stain on his soul worse, though. Besides, wild as Sherry had always been, she'd never had much to do with drugs before, at least before Jessie had gone off to college and she had gotten a job to save for the marriage they'd talked about.

Work, or Jessie's absence, or both, seemed to have changed her. It was not just the PCP. Sherry had always been jealous, but now she seemed to have added aggressiveness. He didn't like it and was about to refuse her offer when her hand found its way between his legs. After a moment he went ahead and took the dust, she with him.

He had her again afterward, his brain kaleidoscoping inside his skull. Her laughter was feral, and after a while she told him, while he was arched up into her saying "Oh God, Oh God, Oh God," where she had gotten the drugs.

"I've been sleeping with my boss," she said. "I think I'm going to have his baby."

One eye.
And dawn brightening.

So much blood.

The sirens and the long way to the hospital.

So much blood—on the walls, on the floor, on him.

And so many pieces.

They had to pry one of her eyes from his hand.

To find that she wasn't pregnant didn't help.

Sitting by the window, looking out at the bright sun and the fluffy clouds that resembled torn pillows. Jessie's hands were praying the rosary. There was nothing in his eyes, only a few compulsive thoughts in his mind.

Jealous. She was only trying to make me jealous because she thought there were other girls at school. I never would have done that. She should have known I wouldn't do that. She should have known....

* * * * * * *

"What's that poor fucker's story," the new intern asked?

The gray nurse looked up from where she bent making the bed, her mouth twisted in a frown at the man's choice of words. She glanced once at the patient, who continued to sit quietly in a chair by the window, before looking back at the intern.

"Killed his girlfriend," she said. "Cut her open in a phencyclidine rage. They say he thought she was pregnant and was trying to find the baby."

"Shit! That angel dust is nasty stuff." Then the man snapped his fingers. "Hey, I read about it, I think. Gory as hell. But why put him in a psychiatric hospital?"

"Don't know really. Maybe because he couldn't remember a thing about it the next day. He had no criminal record, and the act seemed so clearly a glitch. Drug induced. Not likely to reoccur."

"Yeah," the intern said. "I've seen good kids get crazy on that shit. Lucky for this dude organic amnesia is so common with PCP. Better he not remember what he did."

The nurse smiled but there wasn't any warmth in it. "Maybe it would have been better," she said. "But too late now. He got his memory back."

"How's that?"

"An accident. About a month ago. He'd been a model patient so we were letting him ride his bike outside the walls. He got hit by a car and there were some head injuries. Subdural bleeding. Bilateral contusions. He was in a coma for nearly a week and he came out of it in nightmare. An EEG showed localized epileptic activity in both temporal lobes. And every time those miniature seizures go off in there he relives the murder, each and every instant of it."

"My God!" blurted the intern.

"God didn't have anything to do with it," the nurse said.

* * * * * * *

Sitting by the window, waiting for them to leave. Their voices passed out the door and Jessie's shoulders slumped. Sometimes it bothered him that they talked around him as if he couldn't hear, just because he sat quietly and did not speak. He heard every word and understood it. But he knew they had spoken falsely today. God had everything to do with it.

He read the rosary with his fingers and touched the silver crucifix as it winked in the noonday sun. Just this morning he had asked the clinic priest for it, and the man had been happy to oblige a fellow Catholic. Jessie turned the cross around and around until he found the sharpest edge. Then he began digging at his wrists. A seizure broke loose in his brain and his hands blurred with convulsive speed. And the memories started over again, over and over again.

One eye.
"Body of Christ...."

Jessie was sitting happily when the intern came back to check on him at bedtime. He was sitting happily and praying, with all the hauntings running out of him onto the floor. The holes in his wrists and feet were where Christ had been hung with nails, and the beads of the rosary were sewn beneath his scalp like a crown of black thorns.

The crucifix was in his left eye. It had already been in his right one.

WITH EYES LIKE FANGS

1

In the holy forest, they hunt their prey by the scent of weakness that bleeds from its pores. With icicle eyes, prism eyes, eyes like cicatrices, they find the cavern where the weakness lies. Scaled hands and furred ones work spasmodically on weapons. Claws click on steel while in the wet mouths fangs ache with hatred. In a darkling mist, they gather for the kill.

2

In the cavern, the prey stirs awake and lifts her head. A sudden light burns inside her. Through her skin, she sees, and weakness she sheds like a husk. Her mind centers on the forces arrayed against her outside. Her mouth begins a smile; the smile widens until the lips split at the corners and black blood runs.

"Let it begin," she murmurs.

3

The hunters in the woods see the light flare within the cavern. They stir, restless in rage. And when the prey strides free of its hiding place into the rain, they fall upon her with taloned feet and leathery wings, their throats filled with howls and shrieks.

But the prey is not what they thought. They have been tricked. Instead of weakness, strength meets their strengths.

Their bodies shatter upon it. In moments, the clearing before the cave writhes with the dead and the dying.

"Mother!" the bloody ones cry. "Mother! Do not forsake us!"

4

The 'she' looks upon her dying children, and starts to feed while they are fresh. Out in the distant forest, the males begin to call. She hears them even over the crunch of bones. In a moment she will release her own mating cry, will invite the males to join with her at this feast.

Perhaps her next brood will be stronger.

MONSTER SPRAY

Parents use worrying as a defense mechanism against their true fears. It's better to think of their child with cuts and bruises and black eyes than it is to think of them dead, which is what parents are really afraid of. But sometimes a parent's worry can be of a different sort, a colder and harder sort that aches in the dark like an arthritic limb. And maybe that kind of worry is a lot closer to the real terror. It was the second kind of worrying that April Banning was doing about her daughter Jenny.

April had taken enough psychology courses to know that children had nightmares sometimes, and she knew they most often started between ages three and eight. But she also knew, or felt, that a six-year-old should not be having the same terrifying dream night after night for a month, a dream that left her small body shaking and shivering, and her sheets wringing wet with sweat.

April had tried getting Jenny to talk about the dream, tried changing her daughter's diet, tried cutting down on TV. Nothing seemed to work. And lately Jenny had even stopped wanting to sleep with her mom, though that *had* been the only thing keeping the nightmares away. Finally, when Jenny began to lose weight and started to complain about physical pain, April took her to see Dr. Annette Harper, Jenny's pediatrician for the last three years.

April couldn't say she really liked Ann Harper—the woman was only a handful of years older but seemed immeasurably more aloof—but she certainly admired the doctor's professionalism. And Jenny adored her. All Dr. Harper's reticence vanished when she talked to Jenny, or to any child, and the smile that softened her face at such times made her seem years younger and decades happier. Today, as always, April was gratified at how carefully Dr. Harper examined Jenny. But she was also worried. The pediatrician's smile had turned gradually into a frown throughout the course of her probing.

When she finished, Dr. Harper called the nurse to take Jenny to the reading room so the little girl could pick out a storybook to take home. It was a ritual that Jenny enjoyed, one that had long ago convinced April completely of Ann Harper's love for children. Now it only added to April's fears because, until now, the doctor had always gone herself to help Jenny select a book.

"What's wrong?" April asked as soon as the door closed behind her daughter.

"Well.... Jenny has lost some weight. And she is more tense than I have ever seen her. Her heart rate and blood pressure are both elevated."

"What about the pain she's been complaining about?"

Ann Harper's gaze flicked downward and then up again quickly.

"She is having intestinal cramps. I doubt it is anything to worry about right now. But she looks as if she has not been sleeping well."

"She hasn't," April said, as she began telling the doctor about Jenny's nightmares and the things she'd tried to do to stop them.

April was wringing her hands by the time she finished her story, and was surprised when Ann Harper reached out and clasped her wrists hard in a show of support. It helped her relax for the first time in hours.

"It seems I've tried everything," she continued. "I don't know what to do next."

"I think I do," Ann said. "But first let me ask you some questions."

"Okay."

"The answers may be delicate."

"If it helps Jenny, then ask me anything," April said.

"All right then. I believe your boyfriend recently moved in with you, did he not?"

"Yes, but—"

Ann held up her hand. "Allow me a few more questions please."

April closed her mouth and nodded as the doctor continued.

"Now, how does Jenny get along with your new friend? He is acting in the role of her father. Has their relationship progressed to the point where she will stay alone with him?"

"Oh, he keeps her for an hour or two on Friday nights while I'm at the spa. They seem to get along fine then. You don't think her dreams could have anything to do with Keith replacing her daddy do you? I mean, Tom's been dead over five years. I don't think Jenny even remembers him."

Ann Harper smiled, but only slightly.

"I doubt Jenny's nightmares have anything to do with this Keith replacing her father. More likely, they have to do with Keith replacing her as an object for your affection."

"But that's absurd! Besides, I've been dating Keith for a year. The dreams didn't start until just a few weeks ago."

"I know. But these things sometimes build up a while before erupting."

April frowned. She had a fleeting impression that Ann Harper wasn't telling her everything, but it was soon overwhelmed by a fresh wave of worry over her daughter.

"Then what should I do?" she asked. "Tell Keith to leave?"

"No, no. That is not the solution. Get Jenny and bring her to my office. I think I have something to help."

The two of them soon joined the doctor, and April sat down across the desk from the pediatrician and put Jenny on her knee. The girl winced at the contact but April didn't notice. Ann Harper did, and her eyes narrowed for a moment before she mentally erased the small sign of tension and looked up at Jenny with a wide smile.

"Now, Jenny," she said. "Your mother has been telling me

about your bad dreams. They have something to do with a monster don't they?"

"Yes," Jenny said quietly. "But I don't wanna talk about it."

"I understand," Ann said. "I had exactly the same kind of dreams when I was a little girl your age. In fact, the monster told me not to ever talk to anyone about it or he would eat me up."

April's eyes widened. What was this woman telling her daughter? Was it a good thing? But Jenny was looking up eagerly.

"Yes," the little girl said. "That's exactly what my monster said too."

"I thought so," Ann said. "Monsters like that are all pretty much the same. But there is a way to get rid of them."

"How's that?" Jenny asked carefully.

"Well.... All you have to do is squirt them in the eyes with monster spray."

"Monster spray?"

"Yes, *monster spray*! I have my own personal recipe, made just for the kind of monster that is bothering you."

"Really! Do you have some?"

Ann Harper reached into her desk drawer and drew out a small perfume bottle with an atomizer attached. It was about half full of pale green liquid.

"Here it is," she said, holding it out to Jenny. "It's all yours."

"Wow," Jenny said, as she took the bottle into her small hands. "Real monster spray! Is it guaranteed?"

"It's guaranteed. Just spray it right in the creature's face. Aim for the eyes; that really gets them. But be careful and don't spill any on yourself or your clothing. It might stain, and it could even burn a bit. You know this stuff has to be strong to get rid of a monster."

"Gosh," Jenny said.

April caught a quick wink from Dr. Harper and was astonished, both at the wink and at what she had just heard. Still, she couldn't deny the results. Her daughter, who had been so withdrawn for the last few weeks that she'd scarcely smiled, was suddenly her old self again. April wasn't sure how long it would last but she was grateful for even a few minutes of peace.

"How much do we owe you," she asked.

"Oh, the usual for your visit. The monster spray is free."

April lifted Jenny off her lap and stood up to go. The little girl was still engrossed in her bottle.

"Remember to aim for the eyes, Jenny," Dr. Harper said. "And you can always come back for more if you ever need it."

April met Ann Harper's glance and mouthed "thank you" before leading her daughter out to the car.

* * * * * *

That night, after April finished dressing Jenny for sleep, she sat the bottle of monster spray on the table beside her daughter's bed.

"You remember what Dr. Harper said now, don't you?"

"Course, momma. I just squirt that old monster right in the eyes."

"Exactly!" April said, clapping her hands and laughing before she leaned over to fluff her daughter's pillow.

Jenny kissed her mom impulsively on the cheek and April returned the kiss, then gave her daughter a sudden fierce hug.

"Night now, honey. You sleep good tonight. You hear me?"

"Yes, momma?"

"I love you, Jenny."

"I love you too, momma."

April pulled the covers up over her daughter, though she knew Jenny would only kick them off again, and then turned out the big overhead light. The rainbow night-light shed enough illumination so that she could see Jenny snuggle up tightly to her stuffed puppy. It also showed her daughter's smile, and that was enough to loosen the hard arthritic knot of worry that had been tied about April's heart for weeks.

"God bless Ann Harper," she murmured to herself, before

blowing her daughter a kiss and leaving the room.

* * * * * * *

Jenny was fast asleep by the time Keith got home from work an hour later. April heated him some leftover lasagna and sat with him while he ate. She liked Keith well enough, though she couldn't say she loved him. In fact, up until two months ago she'd resisted his obvious desire to move in with them.

April had wondered herself at first if Jenny's bad dreams could have anything to do with Keith. She eventually rejected the idea because the dreams hadn't started until almost a month after he'd arrived, well past the time when the man and child seemed to have adjusted to each other. And, besides, Keith acted genuinely fond of Jenny and was always happy to hold her or let her sit on his lap.

April had to admit that Jenny didn't seem quite as enthusiastic about Keith, but she figured jealousy was the reason for that. After all, Jenny had had her mother to herself for a long time and must find it hard to share. Still, April couldn't really believe that jealousy was the trigger for Jenny's nightmares. Ann Harper hadn't seemed all that sure of it herself when she suggested it. But, if the doctor's theory about the cause of Jenny's dreams was wrong, her prescription for their treatment certainly seemed right. The monster spray was working beautifully so far.

Suddenly, April realized that Keith had asked her something and was waiting for an answer.

"I'm sorry, what?"

"I asked what the pediatrician said about Jenny's dreams today?"

"Oh. She didn't seem to think it was anything to worry much about, though she didn't like how long they'd been going on." April shook her head and laughed. "You know she came up with the damnedest treatment. She gave Jenny a bottle of monster spray."

"She gave her what?"

"Monster spray. I think it's just colored water inside an old perfume bottle. It's got an atomizer and Jenny's supposed to squirt the monster in the face with it if he bothers her again. Dr. Harper told her it was guaranteed to get rid of monsters."

Keith frowned. "I'm not sure it's good to encourage Jenny like that," he said. "She has too much imagination as it is. I'm surprised a doctor would give her such a thing."

"I was too, at first," April said. "But Lord it sure worked. She went off to sleep without a whimper. And she's resting so peaceful you wouldn't believe it."

Keith twisted in his chair. "Well, if you think it's okay. I still don't like it though."

"I think it's harmless," April said, a hint of firmness in her tone.

Keith got the hint and dropped the subject, finishing his lasagna in silence. They tried to follow dinner with a TV movie but Keith soon gave up and went to bed, complaining of a long day. April joined him a little later, and she could sense that he was still awake even though he didn't respond to her murmured "good night."

She shrugged and turned away from him. She knew he was angry about the monster spray, but he would just have to get over it. Jenny was *her* daughter and she would decide what was best for her. She fell asleep trying to remember her own childhood fears.

* * * * * * *

It was just after 1:00 when April woke up to the sound of her little girl screaming. There were other sounds as well, hoarse bellowings and crashings, as if a drunken bull had gotten in the house and was smashing into things and knocking them over. Keith wasn't in bed—probably in the bathroom she figured—but she couldn't wait for him. She leaped up and ran for her daughter's room.

Jenny was sitting straight up in bed when April burst through the doorway. Her screaming had stopped and the bottle of monster spray was clutched tightly in one fist. A humped shape lay on the floor next to the overturned night table. April felt a spurt of irrational fear twist her insides. Or maybe the fear wasn't irrational in the face of whatever was lying there beside her daughter's bed.

"Can't be a monster," April said to herself. "It—"

"I did it, momma. Just like Dr. Ann said. I hit it right in the eyes with this stuff." She held up her bottle and smiled.

"Oh, Sweetie!"

Ready to grab Jenny and run, April forced herself to walk over and kneel down beside the crumpled shape on the floor. It was the hardest thing she had ever done, especially since she could suddenly remember in detail every horror movie she had ever seen, particularly the ones where the psychopathic killer wasn't really dead when he seemed to be.

Despite her fear, however, April managed to get her hands on the body and roll it over. It was Keith, but he wasn't coming back she knew. She recognized him even though he was wearing a Halloween mask and clawed gloves. The mask represented some kind of devil-creature, she imagined. It was difficult to be sure because both the mask and the face beneath it were in ruins, as if some powerful acid had flash-burned its way into Keith's brain, exploding eyeballs and stripping away flesh as it went.

Slowly, April reached out and took the bottle of monster spray from her daughter. She sniffed it and her eyes widened as her nose burned. She looked down on Keith and realized how much she hated him. He wasn't wearing the bottoms to his pajamas and she knew what he had done, what he had been doing, to her little girl. She was glad he was dead.

* * * * * * *

Ann Harper slept late on Saturdays, one of the few indulgences she allowed herself. It was after 9:00 before she carried her first cup of coffee into the bedroom to dress. Seeing herself in the mirror reminded her of yesterday's session with little Jenny Banning and her monster nightmares.

On impulse, Ann reached to the top shelf in her closet and drew down a dusty photo album that had been hidden there. It contained only one picture and it had been years since she had looked at it. The photo showed a smiling blonde woman and a not so smiling blonde child of about six. There was a man in the scene as well, the little girl's stepfather, but Ann couldn't see his features. She had long ago cut out his face.

YOUR NIGHTMARE
OR MINE

The wind blows through a gap-toothed window, stirring the rope into creaking dance beneath the rafter where it hangs. For a moment it seems as if, from the corner of an eye, you see a body dangling from that hempen cord. The image rips your head around. Your eyes fall on the rope. It is empty, swaying, casting no shadow in the gloom-darkened house.

Why are you here?

It is late evening outside, where the wind blows, and it is later still in this room. In the distance the night birds call, in voices full of melancholy, and you know that you must be getting back to your place. You turn to go, but a vague memory stirs feebly in your brain, forcing you to stillness. There is something—your brow wrinkles in thought—something you must remember.

Why are you here?

The rope! Yes, there is something about the rope. It reminds you of a man you once knew. A man who once lived here, and died here, turning slow circles in an otherwise empty house, alone, hanging from a noose he had placed over his own head.

How long ago was it? It could have been ten years, or fifteen years. Was it longer?

"It was twenty years ago," you mutter to yourself. "Twenty years ago today." And you wonder how you know that answer.

Twenty years ago a man hung himself here. It had been a week before they found him, a week in the mid-summer's heat and dampness. How he must have stunk. It would have been much like the odor that seems to roil for a moment in your nostrils, an odor of maggots and rot. Strange how the mind can play tricks, conjuring up some awful stench to fit the imagination that blooms in your head.

But you know that a scent cannot linger for twenty years. Besides, you remember the story now. The man was discovered and taken down, and buried up on the hill behind the house somewhere. Others had lived here then, a young family with one sweet-faced daughter. They had loved the place, until, all of a sudden on a warm summer evening—on a day much like today—the little girl went insane.

Like the stilted figures in a cheap cartoon, the scene spasms its way through your mind. The girl is playing on the side of the hill with her doll. She hears the squelch of mud beneath a heavy boot and leaps to her feet. Her smile flowers into horror; her throat blooms a choked scream. And then other screams are out in the brilliant air, fading away as she flees down the hill, the same screams that went on for days before they finally broke, as if the girl were a windup toy running down. A last note and there was silence, years and years of silence.

WHY ARE YOU HERE?

An abandoned china doll lies on the side of a hill, the image so vivid that you rub your eyes trying to erase it. But the vision remains, of blue eyes, porcelain eyes, staring at you without feeling. It is almost as if you were a witness to the events.

A stone falls, a chair half rocks. The hairs curl more tightly on your neck and panic scratches its fingers against the chalkboard of your reason. You stiffen, and then relax. Surely it was only a loose stone in the old cellar, only the wind through a broken window.

But something is wrong, something about the rope. In a moment it comes to you and your bones creak-crack in their sockets while your skin stretches so taut it threatens to rupture. The rope is not old and yellowed as it should be after twenty years. It is new, fresh and white, still stiff with the memorized coils of the plastic bag that lies beneath it. It hangs there, waiting for a cargo.

Waiting for you?

But then you remember it all and the terror is gone. Only purpose remains. You brought the rope yourself and you *know* why you are here. It's your anniversary.

You step forward, dragging a broken chair behind you until it sits beneath the rafter and the rope. There. Now the noose. Slide it over your head as you climb up. The hangman's knot must be just right, just as it was the first time you saw it, long and long ago.

It's time to kick over the chair, but you stop with one foot lifted. The outside door creaks behind you and you turn to see who it is. The smell is back, stronger than before because it is in the house where the fresh breeze cannot carry it away from you. You don't mind. You've become accustomed to the stench, just as you've become accustomed to the sight that greets your eyes. You've certainly relived both of them enough in your memory.

The lich stands at the foot of the chair, little more now than a sack of desiccated skin wrapped in a few threads of cloth. You recognize him easily enough, though you've really seen him only once before. You take the noose off your neck and climb down from your perch, handing the rope to the dead man. After all, it is his anniversary even more than it is yours.

You don't wait to see the finish. The corpse wants to be alone, and you know what will happen anyway. Instead, you go out of the house and up on the hill. A tattered doll lies almost exactly where you dropped it nineteen years ago. You sit down on the grass and begin to play with it. There's no real hurry. It'll only be a week before you can have your turn with the rope.

A CHOICE OF GHOSTS

I saw her eyes there,
whispering with ghosts of love,
and yet I never noted
how her mandala gaze was stained
with bloody, broken angels,
with blackened wings from which
silver betrayal dripped.

She offered me an easy choice.
Take my own bullet or take her kiss.
And oh that kiss was sweetly warm,
sharp as any venom,
with forever promised in her lips.

It was years before I knew.
I should have chosen the bullet.

OLD BONES

We were bone hunting up one arm of the Great Rift Valley, which cuts down through East Africa like some obscenely stitched surgical scar, when we uncovered a hole in the rock that looked old. There weren't many fossils on the surface here so I'd put a dynamiter to work in the early afternoon among some of the boulder-choked ravines, and by late evening he had blasted open this one little gully all the way down to bedrock. Now, in the last light of day, there was the sweetest little fissure you've ever seen running up one side of the wash. Behind that crack gleamed a deep, thick darkness, a promise I could not ignore.

Where we stood was south and a little west of Lake Turkana in Kenya, at a place called Adawoni. It was a long way south of the Afar Triangle of Ethiopia where Don Johanson had dug up Lucy, the oldest erect-walking human ancestor ever, and it was even south of Koobi Fora in Kenya, which was where Richard Leakey picked up Skull 1470, thus far the oldest and biggest brained of the *Homo habilis* finds. *Homo habilis* was what humans were around two million years or so ago. Lucy was a lot older, around three and a half million, but she wasn't designated as *Homo*. That term is reserved for the known human family. Lucy was an *Australopithecus afarensis*, commonly thought to be ancestral to the human line.

Unlike at the Afar Triangle or Koobi Fora, the fossil deposits around Adawoni were thin. In three weeks of digging we had found only a few horse teeth and antelope horns, one almost intact hyena skeleton, and a monkey's shattered knee joint that had gotten all of us excited for a bit, until we figured out that the graduate student who found it had put the bones back together wrong. He'd joined the two pieces, the tibia and the femur, at an angle, which is how a human knee joint looks, instead of in a straight line, which is the way a monkey's or an ape's joint goes together.

After that disappointment, the deep blues really came up and grabbed me hard. It was *Homo* I wanted, old *Homo*, and I had been in Africa off and on for ten long, dry years while others got the skulls and the glory. But I could feel my spirits lift now. The fissure in front of me looked like it might just be a time portal back to the lost ages I sought.

It didn't bother me that night was coming down; it's always night in a cave. Besides, I had a flash. And I promised myself just one peek. If I found anything interesting then I could always come back in the morning with help. But I knew I was fooling myself. That just wasn't the way I worked. If there was anything here that could be had then I damn well was going to have it.

Billy Taung, my dynamiter, was getting fidgety as the day closed up, so I told him he could go on back to camp. Billy was good at what he did but he didn't know or care much about fossils. In fact, I think they scared hell out of him, and I guess that was understandable. Not many people care to steep themselves in death, but that's just what a paleoanthropologist does for a living. You read in the news about the police digging up bodies under somebody's floor or cellar, and you wonder how someone could live in a house with all those dead things in it, but you go to a museum and that's what most of it is all about— dead things.

Why, I had half a dozen skulls that I carried with me even in the field, and there were a hundred other human bones on my shelves back at the University. I had dug up graveyards and robbed tombs for them. No one minded because they were old, and there was no one left living who could call those bones father, or sister, or grandmother. Oftentimes, when working late at night in my tent, I would take down one of the skulls and look at it, or stroke it for a while as if it were Aladdin's lamp. But I'd yet to find a genie, and despite the six skulls that I had I wanted one more, a big one, as big as Lucy or 1470. Sometimes I wanted it so bad that it was almost like pursuing a lover.

I took a flashlight out before handing my pack to Billy and waving him off. The last sight I had of him was as he trudged off east into the gathering shadows. I picked up my trenching shovel and squeezed through the crack into the cavern night beyond.

There was a pretty decent opening behind the slit and a few quick probes with the shovel turned up something interesting right away, a handful of worked pebbles that might mean *Homo habilis*, or, more likely, *Homo erectus*, the next step up the ladder toward modern humans. I didn't want to take the time right then to map out a few flakes so I didn't move them. You had to record everything that you moved and I had a feeling there was something bigger to be found here, something big enough and old enough to make a few knapped flints look like an embarrassment. Shining the light around showed me where that something bigger might be hiding.

Down at the bottom of one wall was an opening just large enough for a small person to squeeze through. It was a hole worn by water seepage and had not originally been a part of the cave in which I stood. It went on down into the earth beyond this cavern, getting deeper and older with each foot of soil that rose above it. There may have been a sequence of caves built up and torn down over the centuries in this area, and maybe there weren't any remnants of the ones that dated back as far as I wanted to go. But I didn't believe that. And though I would have to get down on my belly to go in that place, it still looked damn inviting. Even the thought of snakes didn't bother me. Well, not much. I dropped down and wormed my way in before the thought had time to bother me some more.

About fifteen feet into the wall I came on to a short slope leading down into a hollowed out chamber that marked the end of the cavern. I could tell by the stone over which I crawled that I was in a much older cave system than the one where I had entered, a system stressed and tortured by the centuries but miraculously intact. It was also about the size of a womb. The roof was maybe four and a half feet overhead and there was no way I could stand up. But I didn't mind. I had laid the flash down on a floor that was made of soft soil, perfect for digging, and the trenching shovel probed easily through the first few inches of earth.

The loosened dirt sucked the light down into it and I quickly turned up two gleaming bones, one a pig's tusk, the other a horn core from an extinct species of antelope. I recognized both species. They had lived side by side with early humans, both *habilis* and *erectus*. I took a deep breath and knelt back on my heels, feeling the old bones gathered there beneath me. I knew exactly what I had stumbled upon, a bone dump, the primitive equivalent to a modern day landfill.

What's more, I knew that *people* were sometimes put into these dumps after they had died, or been killed. Our earliest ancestors saw little need to draw distinctions between the human and the animals that lived beside them. Both were thought of as part of the same whole. But I didn't care how it had happened. The fact remained that there was a skull, and the bones to go with it, down there beneath me right now. It was the one I had been searching for. I *knew* it; I *felt* it. It was down there looking up, dust in its eye sockets, and it wanted me to come down and take it.

As close as I was, though, I didn't want to rush. If ever there was a time for care it was now. I picked up the antelope horn, then held it up to the flashlight to make sure I had the species right. That was when the fear came out of its quiet place inside of me and made itself known. Oh, it was the right horn—a fine horn— but the ceiling, the ceiling where the light reflected, was not... right. It had a draped appearance, like hung curtains, different somehow from the rock that should have been there and the soil that lay beneath. And that ceiling was gently swaying, as if a window had been left open in a house and a pre-rain wind was starting to blow in and stir things about.

I dropped the horn and turned the flash upward, and things began to fall where they were hit by the light, things that had many legs and were as quick and large as a child's hand. They sounded like rain against the old earth where I had been digging. I switched off the light and the rain ceased. The rustling continued on for another moment and then faded out as a new equilibrium was reached. I made no move during that time. I dared not. I just stayed there on my knees in that nighted place, my ears strained with listening. The ceiling was not curtained. Instead, hanging up there above my head like clumps of dried seed pods were myriads of scorpions, an ancient species, fit company for the bones beneath me.

It was horrible there in the dark, but the scorpions did not like the light. It stirred them up, and I had no urge to see the ceiling move and dance over me in a small cavern forty feet under the earth. It might have been different if I had been standing, but they had me on my knees and no one thinks well on their knees. They had me down and they were up there overhead, dangling like rotten fruit.

What if they all rained down at the same time?

I pushed that thought away and began to inch my way slowly out of that chamber, my skin tensed against my collar because the worst thought of all was that one might fall down my neck and come inside toward the warmth.

It took ten long minutes before I was free of the small cavern and the crawl space leading to it. The antechamber beyond was black, the crack in the outside wall faintly visible as a lighter band of darkness. I turned the flash back on and stopped to catch my breath and let my sphincter muscles come unglued. It had been about half an hour since I'd entered the underground and it was deep night outside, a night that seemed welcoming after the shadows of the cave. I started toward the cavern entrance, determined to come back tomorrow with more light and a big surprise for the scuttlers in the dark, and the night's welcome turned into something else.

Somewhere in the deep chamber of the scorpions there came the gentle sound of a plop, as if part of the ceiling had come down to earth. Then there was an almost silent scurrying and rushing, a building, as if one crawler had climbed its way up on another, and another, and another. I stood there and began to wonder what all those scorpions had been doing back there, what they *were* doing. Were they feeding, mating, or something else? And I knew it had to be the something else.

I didn't believe in evil but there was something here in the darkness, here in this cave, back there between the ancient race on the ceiling and the ancient bones beneath. I had been back there digging down but I began to think about something digging up. I began to think about the earth mothers and the half-human shamans that had been buried in the dust with their people, and I began to remember the stories of sorceries worked in the dark, and the whispers of animals and humans who were so close akin in the dawn of our kind that they sometimes shared their shapes. I began to think about light spilling down into earth that had been centuries without it. And I remembered how the light had awakened the scorpions, as if they had been waiting a long time for it.

I began with thinking, and I ended up hearing, hearing something coming up through all those layers of soil, something that had sent out for skin and had the scorpions come to clothe it, something that had been put together all wrong and was pushing its way up through the tibias of monkeys and the teeth of horses, something that was behind me now, right behind me. I turned off the light. It seems I had found what I was looking for.

In the dark, the hand that stroked my skull and turned my head with a gentle touch seemed only a couple of million years away from being human. The kiss that followed was much older, as old as love and lovers, or as predator and prey. After a moment, I heard the rustle of the scorpions as they bubbled up through my lover's open mouth and poured into my own.

WALL OF LOVE

The body wore a rosary that encircled its throat with beads of ivory and a silver crucifix. Kneeling, the young man reached to touch that cross where it draped over the flattened swell of womanly breasts, then bent to lick at the cold, cold metal and at the tissue around it.

A silk slickness greeted his lips and the bitter taste of silver burst ripe into his mouth, mingled with salt and delicate oils from the skin. He could see his reflection in the mirrored metal, could see his gray eyes and bald scalp with its sprouting quills of wire.

"Ugly," he said to no one there. "Ugly, ugly." It was his name after all. At least the one by which he was called most often.

He slid his head back and forth over the body—smearing his face across it—then speared the navel with the tip of his tongue to draw out a tithe of sweet chicory sweat. He could tell by the liquidity of the sweat that the body had not been dead long, though he had blocked from memory whether or not it had been dead when it was first brought to him.

Sometimes Father and Mother gave him a living one. He always thought they wanted him to kill it. He never could. He was doing his best to give them the other things they wanted—demanded. But he couldn't kill. It made him feel bad inside just to watch a body die. Once, he'd even tried to do for one of the dead what he was capable of doing. But Father had been angry. And life was less painful when Father wasn't angry.

After a still moment with his tongue tasting sweat, Ugly

raised his lips from skin and turned his head like a callow bird looking. His eyes scanned the body, registering bare brown flesh, linking soft-edged curves with the stippled patterns of day-old bruises. Ugly knew his Mother's marks. She had created these contusions, and, as always, without harmony.

He sat back on his heels, rattling. The corpse was nude but he was sweetly clothed, dressed in hundreds of alligator clips that were bitten into his eyebrows, cheeks, and nipples, around his belly, in a rood-shaped array on his penis and scrotum. His mind regurgitated a partial memory, a strobe of surgically gloved hands as they parachuted across his muscles, stopping only long enough to snap on black and red clips. He couldn't recall the face, only the razor-hate in the eyes and the sticky lips that writhed over his chest, and lower, the teeth plucking on the clips to sandpaper his nerves.

The memories stopped then, splintering into brittle fragments of fingers, mouths, tongues. Ugly's fist tightened around the rosary and snapped it free of the dead neck. Ivory beads dribbled away, struck the concrete floor and bounced, belling out with such a lonely sound that he wanted to cry.

He stood up instead, clip ornaments chiming, and turned to see the wall behind him. It was his wall. As this was his room—his place. He knew that. But what hung on the wall was not his. It belonged to Father, though it wasn't finished yet. It needed something more.

Ugly bent to the body again, put his hand between the legs to lift the flaccid penis and the skin sack that held the testicles. The prepuce had been removed. And that saddened him. He didn't like mutilation without purpose, without aesthetics. He glanced at his own foreskin, at the matte black and lip-red clips that clustered there, like insects feeding. They even moved like insects, dancing briefly every time his heartbeat thudded through his erection.

He let go of the other's flesh, touched his own. It was cold as love in the room, but his skin was hot and tight and pleasantly curved. As it should be.

A wink of metal caught his eye and he reached and picked up the crucifix where it had dropped to the floor. He noted how sharp the silver sides were, thought how precise an instrument it would be for his purpose. To one side of the room sat a tray of scalpels and drills and hemostats. But the cross would be better because it was spontaneous, natural. With this as a blade, his cuts would be ragged enough to take the edge off a symmetry that could grow too intense unless modified.

The door opened and Father and Mother came into the room.

Ugly looked up. And looked down quickly. He'd seen that they wore their laboratory coats and what they called "scrub greens." Their work clothes. He hated them like this. Because they were two instead of one. When they were one, he liked them better. Sometimes they laughed with him then. Instead of at him. And often they let him sit near, and Mother seemed happy. She was so seldom happy.

Ugly's father was handsome, with cotton hair and a mustache that lent strength to thin lips. His body was lean, the pink skin lying close over delicate bones. Mother was much younger than Father, though the two looked alike. She had blonde hair nearly as white as Father's, and the same gray eyes. Only, her eyes were dull as bullets while his sparkled like quicksilver.

Still, it was Mother whom Ugly watched most. Because it was she who carried the red box, the BAD BOX.

She watched him, too. Her belly was very big. And sometimes it moved.

Father strode to the wall and stood looking at it, his hands clasped behind his back. He spoke over his shoulder, his voice roughened with excitement, with arousal.

"Coming along nicely, I'd say. When do you think it will be finished, Jase?"

Ugly jumped, his clips rattling. It was rare for Father to call him by name. By that name anyway. It meant he was pleased, and Ugly/Jase wanted to keep on pleasing him.

He wished he understood how.

"I don't...know," Ugly said after a moment, his voice a raw

struggle in his throat. It's not easy. To...make it happen."

Father spun around to face him, spoke in a chopped voice that wasn't pleased anymore.

"You've used only five bodies this entire month. If you need more subjects, we've got possibilities waiting." He jerked his chin toward the corpse on the floor. "Not as good as this transsexual freak maybe. But serviceable, I'm sure. If you want them to be. If you'd stop wasting time standing around."

Though the accusations made his chest hurt, Ugly knew that he could afford to ignore them. Unlike Mother, Father was a skilled artist in his own chosen medium. He understood that the elements had to be right if the whole was to be beautiful. Instead, Ugly asked what he needed to ask.

"When do I get what I want?"

It was a stupid question to ask with Mother there, but he had to speak it. He wanted so bad. And the pain couldn't—

But then the pain came. And it could.

As Mother punched a button on the box in her hand, Ugly shrieked like a napalmed animal. The current poured into him through the wires running into his brain, went nova at the point where each clip touched his body. He felt the skin being peeled from his face, being torn down across his shoulders to expose the meat. His bones rattled in their beds of muscle. He urinated on himself in pulses of warmth.

In the next moment the agony was gone and Ugly found himself on the floor in the fetal position. No skin had peeled off his body. His bones lay quiet and still. But the hair of his groin was wet and matted, and he began to cry.

"You don't ask questions, you ugly son of a bitch," Mother shouted. "You never ask questions."

"Now, Angel," Father soothed. "I'm sure Jase understands our frustration with the delays." He looked down at his son.

"Don't you, Jase? I mean, the body has been here over two hours and you've done nothing with it. This was a particularly good specimen. We thought it would be better to have it fresh but you sat here and watched it die. It's very important to me—

to us—that you finish this project."

Father linked his hands together and propped the index fingers against his lower lip.

"There'll be no treat until it's finished," he said. "You know that."

One time, long ago, Father had let Ugly touch one of the things he wanted. It had still been wet and slimy, and he remembered holding it and holding it while he crooned to it a lullaby he'd made up himself. But they'd made him give it back, leaving him with nothing but the blood that had clothed it.

Ugly licked his fingers in memory, then spoke from out of his need, the tears drying on his cheeks.

"I'll...finish...tonight."

And he could. He was close, very close.

He looked up at Father. "But you have to give me what I want," he said. "Not the GOOD BOX. What I really want."

Mother's finger moved toward the BAD BOX again but Father stopped her. He looked at the wall. Even unfinished, its promise had to draw him.

"And this will be everything I demand?" he asked.

"Yes," Ugly said. "Everything."

Father nodded, motioned to Mother. She drew back. It seemed to Ugly that she was reluctant. He wondered if she feared the wall, if she feared it would take Father away from her as she had taken him away from First Mother so long ago.

Ugly knew that it would. And he wasn't sorry.

At the door, Father and Mother stopped for a moment. They glanced back. "Tonight," Father said, his voice a threat. He locked the door behind them as they left.

Ugly did not hesitate. He had known for days what the wall needed—had prepared the bone foundation for placing the final pieces. Only the will and the parts had been missing. The former was here now; the latter would come. He picked up the sharp crucifix and knelt beside the body. It was dead and nothing else would delay his work.

He took off the breasts first. Set them aside. Then the hair.

And the penis. Once in a while as he cut, he reached down and picked up a spilled bead from the broken rosary, putting it on his tongue like a host and swallowing it. The ritual calmed him, as a similar ritual with a rosary had—years ago—seemed to calm First Mother in her fear of Father.

After everything he wanted from the corpse was removed, Ugly carried each separated piece to the wall and slipped it lovingly into the niche that had been readied for it. Next, he began to attach them, and soon the rhythm of creation seized upon him and his hands blurred with speed and blood. Hours passed.

Two more bodies were brought and they came already cold and ready for use. One was a woman with hydrocephalus, the other a murder victim who had been partially cannibalized. Ugly found lips and tongues that he needed. He found ribs and muscles and the sweet bones of the pelvis. From the first body he went back and took the smoothest skin.

In the last hour of his work, when the three bodies lay mined and stripped behind him, and his hands were flowing over the wall like electrical currents, Mother came back to him. She was thin again, as she had not been in months, and seemed wan and drawn. But she carried the black box, the GOOD BOX, and this time when she pressed a button a delicious warmth began to tingle through Ugly's muscles.

Then Mother kissed him behind the ear, and on the shoulder. She knelt, putting her fingers into plastic gloves as translucent as skin. Her lips danced over his body as easily as his hands moved on the wall, and at each place she wet with her mouth her fingers snapped on another alligator clip.

The rattling of the metal clips rang contrapuntal to the slick whisper of tissue in his hands, and the entwined melody tightened Ugly's erection until it bumped lightly against the meat of his creation. After a moment it found an entrance and slid into a mouth that was cool and dry as only non-living flesh could be.

As the last component settled into place, the wall accepted Ugly fully and he shuddered in a necessary orgasm. Mother shuddered with him as she felt his climax vibrate through the clips that now covered his body like scales.

Watching the wall, Ugly felt as if he could visualize his seed spreading along the sinew pathways connecting its nodes. The pieces stirred before his eyes, the movement swirling out from the center toward the edges. Colors turned from sick grays to the delicate pinks found inside the shells of mussels.

Ugly turned to Mother where she knelt in a puddle of sweat. In the aftermath of creation he loved her, and he pressed a red hand to the fevered skin of her cheek. She was staring at the wall and jumped when he touched her. And eyes that had been warm went cold again as she turned off the GOOD BOX and stood up.

Saddened, Ugly watched her leave. Then he went over to his favorite corner and squatted, rocking while he waited for Father to come and view the finished canvas. It was the largest and best he had ever done. The others had been only practice. He could see that now. This one was...right.

When Mother returned she'd exchanged the GOOD BOX for the BAD BOX. But Father was with her and Ugly watched the man this time. He watched the thin-fingered hands rubbing together gleefully.

"Finished?" Father asked. But it was not a true question and Father did not wait for a reply. He closed his eyes and faced the wall, then opened his lids all at once to take in what his son had done. His whole body seemed to fill up with a glow, and after a long moment he turned to look at Ugly over his shoulder.

"Incredible. Beautiful." he said. He looked back at the wall, unable to keep his eyes away. "And it's working?" he asked. "It'll do what I want?"

The other mosaics had not quite done what Father wanted. It had taken a while for Ugly to figure out what Father wanted. Now he had.

"Yes," he replied. "It'll do exactly what you want."

Father only nodded, moved toward the wall, reaching out to caress a circle of breasts. The tissues came alive under the stroke of nailed fingers, nipples growing erect. Ugly knew the flesh would be warm, though it was a false warmth. His Father would not care. Even if he noticed.

Ugly heard his Father's breathing growing louder, harsher. He watched the man strip himself naked and push his body into the soft grip of the wall. Dead hands and mouths attached themselves all over him, fingers clasping, tongues licking. The whole mass of the mosaic began to quiver, old elements converging into new, birthing shapes of utter loveliness.

As Father started to grunt, Ugly looked aside, toward Mother. She was not watching Father; she was watching him. And her still eyes were dead with hatred, her finger moving toward the button of the BAD BOX. She had lost Father. The wall had taken him away from her, would keep him away from her. Just as when she was thirteen she had taken Father away from First Mother and kept him.

Ugly remembered. He'd been seven at the time. And Mother, the Mother in this room, had owned another name—Sister. Now she punched the button on the red box and Ugly's mind cooked. He screamed, dropped to the floor as if he'd been axed. Every metal clip on his body was a bright pointillistic sting, the whole coalescing into a portrait of agony.

Abruptly as it had begun, the pain ended. Ugly glanced up from the floor, blood running from his mouth where he'd bitten his tongue nearly through. With blurring eyes he saw his Father, saw how furious Father was at being interrupted in his act, the purplish erection bobbing between his skinny legs as he hit Mother over and over. She dropped the punishment box, cowered down.

"You stupid bitch," Father was shouting. "We need him to keep the wall alive." And he hit her again. "Stupid, stupid, bitch." And he hit her again and again. She was crying. Ugly had never seen her cry since she'd become Mother. The sight didn't move him, but he struggled to his knees and Father heard him and stopped the beating, then looked toward him.

"You promised me what I want," Ugly said as loud as he

could. "You promised me. You can have the wall forever but give me what I want."

Father's face lost its tautness. He relaxed. Suddenly.

"Control," Father said. "Control, Jase. You'd do well to learn some." He smiled, motioned to Mother on the floor. "Get him what he wants," he told her.

Ugly climbed to his feet, stood swaying, but with the synergy flowing back between his muscles and limbs. He wanted. And the thought of receiving was enough to bring him back from pain.

Mother didn't keep him waiting, as he thought she would. In moments she returned with a bundle in her arms, small and blanket wrapped. She put it on the floor and stepped away, her face ghastly with tears and hate. Ugly ignored her, stumbled forward to kneel beside the covered package, his throat choked with fear and hope. Reverently, he began to fold back the blanket.

Feet came unwrapped first, tiny as minnows. And kicking. It was a baby, and it was alive. Ugly had always wanted a baby, ever since First Mother had promised she was going to have one for him. Before Father had killed her. After she had found out about Father and Sister. After she found out about the "studies" her doctor husband had been running on her son Jase.

Now, Ugly's hands reached out to cup the small warm mound before him and lift it. He stopped; the smile on his face dropped away. The baby stirred, its head coming unwrapped. He saw its eyes, gray like Father's and Mother's and his. And he saw its ears festooned with alligator clips, black to the left, red to the right. Worst of all was the scalp, with the tiny metal wires sticking up through the skin like splinters.

"Electrodes," Father called them.

Ugly remembered. After First Mother had died, Father had put these same kinds of wires in Ugly's head. Then had come the GOOD BOX and the BAD BOX. And the years of doing what Father wanted him to do. Always what Father wanted him to do. Never perfect. Never real enough. And always the pain to keep him in line.

Ugly looked up. Father was grinning. Mother too, her face a rictus. Ugly knew now where her belly had gone. He wished for an instant that she was dead. She had let Father do this to her baby.

And Father! Ugly glared at him, made a choking sound. He bit down again on his own tongue, felt the blood spew over his lips as if he were vomiting in scarlet.

Father's expression changed. He glanced hurriedly to Mother. She was looking at Ugly too, fear blooming suddenly in her eyes. Her hands fumbled...in the pocket of her lab coat... for something. It wasn't there. Ugly knew where it was—on the ground where she had dropped it when Father began hitting her. The BAD BOX was out of reach.

Father lunged for it.

Ugly shrieked.

The wall heard. And obeyed.

Tongues and intestines and strands of silken hair. All of them heard. And reached. Grabbing at Father. Grabbing at Mother. Snapping taut around limbs and necks. Hauling backward. The wall sucked the two of them against it. Teeth clicked in death-dry mouths. Fingernails clawed from dismembered hands.

Father and Mother began to scream. But they couldn't for long. The living wall crushed their vocal chords, tore their joints apart, swallowed their pieces into itself. It found...places for them, keeping them alive in the greater whole.

Ugly never had been able to kill.

But he wasn't thinking of that.

Holding the baby, holding this child, Ugly was thinking only of First Mother, of how she had once promised him an infant. He was thinking of how he—after Father had killed First Mother— had touched her with his little boy hands and brought her back. How excited Father had been to find out that his son could do more than heal bugs and injured lizards. But Father had not let his real Mother live that second time.

Nor the third.

Ugly got up and walked to the wall, still holding the child. He saw Mother/Sister's face form in a swirl of tissue and melt away again. He saw Father's head with the mouth open to scream, a hand growing from the throat in place of a tongue. Ugly reached out, folded the fingers up to push them through Father's eyes. He nodded to himself. The wall of love was complete.

Then he turned away, humming a tuneless lullaby to his little brother. As he plucked the silver wires from the tiny scalp and healed the wounds.

One by one.

TWENTY-FOUR
MILE BRIDGE

MILE 24:

The day's dark and heavy rain began to stomp on the car again as Jan Michaels pulled out from under the protection of the Mandeville toll booth and pushed down on the accelerator of her beat up Toyota. Perched blue against the wet concrete of the right side guard rail, Jan could see the mile marker and could read the white number twenty-four that flagged it. It was twenty-four miles to Greater New Orleans across Lake Pontchartrain on the Causeway Bridge—twenty-four minutes or thereabouts. She wondered if she would survive the trip.

Jan looked over at her passenger. He didn't appear to be watching her. His eyes stared out over the lake to where gray rain met gray water. But Jan knew he *was* watching because as soon as she glanced in his direction his hand moved the coat that had lain across his lap at the toll booth. Beneath the frayed cloth sat a rusted and stained flathead screwdriver. A big one. *Industrial grade*, she guessed. She turned her eyes quickly back to the highway and made sure the speedometer needle sat at sixty-five. As he had ordered.

MILE 23:

The man startled Jan by suddenly rolling down his window and sticking his head out of the car. The ozone smell of the rain swirled in, and at their current speed the impact of the water droplets had to sting the man's face like hot grease. Jan automatically lifted her foot off the gas to slow down. In the next instant the fellow's head was back in the car and the screwdriver was dimpling the skin of her right temple. She gave a tiny, surprised shriek, jerking reflexively at the steering wheel. The Toyota crossed the mid-line before Jan got control again and pulled back into her lane.

Late morning on a Thursday. There wasn't any traffic to speak of. No one had seen. Or cared if they had.

The man took the screwdriver away. "Sixty-five!" he said.

Jan pressed on the gas, felt the car lag for a moment as if it were tired. Then the engine gathered strength and they inched back up to the speed limit. She held it there. The man nodded and stuck his head out the window again, as if the rain would cleanse him of corruption.

MILE 22:

After a minute in the rain, the man drew his head back into the car. "Turn on the radio," he said. "Country." His hair dripped, hung wet and oily black down behind his ears and across his neck. His lips seemed strangely red against the dirty pallor of his face, like strawberries crushed at the bottom of a concrete block.

Jan reached out and twisted on the radio, dialing in 105.7, The Gator, the only country station she knew of. Her father had grown up on a farm and liked country music. She had grown up in the city and didn't. Normally she listened to Easy 101, or to WC2K if she was in the mood for Classic Rock. The man smiled when the station came on, began to nod his head to the wail of a steel guitar. He hooked his left leg over his knee and began to rub the blade of the screwdriver against his hospital issue shoe. After a while, little slivers of rubber sole began to shred away.

MILE 21:

Jan wished she had never become a psychiatric nurse. In the beginning it had been the greatest feeling to get to know a patient as a human being, and then to watch that being walk out of the hospital with dignity restored. Five years of seeing the same failures and diseases, and sometimes even the same *people* returning, had altered things for her. She was only twenty-eight, but even before today she'd felt tired. Through childhood and adolescence she'd clung to the belief that people could be changed and saved, and that scars could be healed. In the last few years she'd started to doubt that, and her soul had begun to callus.

Then came the patient in room 356. She'd wanted nothing more than to end her day at home with a shower and a bed. But when she'd stepped into that room, everything had changed. And now he was here with her, with a screwdriver. She wanted to cry but dared not. The bridge stretched out too far in front of her. Maybe something could still happen to save her, and she had to be ready if it did.

MILE 20:

The sound, when it occurred, seemed as loud in the car as if a cloth sheet had been ripped down the middle by a dull knife. Jan looked over at her passenger, her eyes wide and afraid. Number 356 had unzipped his pants. She looked away quickly, knuckles whitening across the steering wheel, her body hunching forward as if she expected threats and blows.

MILE 19:

"Why are you doing this?" Jan heard herself ask, though she tried to bite back the words even as she spoke them. She only wanted to sit still and small in her seat like a little girl, to drive the car and not be noticed. Instead, her mouth had opened and words had come out to draw the man's attention.

He looked over at her. The whites of his eyes were gray, the lids a raw, infected red around them. "You know!" he said. "You're making me do it."

She shook her head. "I don't want this," she said. "I just...I just want to sleep. Go to sleep and wake up in a month. Or a year."

The man's lips skinned back over teeth that were white and even. Too white. Too even. Although he'd been brought into the hospital as an indigent, he must have had the money in the past to visit a good dentist. Even so, his smile still looked as if something were lacking.

"Too late for *sleep*," he said. "We have to find out who I am."

"Evil," Jan snapped suddenly. "You're evil." Then she shrank back against her seat in fear of what her accusation might evoke.

Number 356 only shrugged. "Maybe."

MILE 18:

The man grunted and shifted position in his seat. "Don't look at me," he ordered, and Jan turned her head to the left so she could still see the road but couldn't see anything to the right side of the steering wheel.

There came a bitter smell, an unwashed smell. She heard the man's breathing get heavy and rapid and thought she was going to throw up.

He can't be doing this.

But he was.

MILE 17:

When the man finished, he reached out and put his hand— the same hand he'd just used on himself—on Jan's shoulder. She bit her lip as his thumb rubbed in little circles across the white of her uniform top. She could feel the pressure through the cloth onto her skin.

"Don't," she said, shifting out from under his grip. The hand fell, bounced on the seat, then seemed to leap like a darting lizard up her arm to close over the trapezius muscle at the side of her neck. It clamped there, wringing a cry of pain from her mouth.

"Don't pull away from me," the man said, shaking her. "I can't hurt you if you don't pull away." His voice seemed almost to be pleading.

Jan nodded carefully. She forced herself to relax, and after a moment the hand went away.

But they always come back, she thought.

MILE 16:

The man was staring intently at his fingers when Jan glanced over at him. He saw her look, made an attempt to explain. "I used...to be a scientist," he said. "I just remembered that." His voice seemed to be testing his words for truth even as he muttered them. "Used to...work with rats. Rabbits sometimes. But mostly rats. You had to tame them first. You bought them young. From the laboratory farms. You had to teach them to hold still when you handled them. Squeeze them a little in your hand when they squirmed. Let up when they calmed. It almost always worked."

He looked at Jan then as if he'd had a revelation. His face bloomed with light until she felt she could almost see through him. She looked away.

They passed one of the crossovers connecting the two spans of the bridge. A gray Causeway Police car sat in the crossover, and for an instant Jan considered blinking her lights or doing something to attract the cop's attention. Then they were past the turnaround and it was too late.

A slow trickle of sweat ran off Jan's neck and burrowed beneath the front of her uniform. Her bra itched. One at a time she took her hands off the wheel and wiped them against her pants.

MILE 15:

Jan watched the man sit in silence, in a sphere of aloneness that seemed to deny her existence. She wished he would just disappear, just evaporate out of his seat. She wished she could *make* him disappear. She didn't think either of those things was going to happen.

Her mouth tasted like bananas and zinc. She swallowed and swallowed but it wouldn't go away. She wiped her hands again.

MILE 14:

The man began once more to bob his head to music. But it wasn't in time with the music on the radio. There wasn't any. The station had gone to a commercial. Another commercial followed and 356 reached out and turned off the power. Only the rain drummed on the vehicle then, but the man didn't stop bobbing his head.

MILE 13:

The rain slackened, fell away behind them, and the silence that followed created a deep well that Jan felt compelled to toss words into. She fought the urge but finally had to speak.

"Will you let me go when we get to the New Orleans side?"

The man ignored her question to ask one of his own, a surprisingly normal one: "You grow up in New Orleans?"

"In Metairie," she said. "What they call Greater New Orleans."

"Family still there?"

Jan bit the inside of her lip. "My mother's dead," she said at last.

"And your father?"

She swallowed. "Yes. Yes. In an accident."

"New Orleans is the center," the man said then. "Everything began there. Love and hate. Did you know that God is dead? I read it in a book once. Came to know it there in Greater New Orleans. At least...," he frowned, "I think I did." He slapped himself on the forehead twice. "I wish I could remember.'

Jan felt the sudden urge to reach out and comfort her passenger. She knew it was a feeling some victims had. She'd had it herself before. It was ridiculous, but the man seemed so vulnerable in this moment. Her fingers even fluttered on the steering wheel as they started to lift. But 356 sat back in his seat before she could move, and he held up the screwdriver and rammed it as hard as he could into the dashboard, impaling her glove box.

MILE 12:

Already, Jan's world had shrunk to the point where only the inside of the car seemed real. Now it shrank even further as the man leaned forward over the screwdriver and began slowly to bang his forehead against the handle. Over and over. Over and over.

"Let me go," he said. "Let me go. I don't belong here. I *can't* be here!"

MILE 11:

Number 356 abruptly sat up straight in his seat, and Jan remained very still while he worked the screwdriver out of her dashboard, dragging it slowly up and through the plastic. The sound was like a saw coming out of wood.

Jan was surprised she'd remained so calm in the face of the man's violence, but maybe it was because she'd finally decided what to do when they reached the end of the bridge. They didn't have to stop to pay a toll there but the speed limit dropped to 35. She'd slow down more than that.

As the bridge ended, she'd see the Causeway Police building on the left side of the double spans. A patch of grass lay between the left and right spans. She remembered it. And when she was going slow enough she'd open the door and jump out toward that grass. She'd jump out and maybe she wouldn't get hurt too badly. Then she'd run toward the police.

If only she could find some way to distract the man. When the time came.

"You asked me why I was in the hospital," 356 said suddenly, and though Jan didn't think she *had* asked, she smiled and nodded her head. *Only ten miles to go.* And if he were talking he wouldn't be doing...other things.

MILE 10:

"They said I was walking and got hit by a car. But I don't remember it."

"Didn't you have a wallet?" Jan asked. "Something to iden-tify you?"

"I had a little girl."

Startled, Jan turned toward the man. "What?"

"There was a little girl with me. She told the people who stopped that I was her daddy, but not her *real* daddy. I think that's why I was in...your kind of hospital."

Jan's throat seemed to clot; she tasted bile in her mouth but couldn't swallow it. She wanted to roll down her window and spit but she couldn't do that either.

For a moment there was silence, and then the man spoke again. "I don't *remember* any of it. But I was told."

MILE 9:

"Who told you?" Jan managed to ask.

"You did," number 356 said. "You read it in my file. You read it to me."

"No!" Jan shook her head. "I don't know what you're talking

about."

The man frowned. Then his face emptied.

"I thought—" he began.

"Well you were wrong," Jan said, clipping the words off as she snapped them out between her teeth.

MILE 8:

The man began to sing very softly. "Happy birthday to you. Happy birthday to you. Happy birthday, dear Jannny. Happy birthday...."

Jan thought he sounded very much like her own father. On her 10th birthday.

MILE 7:

The man scooted over in his seat until he was closer to her. Then he took the screwdriver and placed the tip just below her right breast. Jan began to shake. She wondered if he was going to kill her right then, before she had any chance to try her escape.

Only six miles, she thought. "Please!" she said.

The man didn't answer. He shifted the screwdriver to his left hand and nuzzled his face against her shoulder. His right hand went to her knee and slid back and forth over the rough cloth of her pants. His fingernails were black against the pale nylon. Then he began to work his fingers up her leg like newly hatched spiders crawling.

"Please," she said again, and there were tears in her eyes. But she didn't pull away. He had said what would happen to her if she pulled away.

His teeth began to nip at her shoulder through her uniform, the material already sticky wet with his saliva. She could smell his breath, like mold beneath a water-soaked carpet.

MILE 6:

For a moment, Jan went away from herself, away from the car and the man she both knew and did not know. She went where she'd always gone, that place where she could peer out at the world and do her duty but not be truly touched.

She went there, but the trees were dead and the flowers fallen. The pool was matted with rotting leaves. The skies had grown crow-black and all sweet sounds had been murdered by a bitter wind.

She went. And she came back.

MILE 5:

"Spread your legs for me," 356 said.

"No," Jan said. "Spread yours."

The man looked up from nuzzling her shoulder. She hadn't realized his pupils were so dark, like opened midnight graves. She forced herself to smile into his face, then reached over very slowly to put her hand in his lap. His eyes widened but the screwdriver didn't push any harder against her breast.

His tongue came out to touch his too-red lips. It was roofed over with a green scum, like a little frog swimming under algae, and Jan didn't let herself look away. Her hand began to move against his crotch. His zipper was still down and the metal was cool on her fingers. His penis was hot beneath the cloth of his yellowed underwear and it began to stir.

Only five miles, she thought. *Five minutes.*

MILE 4:

Jan moved her hand on the man as slowly as she could. He grunted and shifted a little to the side. The screwdriver lifted away from her breast but didn't fall to the seat. She lifted his penis free of his pants. It was small and felt strange and awkward in her hand. She encircled it with her palm and began to work it, two strokes and stop, two strokes and stop. It grew quickly until it was hard up against his belly. She resisted the urge to dig her fingernails into the tender flesh and shove downward with all her strength.

MILE 3:

The man was breathing harder now, and quicker. His legs were wide apart and he was lying back against the seat. Jan tightened her index finger and her thumb over the penis head and began to move her hand faster. The man let the screwdriver slide out of his grip and put his filthy fingers against her hip, pushed them up underneath the loose bottom of her uniform blouse to touch the warm skin beneath. Jan shifted her position to let him, and in doing so she lifted her foot just slightly off the gas. The car slowed but the man didn't notice.

MILE 2:

Jan wasn't even thinking about her hand as it moved. The man appeared to be thinking of nothing else. She was looking everywhere, seeing where the door latch was, seeing the gray of the guardrail that marked the end of the Causeway, imagining the grass beyond where she would land when she jumped. She eased her foot off the gas even more. She was below thirty now, her speed still dropping.

"Faster, faster," the man said. But she didn't think he was talking about the car. She began to pump him, and felt his belly muscles tighten.

MILE 1:

The man groaned, and arched himself into Jan's hand. His legs and feet were stiff against the floorboard of the car, his left leg twitching. She felt his scrotum draw up tight beneath his penis.

"Come for me," she said, as she took her foot off the gas pedal completely.

The man groaned, and stiffened further, and she felt his penis spill. They were passing the Causeway Police building now and she cut the wheel to the left, taking her hand off the man and stiff-arming him away. The Toyota hit the curb and bounced back into the street, but Jan had already opened the door and was jumping.

The man grabbed at her and missed, his hand sliding on her right leg. Her knees hit the asphalt, felt as if they were tearing, but her body was over the grass and she hit and rolled forward. As the car bounced into the right lane and surged up onto the curb there, Jan thought she heard the man shriek. But his voice sounded more full of anger than fear.

Jan got up; her damaged knees bought her down again. The Toyota's engine was still chugging but the nose of the vehicle had locked itself into a chain link fence that ran along the border of the highway. The man had gotten out. She saw him with the screwdriver in his hand.

Jan began to scream, began to crawl across the grass toward the pale brick walls of the police building and the Causeway bridge office. She saw shapes there, people rushing out of the buildings. Some had guns drawn.

Jan glanced back. The man ran out into the road behind her, coming for her. His eyes caught hers and he stopped suddenly.

She heard him shout: "I remember. I remember it all! I'm sorry, Janny."

A van coming off the Causeway hit him, seemed to go right through him. Jan screamed again, covered her face with her arms.

Somewhere, brakes squealed. Somewhere she heard the click of guns being cocked. She looked up. The police were surrounding her. Their pistols were pointed at her. At her!

She looked over her shoulder. The man was gone. As if he'd never been.

Then she heard a policeman call out, from where he stood

beside her wrecked car. "Dead man in the passenger seat here," he said. "Screwdriver in his chest. Looks like he's been dead for several hours."

One of the officers squatted to look at Jan. "You kill that man in the car?" he asked.

Jan chuckled, mostly to herself. "Killed him," she agreed. "He'd changed. Thought I wouldn't recognize him. But I did. I did." She raised her voice, began to shout. "Killed you again, daddy. Killed you again."

She looked at the policeman, smiled with a lost mouth. "I'll recognize him next time too," she said. "I promise."

OUTSIDER

The snow falls straight down. Like cold feathers at first. Then in heavy clumps the size of fists. You stumble to your knees. But you're up again swiftly. To stop moving is deadly. Not that there will be time to freeze. That kind of death would be almost welcome compared to the horror you fear. That horror has no easy name. But it follows you. It follows.

You stagger forward through the swirling winds of what threatens to become a blizzard. Wind will cover your tracks, you think. It would be such a boon. But you doubt it will happen fast enough to save you. You doubt that *anything* can save you.

The snow thickens even further. You start to sweat. A book you once read told how dangerous it was to sweat in the bitter cold. The wetness will freeze on you, chill you to death. But you dare not slow down. Those who follow are coming. You hear them, you think. Though maybe it's only the wind's shrill shriek.

Then the world knocks you down. You don't see well without your glasses and in the snow you run head on into...something. Suddenly you're flat on your back with wet white slush piling atop you. Your face throbs. A tooth waggles loose in your gums. You taste salt at your lips, know it must be blood.

Somehow you struggle to your feet. Your hands find the thing that hit you, or that you hit. It feels man-made and you realize it's a wall. It's *the* wall. It towers too high to climb over so you begin to Braille your way along it, knowing there's no time to retrace your steps.

A sound stops you, freezes your blood more than the cold surroundings can. You turn. The followers are there, mere silhouettes through the blitzkrieg of snow. You back away—until your shoulders press flat against the wall and there is nowhere left to go.

Those who follow hone in on your helplessness. They bulk around you, cutting off any escape. You want to cry out for mercy. You would beg in an instant if you thought it would save you. But their soul-less eyes tell you it won't.

One of those who follow holds out something in a bulky paw. Though terrified, you inch slowly forward. The paw resolves itself. It's wearing a mitten. Your glasses dangle from the wool. You reach for them, knowing what will happen. The glasses are released just as you touch them, drop and disappear in the snow. You feel the sting of tears and fight them back.

Somewhere a bell rings. But it's too late. Nothing can end the game just yet.

The other children laugh as they push you hard against the wall, and you hear the crunch as someone stomps your last pair of glasses. You *do* begin to cry then, even though you know it'll make things worse. They love the tears, and they don't care that recess is over. They only care that you're different, and alone with them.

Alone.

Isolated.

An outsider.

GOOD NIGHT;
SLEEP TIGHT

You are lying awake and still in the darkness when you hear the noise, a soft, sticky shuffle, like rotted feet dragging on carpet.

Your heartbeat speeds. Your mouth dries. Who's coming? Who's coming!

The bedroom door scritches back on hinges that need oiling. A shadow bulks in the delicate glow from the hallway lamp. A scream rises in your throat, bulges your lips like vomit trying to escape.

But then you hear Momma say: "Good night. Sleep tight. Don't let the bedbugs bite."

"Yes, Momma," you reply. And: "I love you, Momma."

You think you see her smile. Certainly there is a flash of white in the dimness that could be her teeth.

The door closes and you lie awake and still. But no matter how still you lie, there is movement under the starched sheets. And there is sound, a click-click, click-click, like the tumblers turning over in a lock.

You bite your lip. Your nose itches but you dare not lift a hand to scratch. You must: "sleep tight."

Or else the mandible-clacking little monsters that Momma tucked in with you earlier will rip you to shreds.

BRANDED

I saw the cross of heaven
branded on the face of hell,
where stood a wet-eyed angel,
where danced the discord
of ghosts and God.

I saw the bright electric soul
with ruins red upon its back,
and there were no wings,
no eyes within the wrack.

Yet soft the word bloomed,
scarred etchings on a fossil bone.
Dust to dust we are,
born in blades,
raised to whips and honey.

But the razor will not rend us.
The coffin will not cage us.
Death you will not have us.
For I pillow my head on rock,
and in the night I have seen.

FLOATER

I

She thought about a fruit and vegetable stand she'd stopped at a few days before leaving Earth for the first trip to Mars, the first human trip to Mars. She thought about peaches and pears and grapes, a dozen varieties of each. She thought about cantaloupes and Creole tomatoes, about Red Delicious apples and bananas and thick, tart slices of orange. She thought about watermelons. Sometimes she dreamed about them.

A year ago all Aleksandra Vyshinskaya dreamed about was Mars. Now she dreamed about fruit. The irony wasn't lost on her. The *Gorbachev* was a fine ship and had everything aboard it a human could need, but it didn't have everything one could want. It didn't have a fruit stand, for example. It didn't have snow cones, or beer on tap, or pretzels. It didn't have weather. It did have baseball, but the games were already over when you watched them and it wasn't the same as when you were there in the stadium, screaming your lungs out at a great play and spilling hot dog mustard all over yourself.

Still, Aleksandra was not really envious of the people on Earth. She had something only a handful of them would ever have. She had Mars, hanging huge in orbit below her. And she had five friends down on that red surface. She watched their readouts on her data coms and wondered what they were finding. Sometimes she wanted to be down there with them, but she took seriously the duties that kept her aboard ship.

Though half ashamed of it, Aleksandra was just a little glad the Mars mission planned by the United States for the first decade of the twenty-first century had failed to go out. The collapse of the Soviet Empire during the 1990s, and the resulting era of balkanization and war in Eastern Europe and the Middle East, had turned everyone's mind from space for a while. But, Aleksandra thought the delay had probably been for the best, after all, and not just because of the opportunity it afforded her.

The third decade of the new century had finally brought the cheap fusion energy that powered the *Gorbachev*'s engines. And with the defeat of old enemies like cancer and new ones like the retrovirus diseases of the late twentieth century, there had come a renewed sense that human destiny lay beyond the sweet skies of Earth.

There were still problems on the home planet, of course: overcrowding, shortages of basic minerals, a lack of arable land. Many people thought Mars was the answer to those concerns. It could be mined with robots and long distance fusion barges. Maybe it could even be terraformed. The *Gorbachev*'s crew was to judge the feasibility of such dreams, and Captain Aleksandra Vyshinskaya, Alek to her friends, was supposed to see the crew got to Mars safely and then got home again.

Alek knew she'd been in just the right place and time to be chosen for command of this mission. She'd been born near Kiev in the old Soviet Union, but the civil unrest of the 1990s had driven her parents to the States. There, the daughter of a factory worker had grown up to be a physicist and engineer, and, eventually, leader of a Mars mission that combined the talents of her old country and her new one. It had been a long, strange road, but she wouldn't have given it up for all the beer, bananas, and baseball on Earth.

The intercom's buzz cut through Aleksandra's reverie and she tapped a button to hear the voice of Forest Nance, the ship's astronomer. Forest's work kept him in space as well, and Alek found herself pleased at that.

"Yeah, Forry. What is it?"

"Well...I'm not really sure. I was doing some spectroscopy on the Martian atmosphere and I picked up an orbiting object radiating at about 800 nanometers into the infrared."

"Meaning outside the visible spectrum," Alek interpreted.

"The radiation, yes. But not the object. I found it with the light scopes. It's...uh. Well, all I can say is it's odd. I thought you might wanna know about it."

"What do you mean odd?" Alek asked, the tight coil of her curiosity stirring. Curiosity had gotten her into awkward places as a kid, and though she controlled it pretty well these days it still wasn't hard to arouse.

Forest laughed, the rich, tenor laugh that Aleksandra never tired of hearing. "You'll think I got into the nitrous oxide," he said.

Alek grinned to herself. "I already know about your disgusting drug habit. Now I'd like to know what you think is odd. What kind of object are we dealing with?"

"Well. Offhand, I'd say it was a coffin."

II

"Can we bring it on board?" Forest asked.

Alek had joined the astronomer in the lab after leaving Kim Iverson, the mission tech and last member of the on-board crew, to monitor the landing party. Now she looked up from the data readouts of the *Gorbachev*'s ten million dollar scopes. They had told her the same story they'd told Forest. Just below them in orbit was a rectangular object with the dimensions of a coffin. It seemed to be made of stone and was certainly not typical space junk. It was also hollow according to pictorial scans. Hollow, but not empty. Aleksandra wondered what was inside of it, and knew she wouldn't rest until she found out.

"Is it feasible?" she asked, responding to Forest's question with her own.

"Very! I ran some calculations while you were coming down.

It's only a short distance below us and the energy expenditure needed to match orbits would be negligible. I'll be happy to go out myself and fish it in. As long as it gets named after me, of course!"

Alek was too preoccupied to recognized Forest's attempt at humor. She just asked more questions. "Okay, so it's feasible. Is it wise? What about the potential for contamination?"

"I'd say there ain't any. Vacuum will have killed anything living."

"How about the radiation you observed?"

"It's just infrared. Harmless. I figure it's a beacon of some sort. Hell, maybe it's an eternal flame. You know, like the one that burns outside Gorbachev's tomb."

"If it is, then it wasn't built for our eyes," Alek said.

Forest shrugged. "I'd guess you were right," he agreed.

Aleksandra rubbed her chin with both hands while she thought. "All right," she said at last. "Feed me your calculations once I'm on the bridge and I'll get us close. You bring it in. But I want the outside sterilized. And put it in isolation. We'll open it by remote."

"Aye, Aye, Captain, Sir!"

The decision made, Alek relaxed and grinned at the astronomer. Forest was grinning too, all with the right side of his mouth. But even as Alek watched, the smile slid away and something more serious filtered in. It was a look that had grown steadily stronger over their year-length trip. Aleksandra was scared of it, because so much time had passed since she'd allowed anything personal inside her life. And now was certainly not the time to change, she told herself, though she wasn't sure if that were the truth or an excuse.

Deliberately, Alek tried to change the mood. "Finally you address me properly," she said sternly. "Do continue it, won't you?"

She turned away, pretending not to notice Forest's insubordinate gesture. Joking aside, she didn't really feel much like laughing right now. A mystery always did that to her.

III

Aleksandra had just gotten off the radio to Ivan Brusilov on the surface when Forest buzzed to let her know the object was in the airlock and sterilized. Alek had described the find to Ivan, the leader of the surface team and the mission's second in command, and she could tell her old friend was skeptical. That was just a good scientist talking. Alek didn't know herself what they'd discovered, but she was determined to find out. She left Iverson on the bridge again and went down to help Forest move the object through the ship's corridors.

The thing looked even more like a coffin when Alek saw it up close. Well, not like a modern coffin but more like a stone sarcophagus that might have entombed Egyptian pharaohs. It had that kind of "old" feel, its once smooth surface pitted and scarred by hundreds of micrometeorite strikes. It was also heavy, and they had to lower the corridor's gravity before they could get the thing onto an air sled and down to the chemistry lab, which was the only place aboard with the tools to open it.

Once in the lab, they dumped the object onto a hydraulic table and lifted it up where the robot arms could get at it. Then they activated the quarantine doors to shut the thing off from anything but remote contact through the machines. X-rays were a priority, and once developed they were left with little doubt as to the thing's nature.

"A body in there, all right," Alek said. "It looks human but I can't tell for sure. Why is it so fuzzy? I thought we'd get a better picture."

"I thought so too," Forest said. "Something in the stone must be absorbing the rays. Even allowing for that, the image looks... unformed. Almost as if it weren't quite complete. I'm not sure it *is* human."

"How old you think?"

"Oh. Judging from the amount of micrometeorite damage, and assuming a steady rate of hits, I'd say at least a couple thousand years old."

"Meaning it's not human."

"Unless you want to believe the Romans had space flight."

"Maybe it's a floater."

"A what?" Forest asked.

"A floater. A body buried at sea but without enough weight to take it to the bottom."

"A space burial, huh?"

"Yeah. Maybe. Though I'd guess it was supposed to burn up in the atmosphere. That's only idle speculation, of course. We'll have a better idea once we open it."

"Right," Forest said. "But there's a problem. The robot arms aren't built for maneuvering that heavy lid. They're used mainly for mixing dangerous chemicals, usually in gram-sized amounts."

"True. But they're still pretty strong. And there's a program in the computer to run them simultaneously. We'll just have to get a bunch of them working on the lid at the same time." She reached out as if to touch Forest's arm, then let her hand drop to her side. "You've got the expertise there, I'm afraid. I'll leave you to it."

A beeping intercom interrupted Forest's response and Aleksandra answered immediately, only to hear Kim's voice as it cracked with uncharacteristic strain and emotion.

"Captain! The readouts on the surface crew. They're gone!"

"How could they be gone?"

"They're just gone, Captain! I've got completely empty screens. And no one is answering my hails."

Alek felt the heart slamming in her chest as terror for her friends threatened to overwhelm her. Then her training kicked in and she forced the emotion away.

"Any idea what happened?" she asked, her voice calm.

"None! They were in the Valles Marineris. I talked to Ellen Hector not ten minutes ago! She said they'd found something interesting. You know how she understates things. Then a minute ago their screens went blank."

Alek glanced at the sarcophagus where it squatted innocently inside the isolated lab. She found she couldn't quite believe in that innocence. "What's wrong?" Forest asked.

"We've just lost contact with the surface," Aleksandra replied.

Then she turned and sprinted for the bridge.

<h1 style="text-align:center">IV</h1>

As soon as Aleksandra reached the bridge she saw the empty screens that had once crawled with the surface crew's life signs. The flickering displays were loaded with static, and she felt that static bleed into her own thoughts.

"What now?" Kim Iverson asked, and the same question was etched on Forest's face a moment later as he came out of the stairwell to join them.

Alek looked from Kim to Forest, and back to Kim as she tried to judge how well her two colleagues were handling the situation. Kim didn't sweat much but she was sweating now, the beads shining against her dark skin. Forest was twisting his thumbs together. But they had both practiced for emergencies and Alek didn't think they'd crack. She wasn't so sure about herself all of a sudden, because she had a feeling this wasn't the kind of emergency that could be dealt with rationally. An image of the sarcophagus flashed into her thoughts and was as quickly pushed aside.

Alek released the long breath she'd been holding. "First, we send a message to Earth explaining the situation. Then I take the second supershuttle down to the surface to try and find the crew."

"What about us?" Forest asked.

"You stay here. The both of you. Kim. You'll be in charge. If you lose contact with me for more than one hour, take off for home. And take the object in the lab with you."

"But, Captain! We couldn't break orbit with you and the rest of the crew on the surface. That'd be leaving you to die."

Aleksandra believed Kim would be a good officer one day. But right now she was refusing to admit the obvious. Maybe she was still too young to admit it and remain sane. Forest was almost a decade older than Kim's twenty-eight years, Alek a little more. Both were more aware of their mortality.

"If I'm alive, then I'll find a way to signal you," Alek said gently. "Even if I have to touch off a shuttle engine. But one hour without contact means you pull out for Earth. You won't be leaving anything behind that matters. Besides, if I take the second shuttle there won't be any way for you to get to the surface to look for us.

"Now...." Alek stopped talking long enough to scribble a quick message for Earth control. She handed it to Kim before continuing. "I'm going down. Send this and let me know the second a response comes in. Otherwise, just follow procedures and go by the book. You'll do fine."

"Yes, Captain."

Aleksandra turned to Forest. The astronomer was scared, but trying not to show it for Alek's sake. Alek knew that if she lived through what was happening she'd stop ignoring the feelings developing between the two of them. She could see the same knowledge in Forest's eyes, and the regret that there was no time to speak of it.

"You'll have to get the coffin open as soon as you can," she said quietly. "I've got a hunch that whatever's inside it will shed some light on all our mysteries."

"Yes, of course," Forest said.

Aleksandra grasped the astronomer's shoulder once, hard, then released it and hurried past toward the shuttle deck.

V

The second supershuttle muscled its way easily down through the thin Martian atmosphere and Alek set it down only a hundred yards from the first landing craft. She knew most of the crew had been away from the shuttle when they disappeared, but she also knew at least one member of the party should have been left at the ship. She wanted to check every possibility.

It was eerie crossing to the other shuttle in her oxygen suit, almost as if something unseen was accompanying her. Alek had walked on the moon but that was clearly a dead place. Mars didn't seem that way. It wasn't much different from the deserts they'd trained in on Earth, and it wouldn't have seemed odd to hear a rattlesnake buzz its warning, or to look up and find vultures circling overhead. That last thought was too morbid to dwell on and Alek shook it away as the shuttle's airlock cycled open under her touch. She went in, her palms moist despite the air conditioned suit.

The ship looked lived in. The instruments functioned normally. There was just no one there. Aleksandra hoped all five crew members were out exploring, but she knew that was unlikely. Even if they'd found something "interesting," they would still have followed procedures and left someone at the landing craft. And if that one was gone, what had happened to the other four?

Alek thought of them then, and of the probability that they were dead. Ivan, Ellen, Terry, Mira, Galina. By themselves the names seemed like meaningless files for storing meaningless data. But for Alek they represented friends, five people whose lives were rich and thick, and intertwined with hers. She had to find out what had happened. She checked in with the *Gorbachev*, then lifted off in her shuttle toward a valley named after the first unmanned spacecraft to photograph it—the Mariner.

VI

The Valles Marineris was part of the longest canyon system on Mars, and pictures of it always reminded Alek of Africa's Great Rift Valley. The slope-sided canyons were nearly seven kilometers deep at places, over five hundred kilometers wide at others. The main gorge, along with its serpentine branches, was also a good sign that Mars had once hosted large amounts of surface water. That was one reason the ground crew had come here. Terraforming would take lots of water.

Many scientists also believed the Marineris was the logical place to look for fossilized signs of ancient Martian life. Although no reputable scientist believed complex multicellular organisms existed under current Martian conditions, some held out for simple bacteria. Others thought life could have evolved early in the planet's history. Either way, the huge canyon system seemed an ideal place to search for the signatures of Martian life. It was also where Aleksandra expected to find the signatures of her friends, living, or dead.

The first sign of those friends that Alek spotted was the land rover. It sat halfway down one wall of the valley, at the edge of a rock slide that had closed off its path. The machine seemed undamaged and had apparently been abandoned only because of the terrain. That left the crew on foot, which meant an easy trail to follow once Alek located their boot tracks in the dusty blanket of the valley's floor.

There was no place near the rover to land, however, and Alek had to fly on several kilometers before she could set down. She radioed the *Gorbachev* with her findings and made sure to talk to both crew members. Kim seemed nervous but in control. Forest seemed calm but confused.

"What is it?" Alek asked the astronomer. "You get the coffin open?"

"Not yet. It's locked tight. But I'm using acid on the seal and should have it open within an hour. There's something, though. I took more X-rays and the body seems to have altered in some way. It...uh. It looks more fully formed. It certainly seems completely human now. And definitely male."

Alek frowned. She didn't like what Forest was saying but didn't know what to do about it. She could order her colleague to leave the object alone, but she still felt it was tied up somehow with her crew's disappearance. Besides, knowing Forest, he wouldn't obey that order anyway.

"All right. Keep at it. But be careful. And let me know the instant you get it open. I'll be out on the surface but I'm taking the long distance radio so we won't lose contact. Just hold it together."

Alek signed off and didn't give herself time to think about what she was doing. Mars waited. She exited the airlock before it finished cycling open and was soon moving back up the valley toward the land rover. She interpolated the probable path the crew had followed and was lucky enough to turn up footprints less than two kilometers from her ship.

There were four pairs of boots. Only four! They were pointed south, deeper into the valley's heart. She turned and followed them, and in less than an hour found trail's end at a monstrous outcropping of rock that towered over the plains like a surreal termite mound.

She also found what had attracted the group here. It was a face on the cliff, a face forty feet high. It could not be seen from above and Alek wondered how the crew had spotted it. Then she wondered if, maybe, it could be natural. After all, she had seen similar shapes in clouds.

She didn't really believe her wondering, though. The face was too perfect and too recognizable. She had seen it thousands of times, at home, and in church. Aleksandra had been raised an Orthodox Catholic and knew an image of Jesus Christ when she saw one.

VII

Alek sipped from her water tube as the sweat started under her arms. The face on the cliff seemed to condemn her and she couldn't quite make her mind call the thought nonsense. She wanted to be away from here, but the footprints of her crew led straight toward the wall beneath the face, toward a small cave that made a dimple under the image's chin.

At last she started forward, only to stop again as the radio on her back squawked for attention. She punched the receive button, expecting to hear Kim, and was shocked when Forest's voice burst over the speakers. She was even more shocked to hear the horror crawling behind her friend's words.

"Aleksandra! Please. Get off the planet. He's dead! We'll all be dead!"

Who's dead, Forry? Who's dead?"

"I— I mean— It's...Ivan Brusilov. I got the coffin open and he was inside. Something down there killed him and put his body up here. I don't know how. But that's why the new X-rays looked different. The original...thing had been replaced with Ivan's corpse. And that's not the worst."

Alek closed his eyes and swallowed heavily. "What else, Forry?"

"As I opened the coffin, Kim said four more caskets appeared in orbit below us. I don't think you'll find the rest of the surface party down there, Alek. I think they're up here with us."

Alek looked at the rock face above her and then at the cave below. Her expression twisted between anger, fear, and awe. The anger lost, but so did the fear and awe. Responsibility, and the whip-touch of curiosity, settled in to replace them.

"All right," she said into the radio. "I'm only thirty yards from a cave and I can see where the crew's tracks lead into it. I'm going in. For five minutes! If I don't find anything I'll head back to the ship and we'll get out of—"

Aleksandra stopped talking as she recognized dead air. The radio had cut out. But that didn't change anything. The crew was her responsibility, and the cave was still there in front of her. She started forward, and she hoped the next five minutes would pass swiftly.

VIII

Aleksandra expected darkness beyond the cave's entrance, but she found light instead, a faint, golden luminescence that grew as she stood there. And there was someone else in the cave as well, some *thing* else. In the dim light it appeared vaguely reptilian, though its scales were as fine as snowflakes and its large, copper eyes spoke of vast intelligence. It did not look evil, or as if it were capable of killing, but the footprints of Alek's friends ended abruptly a few feet in front of the rock on which the being sat. And Alek knew they were dead.

Who are you?" Alek asked. "Are you to blame for the destruction of my crew?" She didn't even think about the fact that she spoke in English.

The figure made no overt response, but a smell came into the very air that Alek breathed, as if inserting itself directly into the tanks circulating her oxygen. She recognized damp moss and ferns battening on tarry mud. At the same time, the light brightened against the cavern wall behind the being. An image of the creature's face appeared there, and a voice seemed to speak directly from Aleksandra's headphones, making her jump. It, too, spoke in English.

"You already know the answer to your last question," the voice said.

"For God's sake, why?" Alek demanded. "You had no cause. They did you no harm."

A second odor overwhelmed the first, a dank odor of bursting swamp gas and fetid fish. The image on the wall darkened to obsidian and Alek felt the palpable presence of rage. Even the voice seemed to enlarge with anger, though Alek realized the being's true language probably lay in the odors and that the words were only mechanical translations. Still, she cringed where she stood as the voice exploded inside her helmet.

"DO NOT DARE TELL US WE HAVE NO CAUSE! WE KNOW WE HAVE! Two thousand years ago you gave us cause."

The last words dropped by octaves until they were scarcely above a whisper. There was blood in the scent now, and the wall screen turned gray and red with pain.

"I don't understand," Aleksandra said.

The wall lightened and a blue-green sphere took form there. Aleksandra recognized it as Earth seen from space, though the placement of the continents was distinctly odd. Along with the change of scene came the renewed whispering of the voice.

"Then understand," it said. "Eighty million years past we were born on the world you call Earth. We built a civilization there. And we were destroyed. Your people must know of the extinctions that occur on Earth every twenty-six million years. We knew too, but had no explanation until a nomadic race called the Selkrie came from the void to extinguish us sixty-five million years ago. Only a few of us escaped.

"The Selkrie did not know, but we too had developed space flight, only to abandon it after exploring this system. We understood the limits of metal and flesh, and, unlike the Selkrie, were unwilling to forsake a planet for millions of years at a time. We were unwilling to face the loneliness of the vacuum, perhaps the thing that drove their race mad. Though, a race that could destroy its own home, the planet that once filled the orbit of the asteroids, was probably already mad. Still, we had a few ships in our museums, and some of us slipped past the Selkrie fleet to reach this world. We name it Endirion.

"Here we burrowed deep, hiding from the Selkrie's return. And twice they did return. Soon they will come again. We watched the Earth between their visits, saw the renewal of life, followed the radiation of species and the arrival of intelligence. Your intelligence. We saw in humans a familiar spirit, though you were mammalian and we reptilian. We wanted you to survive, to be ready when the nomads came again. We even hoped your aggressiveness would allow you to stop the Selkrie where we could not.

"We feared that aggressiveness as well, though, feared it would ruin you before the Selkrie ever had that chance. So, two thousand years ago we sent one of our own among you. We are a long lived but nearly barren race, but we sent you a child. We made him human. Almost human.

"It may seem so to you, but this task was not difficult for us. Our civilization was never primarily technological; it was biological. As you would understand it, we altered an embryo's genetics. From the Selkrie we took the last thing we needed, a machine to convert matter to energy, or energy to matter. With it we can transmit materials over great distances, or even insert them inside another object."

"Like putting a body inside my ship," Alek said. "Or even a smell inside this suit I wear."

"Yes. Or sending one of us to Earth. Our volunteer knew he would die alone, but he carried the embryo with him and managed to see to its proper placement. A child was born, from no human union. He was named Jesus. Outwardly, he appeared as one of you, though there were differences in his thoughts and abilities. As he grew, he spoke of peace, and hope, and love. But you slaughtered him with as much savagery as the Selkrie have ever shown. Again we learned a lesson, and though we could not destroy a race, as would the nomads, we could place a warning for you in orbit around this planet, a warning we thought you would understand."

"The sarcophagus," Alek murmured. And the tears began to run on her face, for many reasons and for many losses, but mostly for the death of a lonely being who had deserved better treatment.

The sarcophagus," the voice agreed. "But you ignored it and came anyway. When all we want now is to be left alone."

"But we didn't understand it," Alek protested. "We didn't even detect its radiation beacon until after the surface party had landed."

A smell of cinnamon and sand filled Alek's nostrils.

"A simple mistake," the voice said. "But I do not think our next warning will be so easily missed."

The voice stopped, and at once the radio on Aleksandra's

back began to beep for an incoming call. She grabbed the keyboard, punched the message through. It was Kim Iverson. Alek tried to speak but the contact was only one way. All she could do was listen.

"Captain. I hope, somehow, you get this. I've gotta try. My God, I'm sorry, Captain, but it will be the last thing you hear from us. I sent Forest to the lab. He wouldn't have let me do what we *have* to do. But we're leaving before Mars takes us too. There are three more things in orbit now. Much bigger than the coffins. Fifty kilometers long, or more. My God, they're empty crucifixes. Glowing bright enough to be seen from Earth. I'm sorry, Captain. So sorry."

The message ended and Alek looked back at the being in the cave. Then she looked up, as if she could see all the way through the rock and the atmosphere of the planet into space. She knew why the crucifixes were empty. She knew who they were for. She could already feel pain starting in her hands and feet. And she knew her friends in orbit would not escape.

Forry, she thought.

Then: "Wait!" she shouted to the being. "The child of your race gave his life for others. Let me...too. Let my friends go. Let them live!"

For a long moment there was no response. Then an odor spilled into Alek's nostrils, an alloy of rot and honey. A death odor. A life odor.

She nodded, and smiled.

Aleksandra's last thought was of a fruit and vegetable stand she had stopped at a few days before leaving Earth for the first trip to Mars, the first human trip to Mars.

THE ROAD TO HELL

Part One

Phillip Russo was driving down the off-ramp at the Carrollton exit when the incident happened. Such a thing had never happened to him before, and never would again. But on that day, at that moment, his perception suddenly split into two parts, like a website pop-up on the internet. A teenaged girl stood at the curb just where the ramp curved down to meet Carrollton Avenue, and as he glanced at her out of his window, her image doubled. He saw her standing still, *and* he saw her step off the curb, saw her almost float off the curb into the path of an on-coming eighteen wheeler. And he heard her, the sound she made as she was hit, even over the hissing wail of the air brakes.

Phillip stomped instantly on his own brakes and swung his car past the end of the off-ramp into the parking lot behind the Piccadilly Cafeteria. He slammed back the door and leaped out, knowing that, if he had seen what he thought he had, there would be nothing he could do to help.

But then, maybe he hadn't seen it. He wasn't absolutely sure what he had seen until he was out of his car. Then he realized that he had *not* seen a truck, nor a teenager being run over. The girl still stood at the curb, as whole as ever. Only now, instead of looking at the street she was looking at him. He didn't wonder why. Nor did he wonder why he didn't just get back into his car and leave. He knew. He probably could have explained his sudden vision away as a once in a lifetime hallucination. In time he might even have believed it. But right now he knew that such an explanation would be wrong.

Phillip Russo had never thought of himself as sensitive, in the occult use of that word, but no doubt lingered in his mind that he'd just had a premonition. Some temporary link had been forged between the energy and horror in the girl's mind and his own unconscious, and for a moment he had been able to see *her* imagination played inside *his* head's theater. The curb where she stood was the perfect place to avoid being seen by trucks barreling down the off-ramp, and she had been planning on killing herself there. That he could not allow.

All the Russo's were Catholic and Phillip had been raised to believe that killing yourself was a mortal sin. Even at forty he couldn't escape that feeling, though his excellent education had provided him with knowledge of other belief systems where the right of people to take their own lives was held sacred and honorable. His own beliefs and his own heart would not let him accept that idea. The girl had to live.

Phillip shut the door to his car and started a slow stroll toward the young lady at the curb. She did not walk away.

* * * * * * *

"I just didn't feel like I could live with things anymore," the girl said.

The two of them were sitting in a Haagen-Daz ice cream shop and the young woman was giving Phillip the answers to every question he asked her. He had always been able to get people to talk about themselves, and this girl was an easier target than most. She clearly and desperately wanted to talk with someone. Deep inside the girl there didn't seem much of a wish to die, but that part was well hidden and Phillip figured she *would* have killed herself, more out of some conviction that the world would be better off than out of a hatred for life.

"I even gave my baby away finally," she continued. "Her name was Toni. Like mine. But I gave her away. I knew I couldn't be a decent mother to her. Though I wanted to. It was just that...well, after my boyfriend, Troy, left, the baby seemed to cry so much more. Maybe it was just that I didn't have anything to distract me. No job or anything. And Troy took the TV.

"One morning—" She stopped and chewed her lips for a moment, then spilled another gush of words. "One morning I ground up a valium to put in her milk, to make her go back to sleep you know. So maybe I could get some rest. It's just that I'd been up late trying to put together a work history for the unemployment office, with no work to go on it. But when I found myself by her crib with that bottle, her crying and me crying, I suddenly couldn't remember how much of the stuff I'd put in. And then I wasn't sure if maybe I hadn't intentionally put in too much. Maybe I kind of wanted her to go to sleep and not wake up, 'cause it would be so much easier on me. I started really crying then, and picked her up and hugged her a long time. Then I changed her diaper and dressed her warm, and I took her and left her outside Charity Hospital where I knew she'd be found.

"I already knew what I was going to do. When I was a kid I used to walk past that off-ramp all the time with my grandma. She raised me. She was always afraid of that place, and I guess that just made me notice it more. I don't know if I would have done it right then, stepped off in front of a truck I mean, or if I would have waited until later. I guess it would have depended on whether anything big enough came by or not."

"Then I came by instead," Phillip Russo said.

"Yeah. You came by instead."

"Still feel like you want to kill yourself?"

"I don't know. Maybe not now. Though that could be just because I've unloaded a lot of things on you. I'm really sorry about that."

"I guess I let myself in for it when I stopped."

"Yeah. I guess so. Why did you?"

"An old reason. It makes me feel good about myself when I help others. I'd like to help you some more too. Maybe I could get a few things straightened out for you."

"What things?"

"Well, I know a lot of people at Charity Hospital. I work there as a volunteer. I could probably get you a job there, and maybe help get your baby back. I also know a church where they offer free day care service to single mothers. It might be enough to get you back on your feet."

Toni looked at him for a moment. Then she leaned over her untouched ice cream and started to cry, the good kind of tears.

Part Two

Phillip Russo was fifty-seven years old when he died of a heart attack. He had never married and had no kids, but he still didn't die alone. He was at a friend's house playing bridge when he gave a little twisted smile and fell over onto the table. He even held a great set of cards when he went, and everyone there made a comment about how peaceful he was and how sad it was that the good die young. Of course, they made those comments later, because for a few minutes after their friend keeled over they were too busy dialing 911 and trying CPR. By that time, though, Phillip was already headed upward and would not have wanted to come back.

Seeing the sky open out above him was just what Phillip expected, and the death smile his friends had noted was a reflection of a pretty good feeling about himself. His sins had been mostly small and his life decent. He felt sure he would get his reward. The hours of volunteer work, the charities, the years spent as an educator would all start to pay off now.

The only thing that surprised Phillip was that the road to heaven was so much like what he'd always pictured. He had kind of expected to still be conscious after death, but he had also figured that his idea of heaven would be at least a little bit off. Yet, here he was on a long straight stairway that climbed up through bullet-blue skies into warm clouds. Ahead of him was a glory of light that did not burn his eyes, and then the light began to soften and he heard the first strains of music. He laughed and clapped his hands when he realized it was Mahler's ninth symphony, his favorite.

Next would be the gate, he thought. And there it was, its sweet, sweet gold complemented nicely by the white-bearded savant that leaned on an oaken stave out front.

"Peter?" Phillip asked as he approached.

"Yes."

"Then this really is heaven!"

"One heaven. Your version of it at least."

Phillip didn't quite understand, but that was almost a relief. One shouldn't understand everything about heaven. At least not at first. Besides, none of it mattered now. He was here. He threw his arms wide and spun about, then grinned at Saint Peter.

Peter did not grin back.

"Well what do I do now?" Phillip asked him. "I mean, do I sign something, or just go in?"

"Neither one of those, I'm afraid," Peter said. "At least not yet. You have a piece of unfinished business to attend to."

Phillip felt his heart flutter, the heart that had stopped beating only a few minutes before.

"What kind of business?" he asked. He wasn't grinning anymore either.

"There is someone that you wronged many years ago. If she forgives you, then you can return and enter here. Otherwise no."

"I don't understand," Phillip said. "Who have I wronged? I lived a good life."

"Yes. According to your rules you lived a good life, even an exemplary one."

"Then—"

"What if your rules aren't the right rules?" Peter interrupted.

The saint's words truncheoned Phillip in the face, and his dead heart rippled in his chest, driving him to his knees and doubling him over. Then the agony stilled and he was able to raise his head again. He reached a hand toward Peter. But Peter was no longer there.

The golden filigree of the gate was gone as well, and Phillip Russo found himself kneeling on griddle-hot stone instead of clouds. A roiling darkness ate up his vision, and banshee laughter spun him around to find nothing. And he was struck a sledgehammer blow from behind, hurled forward onto his face too shocked by pain to scream. But a chorus of other screams echoed around him, and that nailed his position down for him. He was in Hell.

Oh My God! he thought.

He was on his belly in Hell. But there had to be some mistake. He'd led a good life. He *had*. No matter what Peter had said about the rules?

A hand stopped his thoughts as it pulled him off his face and rolled him onto his back like a beetle. Something that resembled a photographic negative loomed over him, and he yelled "no" as he held up his palms to ward off another blow. Nothing hit him, but his wrists were vised and snapped down onto the lava-edged rock by his head. The seeming negative suddenly developed features as it knelt down beside him. In form it was a woman, and then Phillip recognized who it was, though both her face and body were bent and twisted with broken and improperly set bones. Only a flavoring was left of the girl he had once known.

Was this who Saint Peter meant for him to reconcile with? But how? He had *saved* this girl. Seventeen years ago he had pulled her out of a suicidal depression and gotten her back the baby she'd given away. He'd even set her up with a job and a place to stay. Of course, he had lost contact with her. Not even a Christmas card for the last ten years. But how could this girl be part of his sin?

"Toni! What is this?" he begged her.

"You bastard!" she said. "You son of a bitchin' BASTARD!"

"Toni! What's wrong. What— Why are you here?"

"Because you saved my life, you shit! You stopped me from killing myself."

"But I had to! Suicide is wrong. I saved your life for Christ.

How can that be wrong?"

"Oh cut the crap about doing it for Christ. You did it for yourself, for your own brand of moral hypocrisy. It made you feel good. You told me that yourself. Only, it didn't work out so well for me. I was sixteen then, still innocent. I'd seen a lot of bad stuff, but I was still a good person inside.

"Then you came along and *saved* my life. And you got my baby back for me. Well.... Ten years later I was a junky. One night I sold my daughter to a pimp for a fix. She was eleven years old and I gave her away for a bag of heroin. They turned her out. They turned her out for a whore and some sick fucking John killed her. I was so far gone I didn't even know about it until days later. I overdosed after that. And this time I wasn't quite so innocent.

"It's all your fault. If you had let me die that day we met, my daughter would have been adopted into a good home and I would have been in heaven to watch it. I know because the Devil showed it to me, showed me all the ways your moment of "kindness" rippled through my life and tore it apart. But now you'll pay. You're gonna roast in this shit-hole with me. And I'll hurt you a little bit more every day."

"But-t-t," Phillip started to say.

"No buts, friend Phillip. No butts except yours in a sling."

She poked him with a finger, like he was a loaf of fresh bread, but he didn't get a chance to find out just yet how she meant to hurt him. A third voice whipped the world into silence.

"BE STILL, WHORE!"

Toni crumpled like a can under pressure, and Phillip saw beyond her to another shape, a statue-huge form that was patterned in light and shade.

"My God, he's got horns," Phillip whispered.

"And a tail," Satan added, as he came forward and prodded Phillip with a pitchfork. "You're not very creative in your afterlife, are you?

"But you know," the Devil continued. "For a long time I wasn't sure I was going to get you. I should have remembered one of my favorite sayings. It's the kind that almost always comes true."

"What saying?" Phillip moaned.

Satan grinned. "The road to hell is paved with good intentions," he said.

And the evening and the morning were the first day.

A CURSE THE
DEAD MUST BEAR

There is no death by natural causes, no slipping peacefully into the grave. There is only torture. Slow, vicious torture.

You who call yourselves the "living" will not believe this. But we who have "died" know the truth. And we curse you for your ignorance. Though, of course, many of us were as guilty as you in our own day. I myself brutalized three people that I claimed to love. First when I buried my father and second when I closed the coffin on my mother. Last when I laid my poor wife to rest. To "rest!" What a cruel term for what I did to her.

I remember when I learned the truth. May 19th, 2010. At the age of eighty-six I still was able to live independently. "Spry," many called me. "How good that you still have your health," others remarked.

But spryness could not save me when, in coming down my stairs, I tripped over a toy left by my grandson and plummeted headlong into horror. Notice that I do not say I plummeted to my death. For I did not die.

To all appearances I *was* dead. The fall broke my neck, and when I landed in a position that should have been face down my head was twisted so hideously that I gazed back over my own shoulder at the ceiling. My last breath had already come and gone, and I breathed, and sighed, and spoke no more. My heart did not beat within my chest. But my mind lived somewhere deep within its core, and through my still opened eyes that mind could see.

For almost a day I lay there, and no muscle in my body would stir at my command, no matter how strident and violent those commands came. My son found me. My "loving" son. He fell to his knees beside my body. He did not touch me, perhaps because of how grotesquely I lay. But he demanded and cajoled and wept for me to get up.

I could not obey, though I strove harder than I had ever strove at anything in my life. And I could not speak to him, though I heard his words clearly. I *heard* his words clearly. And I could *feel* his tears as they spilled on me, could smell the cologne he had put on that morning and the chicory in the coffee he'd drunk at noon. Every sense was so exquisitely intense, far more than in what is called "life." Such a curse, the dead must bear.

Finally, my son's tears ceased. He rose from beside me and went to the phone. I heard him make the call that he, of course, felt he had to make. Until that moment I had wept inside for his sadness, had ached with the need to reach out to him, to brush back his hair as I had done when he was a child. But now my empathy for my son turned to terror for myself.

What were they going to do with me now?

And I knew. My God, they thought I was dead. They thought I was *dead*!

Only moments before I would have sworn that I'd used every bit of strength I had in trying to speak to my son. Now I truly understood how little I had known of my own capacity. I fought, I tore, I raged, I shrieked. And still I did not move. I did not even blink. I only felt, and thought, and begged, and prayed. To no avail.

An ambulance came. Someone pronounced my death and the words were spikes that would see me nailed into a coffin. Another closed my eyes. I was blinded. But I felt every bump of the journey to the morgue. I felt the cold table upon which I was laid, and every moment was agony as my blood was exsanguinated and my organs pumped full of formaldehyde.

Yet, even embalming doesn't kill you. Doctors and coroners cannot accomplish that act.

It is left next for your loved ones to try.

They see you placed in a coffin. They give you flowers and weep. They watch you lowered into the dark meat of the earth. And they go away and leave you, no matter how hard you try to scream. And for that your love turns to anger, to hatred. You think of a hundred ways to seek revenge. But none of those are within your reach, anymore than it is within your reach to force one last palpitation from your heart.

But even hatred cannot survive for long with nothing to push against in the darkness. Only *you* survive. Only you go on. And on. For a hundred years? For two hundred? For more? Perhaps the total dissolution of my body will end me. I can only hope so. I can only hope that being buried alive will one day kill me.

Do not die. Do you hear me? Do *not* die! Or if you think you must then have yourself cremated. Burn yourself to ash. For you have no idea how ghastly it is to lie quietly moldering in the grave, with the feel of silk decaying around you and the smell and taste of your own slow rot as thick as mud in your nostrils and mouth.

You have no idea how it is to lie there and listen to a dozen, to a hundred, to a hundred-thousand voices just like yours. All of them trapped in bodies that will not move, that cannot escape their oblong prisons. For there is neither a heaven nor a hell to escape to. There is nothing but the ever present whispering and moaning that only the ones you call dead can hear, the lamentations of mothers and fathers buried years before, of husbands and wives whose crypts lie so close.

No, you have no idea.

But you soon will.

SMOKED MEAT

After the short battle with the Shadowones was over and won, me and Gunner and the Commander popped open the turret and climbed out on the shell of our Mako tank, where the wind could ease our sweat. We still had a few piss-warm beers we'd brought through the portal from Earth and we drank 'em for the fluid content. I sure missed the electric cool-cans from home, but none of that high tech shit worked here on World 1470.

Hell, even the Mako was old fashioned. One mean lady, don't get me wrong. But she was as primitive as a stone knife. I mean, she had diesel engines for Christ's sake, modified with mechanical strikers and crank-started to avoid the need for batteries. Even her guns were aimed by hand. Nothing fancy on this female.

A scientist type had once tried to explain to me why an electric gizmo couldn't go through a parallel world portal without frying itself. I understood about as much of what he said as he did about fixing the guts of diesel engines. That's why I was here, to drive the Commander's tank and to cure stuff that broke, like replacing the strikers every time that damn diesel fuel gummed 'em up.

Come to think of it, though, being in a stone age tank fit well with the theme on 1470. This world was parallel to a long time ago in Earth's past. There were few flowering plants, and absolutely no birds in the reddish sky. There *were* dinosaurs. Our battle had been fought amidst a migration route for 'em and the crew of one of the other Makos was even now taking pot shots at a distant Triceratops herd.

The Commander was still pretty new and was watching the circus through his binoculars. I couldn't care less about it. I'd seen the huge damn things get explosive rounds down their gullets before. Take a rat, shoot it in the head with a .357, then swell it up to about eight tons. That'll give you an idea of the result. Even from where we sat I could hear the big things screaming as the 125 millimeter shells popped them open like ripe watermelons. The sound was amazingly high pitched for such large bodies, and I could picture the volcano of meat and blood that brewed up when the rounds hit.

I'd much rather shoot a Shadowone than a Triceratops. They didn't leave nearly the mess. No mess at all, in fact, just a dark and hazy silhouette that disappeared completely about a minute after you killed it. Earth Control had told us that no living thing could stay in a parallel world after it died. I'd certainly seen *our* dead pull the same fade out, and I knew those bodies showed up back on Earth.

The thing is, you see—and this I *could* understand—the warping of the natural order used to open a world-portal did strange things to physical laws. For example, though I hardly noticed it anymore, it had taken a while to adjust to having everything on a new world look like it was on the other side of a bonfire from me. That wavering distortion doubled if what you saw wasn't native to the new world either, and the result was a Shadowone. That meant, to our enemies, *we* were the shadow ones.

All our senses were bugged to some extent, but weight and mass weren't affected at all. An enemy tank would be just as heavy as ever when it rolled over you, even if you couldn't see it as anything but a patch of darkness. Fortunately, explosives worked too, as I'd seen enough times. So we weren't forced to rely solely on running the enemy down with our tanks.

A scream of pure rage broke my thoughts and I grabbed my binoculars to have a look toward the shooting gallery. A

Tyrannosaur had joined the game, attracted by all the gore no doubt, and my buds in the other Mako had put a round into his upper torso. The huge predator wasn't dead when I first glimpsed him, and I could almost feel the violence pouring off his hide. Then another shell churned his skull into confetti and a weirdness happened. As twenty-five feet of headless sinew fell backwards, a transfer portal opened up and took the Tyrannosaur right out of World 1470. Behind that portal, for just a second, I saw an acid black sky, a thousand fires, and the movement of what could have been people...or Shadowones.

I lowered the binocs and looked at the Commander. He was looking back at me, surprise dripping from every pore. It was like the guy upstairs had suddenly dropped a turd on his head. The Commander had never seen a maverick portal before. This wasn't what caused the fade outs our soldiers took; these were actual world-gates. But they opened on their own instead of through the actions of Earth Control

I'd seen such portals twice, once when we'd brewed up a Shadowone tank and the smoke rising above it had gotten sucked into the lungs of a void, and again when I'd shot an enemy creeping in on our laager and had watched him spin around and fall into nothingness. Each time I'd seen the same black sky and the same fires burning. I figured it was Shadowone territory.

Now, our forces had been looking for the Shadowones' stomping grounds for a long time so we could go in and clean them out at the source. The problem was we could never find their permanent world-gates. The brain boys knew about the temporary portals too, of course. They thought such wild gates might explain the strange disappearances of people like Amelia Earhart, John Carter, Esau Cairn, Dray Prescot, and Ruenn Maclang. But the scientists didn't waste much thought on the temp portals because there was no way to control them. I suddenly had an idea about that.

I figured what I'd been seeing was those same temporary portals. I figured the reason I'd seen so many was because World 1470 didn't like having us and the Shadowones on it.

It was starting to twitch its hide to get rid of us, like a horse shooing flies. To me, that meant the temp portals would open in one of two places, Earth, or the home world of the Shadow guys. I didn't think it was Earth I'd seen in the hole behind that Tyrannosaur's ass.

I was pretty proud of myself for all the mind sweat I'd been shedding, but the kicker was even better. I'd figured out something the science guys never had, how to control a wild gate. Every maverick gate I'd seen had opened when something got killed, and the size of the gate depended on the size of the killing. The Tyrannosaur's death had opened a hole big enough to drive a tank through.

My thought was: *Why not?*

The Commander's eyes got bright and round as I told him my thoughts, and then he slapped me on the back and congratulated me on "an historical discovery." He also piggybacked on my ideas quickly enough. I'd imagined a reconnoiter, but the Commander just said: "Why not kill enough dinosaurs to open a really big gate, big enough to take the entire regiment through?"

That was eighty tanks.

I didn't much like the idea of wasting all those dinosaurs but I couldn't see any way around it if we wanted to follow up on our discovery. And I knew enough about the Commander by now to know I wasn't going to talk him out of it. He quickly called in the other crews and went about planning our invasion. Nobody mentioned that we'd be outnumbered, which tells you how drunk we were on the idea of being the first shit-kickers to barbecue in the Shadowones' back yard. Our main concern was whether we had enough explosives.

The next morning broke bright and sunny, as most days did on 1470. The tank crews were pissy after staying up half the night setting charges along the dinosaur migration route, but the reddening of the sky lifted their mood. We'd found that the dinos didn't travel in the dark so we'd had plenty of time to set up a logjam of tripwires and delayed fuses, and then to circle around behind a Triceratops herd and brace ourselves for moving time.

The big females started first and the others followed, the bulls reining in behind. Tank engines caught almost as one and we began to crawl along in the herd's wake as soon as the crank crews were back in the turrets, gradually raising our rpms a notch at a time. The bulls began to get nervous with us at their heels, but they kept on straight until we reached jogging speed. Then the inevitable happened. One bull got pushed too far and turned to charge, dragging four of his fellows along. I heard the order to fire and looked up just in time to see the lead bull's head cave in with an armor piercing shell. It looked like someone had punched a soft clay sculpture with his fist.

Since we had no radio, the other crews had been waiting on our gun. They followed fire, but only a few concentrated on the charging bulls. The rest hurled incendiary rounds into the herd's rear. Nothing but a stampede could follow that flaming, and we pushed our tanks up near top speed to stay with the crowd. Any portals that opened were ignored. I kept my eyes on my driving and tried to forget the turbo-engine shrieks of burning reptiles falling away to either side. Despite the losses, though, there were still over a hundred animals alive when they hit the tripwires. We were close enough to smell the exhaust from their assholes.

The first explosions ripped open the bellies of the lead animals and spilled a hundred tons of guts onto the soil of 1470. Then the delayed charges went off throughout the herd, throwing up geysers of blood and dirt, and chunks of smoked meat. Another two dozen reptiles brewed up. The squalling and stinking were bad enough, but the look of absolute glee on the Gunner's and the Commander's faces was even worse. It was easy to imagine that look on every face in the regiment. I told myself we were killing the beasts for good reason, but that didn't stop the vomit from filling my mouth and overflowing onto the deck of the tank.

It was only the changing of the world that drew my thoughts away from sudden guilt. A shimmer of florescent yellow light threw a caul over tanks and dying reptiles alike, and the sky switched from reddish to black in an instant. We had gone through a gate, zippering ourselves into another world as easily as sliding into a well-known lover.

I saw right away that we were into something we hadn't expected. For one, there was absolutely no sensory distortion, which was supposed to be impossible as long as you were on any world besides your own. For two, the sky was black because of smoke from the fires we had seen, and the fires were coming from huge concrete ovens and from pits where bodies were burning by the thousands. For three, there was a gray hole floating in the air between the pits. A Shadowone world-gate!

It looked like someone else had learned to open gates with death. That's why we'd never found any permanent portals for the Shadowones; they didn't need 'em. They just killed something whenever they wanted a doorway. Of course, dinosaurs would have been a hard fuel to transport for that purpose.

Human beings worked a lot better.

The worst thing from the regiment's standpoint was that the Shadowones were waiting for us. They knew something we didn't, that temporary gates, unlike the permanent kind, are attracted to each other. They knew if we ever opened one we'd come out facing their own portal. That let 'em chop us to shreds as soon as we arrived, before the battlefield even cleared of the dead dinosaur chunks that had come through with us. The three of us in the lead tank *did* get spared. For questioning, they said.

Strangely, the Shadowones didn't seem to mind answering *my* questions too. Must have figured I wouldn't be tale-telling. The first thing I asked was who they were, since it felt strange referring to perfectly normal looking human beings as Shadowones. I should have been able to guess, though. After all, I'd read a lot about Adolf Hitler and his thousand-year Reich. That was one seriously death-conscious dude.

My second question was why there was no sensory distortion when we looked at each other. I'd always thought that was impossible on any parallel world. Their explanation kicked my nuts all the way into my lungs. I was on *my* Earth, just further back in the past because the temp gates are also time gates. And, in one of those paradoxes that'll make you sterile if you think on it too long, they'd learned how to open the portals from us. I mean from *our* regiment. I can't explain it.

That was when I asked for paper so I could write my memories down just the way they'd happened. They agreed like they thought my notes were for them. Well, they are. One set anyway. You see, they gave me an old fashioned stylus to write with, and there was something I'd learned as a kid about those metal tipped pens. With a little skin scraping you can make a nice tattoo, words and everything.

I wrote a second set of notes all down the insides of my thighs where the guards weren't likely to see. Gotta warn somebody. Somewhere. Somewhen. Our regiment changed history. That has to be corrected.

The Commander and Gunner like it here. They've joined the Waffen-SS where they belong. I'm going off tomorrow to a concentration camp to be burned as gate fuel. Today, though, I get to walk in a garden for the last time. It's a closed garden, with a nice big fence around it—an electric fence.

One minute after I die I'll be fading out for home, for my own time. I just hope someone back there reads between my legs before they bury me.

OLD DEAD WOMAN

overdose draped in a cold white shroud
hydrocephalic cranium, cleft palate
sine-wave shattered, flattened
no currents flowing
old dead woman
homeless
autopsy

latex-gloved doctor gowned and masked
bright scalpel fits an easy palm
spoiled blood decanted
syphilitic host
old dead woman
fifty-two
abortion

sutures tucked in the fruit of her womb
inflamed long ago, scarred ugly
pathological spawn never born
placenta devoid
old dead woman
stone fetus
burial

sky yellow and lifeless, burning hot
headstones different but alike

no stone for them
the earth sweats
old dead woman
dark hole
mother

And child

ALL GOD'S CHILDREN GOT GUNS

1

Drake Banning was rolling down River Road in his patrol cruiser when he saw the horde of teenage boys gathered on the levee. There were maybe eighty of them standing up there in the early morning, all dressed in primary colors and carrying what looked like rifles—short, chop-nosed things that made him think automatic weapons. Drake had been a cop for six years but he had never seen anything like it. Kids with guns, yes. But never so many in one place at one time. He figured it had to be gangs; New Orleans had its share of those.

Gangs or not, Drake wasn't going to drive right into the middle of whatever was brewing up there alongside the Mississippi River. He pulled over to the shoulder and was reaching for his radio when the sun caught just right on the automatic rifles and Drake saw a flash of fluorescent yellow peel away. He knew that flash of color. He'd seen it at home, in the arms of his six year old son. He dropped his head back on the vinyl of the car's seat and blew out a breath of air that was half bark of laughter.

These gangs were heavily armed all right, with squirt guns. Super Soaker water rifles to be exact. The Super Soaker toys had bright plastic bodies and oval tanks that seemed to hold most of a gallon of water. His son's rifle could squirt a liquid stream for almost fifty feet. Drake had been seeing a lot of kids with them lately and was damned glad he hadn't called in a report on these. He could hear the "Drake's War" comments now.

About twenty-five yards ahead of his cruiser was a dirt road that gave access to the levee, and Drake turned into it and drove up the slight rise to where a decidedly non-vicious gang-war seemed about to take place. The boys were all younger than he'd thought at first, maybe eight to thirteen. They didn't move as he came up to them, just stood still with their oversized water guns and their sweat-shiny faces that expected to be rousted.

Drake rolled down his window and leaned out into the moist river air. "How you fellas doing? Getting in some target practice?"

The biggest of the boys was wearing an earring. He held up his water rifle and shook it so that the liquid in the tank sloshed. "No, Sir, Mr. Officer. We gettin' ready to invade N'awlins." Then the boy smiled and Drake grinned back as he cracked a short laugh. It felt good to exchange pleasantries instead of anger.

"Well, keep it clean," he said, by way of making a small joke. None of the boys laughed, though some of them were wearing fat and sassy grins.

Drake turned the cruiser around and headed back toward River Road. In the rear view mirror he saw the leader waving goodbye and returned the gesture with a backhand motion of his own. It was moments like this that gave him hope for his city.

2

A half-hour passed before Drake cruised back by the levee battlefield. There were only two of the youngest boys still around and they had walked down to the main road where they were taking turns spitting and pacing. On impulse, Drake turned in the access road and pulled up to them. He rolled down his window.

"War over already?" he asked.

"Naw," one of them said. "We just the rear guard. We supposed to watch this road. Stop the enemy from bringin' up reinforcements."

Drake started to laugh but checked himself. It was funny as hell, but these boys seemed to be taking their game seriously and he didn't want to hurt their feelings.

"Right, then," he said. "Well, I'll keep my eyes open for the enemy and send them your way if I find them."

He turned to look over his right shoulder so he could see to back up, and a spurt of cold liquid flooded against the side of his head and poured down under the collar of his uniform.

"Hey!" he said, spinning around in his seat to face the two boys. Both of them had big eyes and both of them looked scared. That didn't make them run, though.

"You *is* the enemy," said one, and squirted him again, in the face. At a distance of only five feet, the liquid stream from the Super Soaker was strong enough to sting. And the water was as black as if it had been churned up from the Mississippi River bottom by a catfish on a hook.

Drake sputtered, then slammed open the cruiser door and bolted out in anger. He wasn't sure exactly what he was going to do besides take the water guns away, and he quit thinking about it before having a chance to make that decision. A sound rolled up out of the city at his back and stopped him cold two steps from the boys. It was a sound that didn't fit the bird-chirping, coffee-drinking image of early morning New Orleans.

The city had started to scream.

Drake reached up to his cheeks to wipe away the water from the toy guns. His eyes were on the boys and were full of just one question. The two youngsters answered almost as one.

"Ain't just water," they said.

Drake's skin began to fall off.

CRYPTO

Eight protestors were killed when the front wall of the National Academy of Sciences in Washington D.C. exploded, spraying razored glass into the gathered throng. Four more were ground underfoot in the human rodeo that followed. But fifteen deaths were only a flavoring of what happened when the "thing" smashed its way up out of the rubble of the building and stomped headlong through the crowd, flattening the frightened mob into sail-the-human Frisbees.

None of the protestors had realized exactly what they were protesting against until it began stepping on them. They only knew that they didn't like the wholesale fiddling with the stuff of life that had been going on ever since the President had signed the huge DNA Project into law back in 2011. The scientists had started with natural DNA in an attempt to find out how one unique chain of chemicals had come to play the role of director in so many different theaters of life.

They didn't stop there, though. When their questions about fleas, ferns, and fungi were finally answered, those same researchers began creating brand new laboratory DNA, and then they started phasering it with fission radiation until it twisted around on itself to form...new things.

Up until today, however, the protestors had only been warning of potentialities, because no experiment with the mutated DNA had worked well enough to cause trouble. Now, such an experiment had worked only too well, and the result, minus the statistics and tables of a good scientific publication, was crushing people and cars as it moved up the Mall toward the Capitol building and the seat of U.S. Government.

Some wit quickly dubbed the DNA beast "Crypto," for cryptozoology, the study of fantastic creatures that might just exist. The name was apt because Crypto was indeed quite fantastic, and it did most definitely exist. It stood one hundred and eighty stinking feet tall on its seven legs—which was why it was able to step on so many people at the same time—and those thick, fluted columns of flesh supported a body resembling an upright stack of lopped off body parts, as well as the torso and head of a not unattractive middle-aged matron with a mild case of hydrocephaly and a bad overbite.

The military responded quickly to the threat, even though most of its units were in Europe fighting a neo-communist uprising in the old Soviet Union. The 113th airborne, which consisted only of individuals whose thinking was politically correct, were helicoptered into the city, tanks and all. They caught up with Crypto just as the monster walked through the flags around the Washington Monument and took a bite out of the building's side, spewing out chunks of stone and chunks of people pretty much at random.

The army's tanks opened up as soon as their treads touched the ground, and the explosive shells cross-stitched flowers of blood up Crypto's bright pink hide. Then the creature's mutant DNA kicked in and its skin segued from the merely shark-tough to the diamond-hard of overlapping bony plates. The remainder of the military's ordnance bounced off.

Crypto's feet did not bounce off, not off a single helicopter, tank, or armored car, and the soldiers who weren't crushed outright had a little time to reconsider their political ideology. Just one dirty joke in mixed company and they could have been killing interesting people in Russia instead of getting stepped on in the good old U.S.A.

The horrendous panic engendered by Crypto's swift and violent advance from the Washington Monument through museum row triggered a traffic jam that piled up for miles along

Constitution and Independence avenues. The gridlock soon reached neutron star density directly around the Capitol, and even U.S. Senators and Representatives couldn't pull rank on cars that were unable to move at all. In fact, most of Congress was still in chambers when Crypto cracked open the dome and began using its upper appendages like a pair of lobster forks to chase human tidbits through the marble halls. The creature must have eaten the whole Senate and half the House of Representatives before the air force arrived to take over from the army.

To the detriment of the Department of Defense's annual budget increase requests, however, the air-to-ground missiles of the fly boys couldn't get through Crypto's tough exoskeleton any better than the army's tank guns. They did knock the creature down the steps of the Capitol and flatten it on its keister in the reflecting pool, but all that did was brew up a small tsunami that surged its way up to Union Station, drowning several hundred people who were waiting there in panic for the trains.

The air force later claimed that their missiles did have one more substantial effect. But the scientists were never in agreement. For whatever reason, about the time Crypto got hit in the solar plexus by a sidewinder, there started an upwelling of gas in the creature's gut that erupted as one helluva belch. That blast of foul air knocked down fighter planes left and right and blistered paint on buildings across the Potomac.

The remaining jets pulled off pretty fast, which should have left the Supreme Court open for Crypto's attention. But Crypto didn't move, and its matronly face twisted in sudden agony as a burst of cramps rocked its belly. A couple of aborted belches barely ruffled the surrounding trees, and then, according to more than a thousand witnesses, Crypto's armor-plated abdomen bulged outward as a gargantuan bubble of gas propagated down through its intestines toward its anus. Unfortunately, while everything else in its body was greatly enlarged, Crypto's excretory system was the exact same size as that of the side-show short man from which the anal DNA had been taken.

Even so, everything might have been okay if Crypto had not eaten so many politicians. The resulting buildup of bad gas was so strong that when the fart finally cut loose it propelled Crypto's considerable bulk skyward on a column of highly compressed methane. Crypto's natural jet propulsion system cut out only a few minutes later, but by that time the creature was twelve miles out over the Atlantic Ocean. The cold waters swallowed its bulk forever.

The air force always claimed afterward that it was their missiles which made Crypto fart. The scientists said it was only a design flaw. The American people didn't care one way or another. They were only relieved that one more threat to our great way of life had been averted.

Luckily, few people outside the President's inner circle ever found out just how close to true catastrophe we had come. They didn't find out because they lacked two crucial bits of information. First, scientists never published the fact that even a slight increase in gas pressure would have caused Crypto to explode in the stratosphere, ultimately blocking out enough sunlight over the Northern Hemisphere to stop plant photosynthesis. Second, the media overlooked the presence in the Capitol building that day of the four biggest televangelists in the U.S., Jimmy Strident, Jimbo Tripwell, Jim Canker, and Jimmy Dean Roberts, who had escaped being eaten only by hiding in the stalls of the lady's first floor bathroom.

Those in the know were grateful that Crypto had failed to cross paths with even one of the evangelists. They didn't like the idea of what Carl Sagan would surely have called Monster Winter. The Surgeon General summed it up best, though, when she told the President that the near disaster had reaffirmed for her one of the great truths of American Democracy.

"Never mix church and state," she said. "Especially not for dinner."

DO AS I SAY...

Bobby Tafaro squirmed as the seat belt was pulled snugly around him.

"Not so tight, Daddy," he protested. "It's too tight!"

Clay Tafaro frowned. But he didn't relent. It was the same every time they got in the car. Bobby hated wearing his seat belt. Now, the five-year-old even tried to push Clay's hands away as they pulled the slack out of the belt.

"Son!" Clay snapped.

Bobby jerked back as if he'd been burned. His lips trembled.

Clay winced. *Idiot*, he growled at himself. *It's not his fault. Just because you don't like how your life is turning out these days, don't blame your son.* He lifted a hand and tousled his son's hair.

"Hey, Buddy. I'm sorry. Didn't mean to yell at you. But you have to be a big boy and wear your seat belt. Your mom would never forgive me if something happened to you. I wouldn't forgive myself. And there are too many crazy drivers on the road these days."

Bobby straightened back up in his seat, but his face was still sullen. "I wish I was really a big boy," he said. "Then I would never have to do things I didn't want to."

Clay shook his head. "That's not true, Bobby." He glanced out at the dreary sky through the dust-speckled window of his '87 Corolla. The dashboard was cracked, the maroon paint on the body faded from years of sun. "Even big boys have to do what they don't want to sometimes. Even Daddies."

Bobby drew his eyebrows down in the way he did when he was going to be stubborn. But he didn't say anything.

Clay slipped the car in reverse, backed out onto Peach Street. In a few minutes they were merging onto I-20. In fifteen more they'd be at Lincoln Elementary where Clay had taught sixth grade math for the past nine years.

Mercifully, Bobby had stopped fighting his seat belt. He was staring out the window.

"You OK, Buddy?" Clay asked.

Bobby turned to look at his father, his blue irises so pale that they were almost silver. "Are you going to do something now that you don't want to, Daddy?"

Clay started, glanced guiltily at the glove box where it was easy to imagine the crisp white envelope that he'd slipped in there when they'd gotten into the car.

"Why do you ask?"

Clay had chosen his words and tone carefully, then immediately felt ridiculous for doing so. It wasn't like he was trying to keep any secret from Bobby.

The traffic had picked up on the freeway as they got closer into the heart of town, and Clay had to keep most of his attention on the road. The little Corolla rocked and shuddered as eighteen wheelers passed them, but Clay didn't want to drive any faster on the worn tires that he knew needed to be replaced. Still, he caught the shrug of his son's small shoulders.

"Has Mom been telling you about my new job?" he prodded.

"Mom said you were gonna get paid more. But that you wouldn't like the new job 'cause you just had to push papers all day. Do you get to color on them before you push them? I might like that kinda job."

Clay chuckled, but the chuckle quickly withered. "Pushing papers just means I'd have to spend my days reading numbers and adding them up, then sending them to other people so they can add them up again. And no, unfortunately, I don't get to color on them."

"You wouldn't be teaching math no more?"

"Any more," Clay said. "It's *any* more. And I wouldn't be teaching at all." He glanced once more at the glove box, thinking of the single sheet of white paper nestled inside the white envelope there. "That's where we're going today. I'm resigning from Lincoln Elementary and I have to turn in my letter to Mr. Farnham so he'll have time to find a replacement before the fall term. So, I guess I'm doing something I'm not *sure* I want to do."

"Why?"

Clay changed lanes to get out of the way of a semi that came barreling up behind him. But as luck would have it a State Trooper chose that moment to merge in with the freeway crowd, and the truck driver slowed immediately in fear of a ticket and shifted into the right lane directly in front of the Corolla. Clay dropped back, giving the big rig some space.

"Why, Daddy?" Bobby repeated.

Clay spared a glance at his son. "It's money, Bobby. We need a new car. Well, we need a lot of things. Stuff for the house. And we have to save for your schooling. All of that takes money and teaching doesn't pay enough. I'll be making more than twice as much at my new job."

Bobby frowned. "Will I have to push papers when I grow up?"

Clay might have found the question funny at another time. Not now. A drizzle began to spatter the windshield and he switched on the wipers, though mostly they just smeared the dust around. They needed to be replaced, too.

"I hope not, Bobby," he said. "Maybe that's part of why I need to take the new job. To make sure you have some choices later in what you do."

"But won't you be sad not teaching? Mom says you will. She says you're bestest at teaching. If I give you the money in my piggybank, would you not have to push papers? I don't even want a new car. I like this car."

Clay's heart hurt itself against his ribs. He swallowed, then reached to squeeze his son's knee. "I *do* like teaching, Bobby.

But I'll adjust. Like I said, we all have to do some things in life that maybe we don't really want to do."

Bobby sighed.

The rain started to fall harder and the traffic began bunching up again. Clay was glad that it was only another few minutes to their exit.

"It's not fair," Bobby said suddenly.

No, it isn't fair, Clay thought. *You spend years working with kids, learning how to teach, learning how to learn.* He'd always thought it was the most important job in the world next to being a parent. But the world didn't think that way. And if you wanted to get along you had to start thinking like the world.

Didn't you?

He looked over at Bobby, then toward the glove box. His hands clenched on the steering wheel. *But what am I modeling for my son?* he wondered. *That you should go for the buck? That you should give up on doing the things you* know *need to be done?*

And did they really need a new car? A bigger house? They could get by. Maria didn't care. She'd tried to talk him out of resigning, anyway. And maybe he could find some other way of making a little extra. He could tutor. Or write. A sense of relief suddenly washed over him as he reached a decision. For the first time in days a genuine and deep smile curled Clay Tafaro's lips.

"You know, Bobby," he said. "You're right. And your mom is right. Sometimes we should do what we want to do." He ruffled his son's hair. "I think I'm going to tear up that letter. Let's get Chinese instead and surprise your mom."

"But that doesn't mean—" he started to add. And he heard a click.

He frowned, looked down.

Bobby had done what he wanted to do. He'd taken off his seat belt.

On the rain slicked road, the driver of the eighteen wheeler in front of them slammed on his brakes.

ONCE UPON A
TIME WITH THE DEAD

Alkali dust under the white blaze of an Arizona sun.

A town stands idle on a ghostly quiet day.

Then riders emerge from a haze of heat. Past a sign reading "Welcome to Comfort," those riders come. A whirlwind swirls up the street before them.

But the town is not as idle as it seems.

From the tower of the adobe church a lone bell rings once and is stilled. From a blank window in the mercantile comes a wink of silver. From the cantina comes a click-click snap. Men are waiting for the riders, good, honest men who have been warned that an old hatred is sweeping across their land. They believe themselves to be ready.

The riders drift into the town square, long gray coats flapping in the dry wind that moves the dust. There are five of them. Known men. Wanted men who covet what doesn't belong to them. They are men with strange, dangerous names like Doc, Clay, Jesse, Billy, Ringo. Their eyes are an empty black, colder than the single-action Colts at their hips. The leader is Jesse. He dismounts, spurs chinking on the stones that pave the square.

Jesse's movements are a signal to those who watch. The church bell rings again, pealing out like the voice of a frightened god. From the windows of the town rifles speak smoke, and the rolling crack of gunfire hammers the brilliant sunshine. Bullets tug at gray dusters. A horse drops, and another, their riders leaping free, hands diving for pistols, coming up belching fire.

Jesse takes a shotgun slug to the chest, a 44 round through his shoulder. But his own guns are banging. Splinters and glass fly from the building above him. A man tumbles through a broken window, crashes through fleeing pigeons to the ground. Another man staggers from the cantina and falls bleeding red in the street.

The townsfolk are outmanned. This is not the evil they had expected. Their bullets tear holes in pale flesh and tattered gray, but it is only the defenders who fall, until they all lie crimson and still against a canvas of light and stark shadow.

But the gray riders?

They do not bleed.

They will not lie down to die.

Though the grave has been their friend before.

ALTAR

I pray her eyes closed
Offer a chalice of sleep
to her lips
Watch her skin fade in blue

Sacrificed beauty
On an altar of light and reason
Joined to me in knives and love

And I kneel her in red lace
Take her hand as we worship

Secret gods

SCRITCH, SCRITCH, SCRITCH

Scritch, scritch, scritch.

The smile that Desdemona Howard had put into place for the two police officers sitting on her living room couch slipped a little. Neither of the two saw that slippage. Ray Miller, the older officer, was busy tapping at his laptop's keyboard as Desdemona responded to his questions concerning the disappearance of her husband. The younger policeman, Jason LaFrance, seemed to be cataloguing the glass eggs, porcelain thimbles, crystal angels, copper bells, silver spoons, and numerous other knickknacks that cluttered the room. The men's distraction gave Desdemona time to cast a surreptitious glance around for the source of the scratching sound.

Scritch. Scritch, scritch.

Desdemona almost jumped as the noise occurred again; she almost let out a tiny shriek. She managed to control those impulses, though she couldn't help staring for just a moment at the north wall of her living room, where hung a large, recent portrait of her husband—Dale Howard.

It seemed as if that portrait vibrated faintly against the dark paneling. Desdemona started to shake her head to deny that notion, but quickly arrested the gesture and forced her gaze back to the policemen. Both of them were looking at her now, and she smiled sweetly. LaFrance returned it and Desdemona felt a brief blush color her cheeks. The young man was quite handsome, she decided.

Scritchhh.

Desdemona coughed to cover the sudden noise, then, oh so casually, rose to her feet, uh-huhhing and unh-unhuhhing to Officer Miller's questions as she drifted toward the television, making sure her sensible heels clicked loudly in the, to her, unfortunately funereal hush of the room.

Scritch.

"I hope you don't mind...," Desdemona began, rather too loudly before catching the incipient hysteria in her voice and softening it, "if I turn on the TV. I've become so used to its company whenever my husband is gone that I can scarcely think without it."

Miller paused in his questions. LaFrance frowned.

Desdemona didn't wait for an answer from either man, just smiled and flipped on the ancient set. It stood directly below her husband's portrait and was tuned to truTV, the court channel, which she'd taken to watching of late. She quickly switched the channel to something else and then moved back to her chair near the policemen. The set was on a little louder than she normally kept it, but, of course, a sixty-plus-year-old woman might be expected to have a little hearing trouble.

No need for the officers to know that her hearing was actually exquisite.

"So you and Mr. Howard have been married about five years?" Officer Miller asked.

"Yes."

"And he started having trouble just this last year?"

"About that."

Desdemona was aware that the young Jason LaFrance had been studying her rather closely and now he asked a question of his own. "Are you all right, Ma'am?"

She smiled again, even though she sensed she was smiling too much. It was just that this young one was indeed good looking. Like a twenty-something Kevin Bacon. And she was beginning to think from the way he watched her that he found her attractive.

She tidied her bun of gray hair toward Jason and nodded. "Oh certainly," she said. "I'm perfectly fine. Sorry about the TV but it just helps me concentrate. I don't know why." She put a suitably fragile look on her face.

"No problem," LaFrance said hastily. "Just making sure you were OK."

"Yes," Miller added. "Whatever makes you feel comfortable, Ms. Howard."

"It's Mrs.," Desdemona Howard said.

"Eh?" Miller asked.

"Mrs. Not Mzzz. I'm very proud to be married to my Dale. I even gave him a child. Though God did not see fit for it to live. It wrecked me, but through it all Dale was just wonderful. Although now.... With the Alzheimer's...."

She sniffed a little, drew a lacy handkerchief from her sleeve and dabbed at her eyes. Though the lace of the handkerchief said "old woman," the royal purple border of the cloth suggested a youthful if mature style. She felt that the handkerchief perfectly reflected an age that should be judged at precisely two decades younger than her 84 year old husband.

"We understand," Officer Miller said. "And we're very sorry for your loss. It's hard losing a child. And now with your husband missing. I'll...we'll be out of your hair in a moment. Just a.... Let me see where I was with the questions."

Scritch, scritch. Scritch, scritch.

Desdemona smiled a little more broadly. The scratching was barely audible over the yammer of the TV. If her hearing had not been so acute, so much better than that of the policemen, she wouldn't have heard it at all.

Then a thought struck her. What if the men's hearing was better than they were letting on? What if they *had* heard the sound? Perhaps they'd heard it and just not paid it any mind. *Or,* perhaps they had heard it and were playing it cool. Pretending *not* to hear it, to not know what it meant.

SCRITCH, SCRITCH, SCRITCH.

Desdemona jumped slightly, then twisted her body into a

cough to cover her momentary lack of control. She blew her nose delicately, but kept watch on the two police officers over the bunched lace of her handkerchief.

Was the young LaFrance looking suspicious? The sound seemed to have gotten louder, as if compensating for the TV. Surely at least the young one had heard it. Was he toying with her? Was he like Kevin Bacon in more than appearance? Was he acting? Why didn't he ask about the noise? Why?"

Officer Miller murmured another question. Desdemona heard only: "...kill your husband."

"What? What!"

"Did you try to call your husband, Mrs. Howard?" Miller repeated, louder this time. "I believe you said you always put his cell phone in his pocket when you helped him dress for his days."

"Oh, oh, yes. I'm sorry." Her momentary lapse of concentration irritated her and she hoped she didn't look as flustered as she felt. "I misheard you. I did call him. Quite a few times. It rang and rang but he never answered. It's not in the house though so he must have had it with him. But perhaps he...lost it. I'm sorry. I seem not to be handling this well."

She dabbed at her eyes again.

Young LaFrance suddenly stood and said to his partner. "Maybe we should let Mrs. Howard get some rest, Ray. She's obviously a little frazzled at the moment. We can check back later."

Such a dear, Desdemona thought of LaFrance. How could she have imagined only moments ago that he was suspicious of her? She wondered if he wanted...to do things to her.

"Ah, of course," Officer Miller said. "I'm sorry, ma'am." He quickly saved his document and closed his laptop. "We'll get this report filed on the way back to the precinct. There'll be officers on the lookout for your husband right away. If he's wandering because of his Alzheimer's someone will spot him and pick him up. We'll be in touch. But in the meantime...." he drew a business card out of his shirt pocket and handed it to her, "you call us if you hear anything from him. Or if you think of anything else that might help us."

She took the card and stood up.

Scritch.

Her eyes darted to the wall behind the TV, then back to the officers. Miller was busy with his packing up but LaFrance was watching her. And once more he failed to appear as innocent and sweet as he had at first. He even looked a little...piggish.

Desdemona licked her lips and moved toward the door as if to usher the men out. "I certainly will call if I think of anything else," she said.

Scritch, scritch.

She laughed quickly, almost gaily. "I already feel much better for speaking to you fine men. I just know you'll find my Dale."

They moved toward the door. "We'll try, Ma'am," Miller said.

Scritch, SCRITCHHH.

Desdemona stumbled, just slightly, and caught herself. Officer Miller put a comforting hand on her arm. Or *was* it comforting? She realized that he wasn't smiling; he seemed to be frowning down at where his fingers grasped the muscle beneath her dress. She straightened up, pulling away from him without seeming to do so.

And now he *was* smiling.

But what did the smile mean? Did the officer really want to reassure her, or only throw her suspicions of the two policemen off? Why had he frowned when he clutched her arm? And what about the *sound*, that god awful, horrible sound? Was she really to believe that they hadn't heard it? How could they not?

But by then they were on the porch, the three of them, and she pulled the door closed behind her. Faintly, she heard a "scritch," but it could easily have been some random slash of sound from the TV.

Her heart quieted. That's when Officer LaFrance turned back toward her. "Oh," he said. "I almost forgot to ask. Do you have a picture of your husband we could take with us?"

Desdemona blinked. For a moment her mind simply would

not work. "A...a picture?" she murmured.

"Yes," LaFrance said. "To help our officers identify him."

"Uhm...I don't. I don't know...about anything recent. I...."

"What about that portrait above your TV? We could have one of our sketch artists reproduce it for us. Smaller, of course. I assure you we'd return the original without any damage. It would really help us find your husband. You *do* want us to find him, don't you?"

LaFrance was smiling, but at last, clearly, Desdemona could see through his act. He knew! She looked at LaFrance's partner, Miller, who wore an equally vapid grin plastered across his lips. They both knew!

Something clicked inside Desdemona and she drew herself up to her full height. "Of course," she said. "Whatever it takes for you fine officers to do your duty."

She turned and opened the door to her house, then stepped back to allow the policemen to enter ahead of her. Shutting the door behind them all, she swept around the two men toward the TV and Dale Howard's portrait above it. The officers followed, and though she didn't look at them, her exquisite hearing told her exactly where they were.

She leaned over the TV for a moment, as if searching for something behind the set.

"Ma'am?" Jason LaFrance inquired.

She clearly heard his suspicion then. But it didn't matter. She turned and fired four shots from the silencer-equipped 9 mm Sig in her right hand. Both men staggered back. LaFrance grabbed toward his throat where one of the slugs had caught him above the edge of his bullet-proof vest. Then he was down. Miller scrabbled for his service revolver and Desdemona fired again, a double-tap into his skull that took all the life out of him.

Holding the Sig ready, Desdemona moved cautiously over to stand above Officer Jason LaFrance. The young man's pupils were huge amid the rind of white in his eyes. He lifted his head but it dropped back again, banging on the wooden floor. Blood poured from his mouth and Desdemona squatted to watch him choke his way into death, making sure to sweep the long lace skirt of her dress back from the pool of crimson that spread slowly out around him.

Not so handsome now, she thought.

Scritch, scritch, scritch.

Desdemona turned her head to look toward the wall where the sound came from. She rose and moved in that direction. Shoving the TV out of the way on its wheeled cart, she reached up and took down the portrait of Dale Howard and set it aside. Behind the portrait was a small latch and when she twisted this open a large panel of the wall slid back to reveal a glass enclosed room about five feet square.

Scritch, scritch, scritch, scritch, scritch.

"Couldn't keep quiet, could you?" Desdemona demanded. "Just a little quiet and the cops would have gone safely away." She shook her head. "Well, I suppose you're hungry again. Don't worry. I'm going to feed you even if I *am* angry." She laughed suddenly. "I hope you like...pork."

Scritch, scritch.

"Now don't look at me that way. The situation was inconvenient for us all. But you could hardly expect me to explain to everyone that I was living a lie." Her left hand went up and pulled off her gray wig; the years seemed to fall away as blonde hair cascaded down to her shoulders. "And I guess I *am* partially to blame for today," she continued. "That Officer Miller figured out when he grabbed my bicep that I wasn't any sixty-four-year-old. But if they'd been paying attention, they'd have caught my earlier slip about you anyway."

Scritch, scritch, scritch.

"I was nervous. OK? I told them I'd had a child. *Since* I was married. I was supposed to already be nearing sixty when I married your father." She looked over her shoulder at the dead policemen. "It doesn't matter now, though. The evidence will all be gone soon."

Desdemona turned back to her four-year-old son where he pressed his dirty, hungry face against the glass wall of his secret room. Just behind the child lay the remains of Dale Howard, the bones picked clean.

"I'm sorry about your father," she said to the boy. "I really am. I was going to wait for him to die of old age but he found out about you. I couldn't let him report me to the police. Or divorce me and keep all his money for himself."

The boy's mouth opened and closed above the scar in his throat where his mother had long since sliced his vocal chords. His hands found the glass wall; the long hard nails came scritching down, scritching down.

Desdemona winced at the sound. "Save it for the cops," she snapped.

SPOT

Spot is my pet and I love him. My daddy brought him home last week, but already we're inseparable. He sleeps on the floor by my bed and I feed him scraps from the table when no one is looking.

I love my daddy, too. And not just because he brought Spot home after my dog, Rover, died. Daddy knows everything. He teaches at a *major* university and is a doctor, though I'm always sposed to remember he's not a "med doctor" but a doctor of Sperimental Psychology. He says med doctors are just plumbers.

I'm seven years old and one thing that worried me at first about Spot was that he was older than me. So was Rover. But when I asked Daddy if he thought Spot might die soon from old age, he said not to worry, that Rover had died from barking too much and Spot doesn't bark.

Spot plays all the games I like, as long as I give him clear orders. I specially like to play fetch with him, and he never gets the ball all slobbery like Rover did. The only thing I don't like is that he's not as much fun to pet as Rover. Part of it is cause he doesn't have Rover's soft fur, but I think a lot of it is the ugly black box attached to his head. It gets in the way a lot.

Daddy says the box is real important, though. He says it has lectrodes that control Spot, and that without it Spot would run away. I don't want that so I'll just have to live with the box, I guess. I sure wouldn't wanna see Spot's picture on a milk carton like those other lost kids.

THE LITTLE THINGS

April 1: Dear Diary.

My baby, my little girl rather since she is in fourth grade, was bad last night. She had a dream or something that woke her up and she wouldn't go back to sleep. And she kept ME up till early morning. And I had to go to work too. I gave her a little milk to sooth her but forgot how milk just runs right through her, and she got my bed and my new nightgown all wet. That would make any mother angry and I really wanted to shake her to make her shut up her whining. I didn't, of course. Children are such little things to be such pains in the ass.

Whoops! I better mark out that word. I wouldn't ever want someone to read this diary and find out I used it.

Anyway, I was really tired and wanted to sleep late the next day—the baby was sleeping late 'cause she had been up so long the night before—but my mother called me real early and wanted to know if I wanted to go to the mall with her since it was Saturday. I wanted to say no but I don't like to make my mother mad. She was pretty insistent anyway so I got dressed real quick.

We did have a good time at the mall, though. Mostly. Mom bought pizza and soda for all of us and we got along pretty well. It was the baby who ruined it. She had to go to the bathroom and just couldn't hold it till we got home. I didn't really want to spank her for it but children are coddled way too much these days. That's what mom says and it's what I say too. So

I spanked the baby and she had to go to bed early that night, without anything to drink since she had wet herself. But she slept OK, I think. At least I didn't hear her.

Well, gotta close for today. It's time for me to go to bed too.

April 3 Dear Diary:

There were lots of papers and stuff to do today and I had to work real hard. But, of course, as soon as I got home I had to fix the baby something to eat and give her a bath. I hadn't bathed her in a couple of days and felt a little guilty. Then she didn't want to go to bed. She was up till nine and I finally had to give her a little of that nerve medicine the doctor scribed for me last year. She went to sleep pretty soon after that, which was good because I really had a lot of work to do. I kind of hated giving her the medicine but I had to get that work done. Sometimes I wish I didn't have to work so much but that's just what mommies do I guess.

April 4: Dear Diary.

Not much happened today. I worked late and my little baby was sleeping by the time we got home from the sitters. That's where she always goes after she gets out of school. I just put her to bed and took a quick bath myself, and now I'm going to bed without even eating. I'm too tired to write more now.

April 7 Dear Diary.

It has been pretty quiet for a few days but this evening the baby was bad. If I just wasn't so tired from working. And if that old bassard that fathered the baby hadn't left me. And if he would at least send me some almony.

We had no sooner than gotten home from the sitters when she was marking on her table with some new colored pens they got at school today. I was so mad I was seeing red and I really tanned her little bottom for her and sent her to bed without any supper. Afterward, though, I felt bad and took her a cheeze sandwich and a glass of milk. I told her I loved her and I never wanted to hurt her.

She said she loved me too. She said: I love you, mommy. I told her to give me a hug and it would all be forgotten. I think I'll let her sleep with me tonight. I should never have spanked her so hard over some ink marks. But then, it's always the little things that drive you crazy. I guess you know that.

April 16. Dear Diary.

Another good day. Its Sunday and we got all dressed up for church. My baby, my little angel, looked so cute and I took a picture for my purse. We had breakfast after church and she didn't even get anything on her dress. She was extra special careful. Then we went to the park. She was really good and we had popcorn at the park and fed some to the ducks.

April 17

Everything's gonna hell again. The baby was so good yesterday and so bad today. She said she was sick and needed to stay home from school. Well, I had to miss half a day of work, which we can't afford, and then you know what I caught the little bitch doing. She was sticking the thermometer up against her nightlight to make like she had a temperature. Well, I just exploded. I made her go to school after that but I blistered her little hiney good first. Sometimes kids don't understand anything but a strap.

April 18

The baby's sitter looked at me real funny this evening when I came to pick her up. I guess she had seen the welts on the baby's bottom. Well, I didn't hit her that hard. Her skin just makes welts easy. She makes welts if you just touch her. I didn't say anything to the lady at the sitters and I know the baby didn't either. She tried that once with her grandma and got her television priveledges taken away for two weeks.

Anyway, she needed sleep when we got home and I had to work so I gave her a little bit more nerve medicine to make her sleepy. That's all for tonight. Gotta work.

April 19. Dear Diary.

The dog got ahold of the baby today. In the evening. I had gone upstairs for just a moment and when I came down I saw that the dog had one of the baby's legs in its mouth and had a paw over her face. I started crying and grabbed up the baby and ran as fast as I could to see my mother. I didn't know what to do but my mother told me to shut up so she could work. I said we should take the baby to the hospital and she shook her head at me and got up from work to take the baby. She said: No. I can fix her right up.

She put some bandaids on the baby's scratches and that made her quit crying after that. Later, I put some andiseptic on the scratches and held her and rocked her. Then I began to get a little bit afraid. I mean that sometimes it seems that everything that happens to me happens to the baby and I wondered if it ever worked the other way around. I stayed away from the dog the rest of the day. My mother said I was just silly and that this would teach me to leave things lying around where the dog could get at them. I started crying then. But I did it in my bedroom where no one could see.

April 20 Dear Diary.

I took the baby to the doctor's anyway today. I was worried because she wasn't eating or sleeping much and she had started to wet the bed again like she used to. The doctor was real nice and he looked kind of funny when the baby flinched away from his stethyscope. My mother was with me and the doctor looked at her kind of strangely too when we got ready to leave. But I liked him. He gave the baby a lemon sucker to take home with her.

P.S. The dog kind of growled at me this evening and that really scares me. Like everything that happens to the baby is going to happen to me. My mother just says I should grow up.

April 21

I grabbed the baby by the arm today—to keep her from falling down—and I guess I grabbed too hard because it tore her dress and bruised her arm enough to make her cry. I felt really bad, but she wouldn't stop whining after that. She just kept on whining and then she spilled the soda pop I gave her to quieten her down. I had to walk away from her to keep from hitting her. I told her that. Then I just had to get out of there. I left and went and took the car to the store. Oh don't worry. I locked the door behind me and she's too little yet to get out.

I wasn't gone that long—I just talked with a friend for awhile—but the baby was asleep on the floor with a pacifier in her mouth when I got home. Lord knows where she found that damn thing. I thought I had thrown them out years ago. I guess I carried her up to bed. I don't really remember but she was in her bed in the morning.

April 23 Dear diary.

Sent the baby to her grandma's for the week. I need a break from the kid. Her teachers are on strike this week anyway.

April 29 Dear Diary

Went to grandma's for the baby today. Grandma was nice, for a change, but the baby didn't look at me. I think she was angry with me for leaving her. Well, she's gotta learn to be more indapendent I told her. She's growing up now and needs to stop acting like a baby. We can't always have what we want. I don't EVER get what I want.

April 30.

Mothers don't like the stupid dolls that kids carry around sometimes. I told baby that and she cried. Lord she cries about everything. You'd a think I didn't do everything in the world for her.

April 30: Sunday.

Diary, my mother tried to take my baby away from me today. She said that I was too immature and that she didn't have any social life left except work. I yelled at her when she said it about the baby and she hit me. She grabbed the baby and I tried to grab her back. The baby was crying and I wanted to spank her to make her be a good girl, but my mother just held the baby out of my reach with one hand and hit me with the other. She just kept on hitting me and I was screaming. Finally, I ran and locked myself in the bathroom.

My mother really got mad then. She screamed that I better open the door or else. She said I better come out and take my punishment now or it would be worse later on. I told her that I wouldn't come out until she gave me my baby back. She said she'd give it back all right and that scared me. I heard an odd sound and then my mother left the door and went upstairs.

I still didn't open the door for awhile. When I did the baby was laying on the floor. She wasn't crying or anything but how could she. My mother pulled her head off and left it there. I screamed then. I thought of the dog biting the baby and then growling at me. I saw the baby's head on the floor in one place and her body in another. I screamed and screamed.

Then someone was banging on the door to our house. I started to open it but my mother came downstairs and told me to get away from there bitch. There were police when she opened it. They looked pretty mad and they took her away with them. She was yelling a lot. She said it was all my fault but I knew it was the baby's fault.

Another lady came then. She said she was a social worker. I liked her, though I was kind of shy at first. She looked me over real good and said I was probably fine cept for some bruises and a cut or two. She gave me some chocolate milk and sat down with me on the stairsteps. I was holding my baby and she said she could fix it. I started to cry then. She hugged me and took the baby.

See she said. The head just snaps back on.

Then she gave me back the baby and I told her thank you maam. She gave me a kiss and said she had a little girl just about my age. I asked if her little girl had a baby and she said yes. She said that sometimes her little girl would punish her baby just like she got punished and she wanted to know if I ever did that. I told her that you had to make babys behave. She asked me to show her how I made baby behave. So I told baby she wasn't going to have any supper and that if she didn't shut up that whining I was going to use my belt on her. I told her I was gonna send her to live with her bassard father and he wouldn't even care if she lived or died.

The lady was crying then so I started crying and baby started crying. I shushed her real quick. You better be good, I told her. I didn't want her to make me punish her. That's what my mother always said I did. And they took her away for it.

THE GRAY MAN

He came frequently to the library. The gray man.

He was of average height but well above average weight. His hair had gone missing except around the edges and was a lighter gray than his skin.

The man's color looked bad to me. At first, I thought him constantly on the verge of heart failure. But over the next few years I saw him at least once a week, often more, and during that time he scarcely changed physically except for losing a few pounds here and there.

When I first arrived at the university library, people spoke of the gray man with an intense dislike. He was retired. An ex-professor. But he seemed not to have recognized the "ex" part. I had heard that he would pontificate and exasperate. He was said to demand services, in a loud voice. Staff members were sent scurrying after articles and tomes that he sought. And he never said, "thank you."

Always as the gray man made his slow way in through the doors, the library folk would watch him with hooded eyes. It was those eyes that made me listen so closely for talk about him. And I heard. I got an earful. No one liked him. They wished he'd retired to Florida. Some said, "to Hell."

But the gray man's "loud" days must have been behind him by *my* time. I rarely saw him speak, and then only in a mono-tone, almost a stale whisper that seemed asthmatic in passing. For years I saw him come in, saw him remove papers and volumes from the small black satchel he habitually carried and spread them out around him on a library table. I saw him rise ponderously on occasion to fetch more books and journals from the shelves.

For years I saw him scribbling notes on the various legal pads he owned. I saw him transferring snippets of information from one place to another. I never heard that he published an article from it, or even that he'd put anything together to submit. I thought, perhaps, that he was working on a book, but the research materials he used were too eclectic to reveal a subject. During that time I scarcely saw him interact with the library staff. He generally spoke only when spoken too, and then not at length. I never saw him demand anything but to be left alone.

Over the years, the looks the staff gave the man changed: from irritation, to resignation, to tolerance, to pity. Eventually, they seemed not to see him at all. But I could see him. He became as gray and ephemeral as a passing rain and I knew then that I could finally approach him. For he was as dead as I, and would not be afraid.

COLD AS LOVE

She walks in a bitter harvest
of want,
in a winter of axes and scorpions,
cold as love.

Tired of the wine chill
of her life,
she rivers her hate,
caresses her heart to oblivion,
with a bullet.

I CAN SPEND YOU

They all looked up at the sound, the clink-clank-clunk of heavily laden saddlebags striking the doorframe as the prospector stepped into the eatery. Their eyes registered both the prospector and his bags, but it was on those worn leather satchels that their gazes lingered, that of the bartender and the cook who had come out of the kitchen to talk, that of the waitress with her thin, angular body and her attractively regular features, that of the few customers: a father and his little one, a couple who were courting, an orbit-trucker who sat humped over his table with a cup of steaming black in front of him. It was a negative ion sort of night, and business was slow at Memory's Place.

Limping on what appeared to be two damaged feet, the prospector warped his way over to a table and sat down heavily. He seemed deliberately to choose a site in the middle of the room, as if he wanted everyone's eyes upon him. He needn't have worried. The punctuated thud of the saddlebags striking the floor beside him made sure he had all the attention anyone could wish.

The waitress, who had long cultivated a highly refined sense of boredom, suddenly developed a swift and animate sparkle in her gray orbs. It was perfectly logical to assume the prospector had hit it big, and that meant the likelihood of a generous tip. She was beside the fellow's table and offering him a menu disk before his chair even had time to cough up all its creaks and cracks. It almost offended her when he waved the proffered disk aside, but she quickly erased the semi-feeling as the prospector leaned back in his chair and began to recite a list of foods that had obviously been ritualized years before.

It was a long list, but the waitress didn't write it down. She had a near perfect memory and never needed to. But even if her memory had been awful she would not have forgotten this order.

The old foods, she breathed to herself. *The old and very expensive foods.*

She did not look in the direction of the bulging saddlebags, but she knew, as everyone else in the room knew, exactly where they were located. Then she turned away from the prospector's sharp-planed face and went to put in his order, her precise mind clicking over T-bone steak and lemon chicken, over scrambled eggs and buttermilk biscuits, over strips of crisp bacon and long-link sausage, over blackberry cobbler and ice tea.

Ice tea for Memory's sake. When was the last time anyone ordered ice tea?

Of course it was on the menu. All the foods were. Memory had kept them on because they were a link to a past that everyone needed to be reminded of occasionally. But no one ever ordered them. Or if they did it was for a lark, a little late night fun after a few too many quantum bourbons and neuronal fizzes. The waitress had no ability to question the prospector's choices, though. She wondered at them, but all she did about it was recite the list to the cook as she went past him into the kitchen and began laying out the ingredients from the store vault.

While he waited for his order to be readied, the prospector reached into a pocket and pulled out a silver flask that bore the marks of long use. The flask's cap acted as a shot glass for the thick liquid he poured into it, a liquid as amber and viscous as new oil. The drink was a reward, a repayment for years of deprivation. It went down far more smoothly than it looked.

The food was another repayment the prospector wanted, and by the time he had savored his way through a second shot of liquor the food began to come. It was just as he remembered, maybe better than he remembered, which surprised and frightened him a bit because of what it told him about his memory and the world it lived in.

Still, the forgetting didn't really matter, because he soon began to learn the tastes again. Reconstituted or not, the steak was thick and dripping with juices. The chicken was creamy soft on the outside, puffy and air-light on the inside, like foam packing miracled into something delicious by all the spices of heaven. Best, though, were the biscuits. He could have written odes to their golden layers, though he preferred popping them buttered and whole into his mouth where they could be chopped into crumbs and washed down by sweet draughts of tea.

The prospector had thought that he remembered all his favorites among the old foods, but eating the bacon reminded him of fried ham, the sausage of jam-spread toast, the eggs of mushrooms and cheeses. He sent the waitress back for all the new/old things that came into his head, and he yelled after her for more tea, and for bread to sop up the juices.

And then he moved into the rhythm of eating, knife-slicing with one hand and forking bites of food to his mouth with the other. When he was finished with the main courses he used the fork to punch in the top of the blackberry cobbler and drag out thick rafts of crust and berries, the size of the bites limited only by the width of his fork and the width of his mouth.

There came a moment, though, when the last berry went the way of the last scrap of bread, and the prospector sat back in his chair with an audible thump. He swallowed a belch, then looked around the eatery to see that no one was making even a pretense of not staring. They were watching him openly and with amazement, with what he knew to be a bit of disgust at his choice of foods and his table manners, but also a little bit of envy. And, of course, he knew why they were *really* watching him. They had to see how he was going to pay for his meal. They had to see what was in his bags. He made them wait just a moment longer.

The waitress had come to clean the table and to stand by expectantly. The two lovers had fallen silent, and the father and son were leaning forward in their seats. The bartender had been polishing the same spot on the same glass over and over, and even the trucker looked up from his fourth cup of black.

Inwardly, the prospector smiled, though it didn't show on his face. He stood, and hefted his bags. The table had been cleaned but he took a preliminary swipe across it with his arm to wipe away imaginary crumbs, and to heighten the tension. Then he upended the bags, first one and then the other, and the riches spilled out in a glittering, clinking heap. The waitress gasped, and so did some of the others, and their eyes seemed held to that pile as if grabbed by the juice in an electric socket.

The prospector rooted around in the imbroglio until he came up with half of a short rib-bone that he handed to the waitress for payment. Then he tossed her a smoothed white knuckle as a tip and watched as she caught at the precious thing with both hands and still almost dropped it.

An entire skeleton, the young father who was watching thought to himself. An entire human skeleton. And it seemed new and fresh, not as if it had been dug up out of some long overlooked cemetery. He had never scanned so much raw piled wealth, not up close anyway. Of course, they had all seen videos of the national treasury, with its neat and overwhelming stacks of bones. But that was not like having the real thing poured out in front of you while you sat nibbling at your cation salad.

The other watchers seemed just as stunned, and all of them sat frozen while the prospector scooped up the remainder of his loot and left. Then they unfolded and reached for their things. The lovers were the first out the door, and the trucker took only as long as it required to drain the dregs of his polymer coffee before heading to his rig. The father watched them leave as he paid for his order with a few small bone coins. Then he walked over to where his son was standing beside the prospector's empty chair. The young eyes were irised wide as if they could still see the jumbled tibias and femurs, the mandible and the ribs, the ilium, sacrum, radius, ulna, the carpals and metacarpals, the phalanges of the fingers.

"Did you see it, father?" the youth asked. "Did you?"

"Yes, son," he said. "I saw it."

"A real human skeleton, father. Just like on the viddisks. It was incredible."

"Yes it was."

"You know, 00101's father says that there are still bio-humans out there. Is that possible?"

"No, son. That rumor's been around a long time, but we hunted down the last bio over twenty years ago now." He reached out to pull his son close with steel-framed hands that could crush diamonds, but his touch was soft as a silkworm's tongue. It seemed as if a nova of fizzing electrons had been loosed inside his co-processor, and a quick diagnostic could not tell him what was wrong. He wondered for a moment if it had been a mistake to kill the humans. He wondered....

* * * * * * *

The prospector stopped for the night on a hill where he could watch the ribbon-shiny streets of the android town spread out before him. At this distance, the swiftly moving transports looked like flowing jewelry, or maybe like the chasing lights his wife used to put up on their Christmas tree every year. He took a chance and built a fire, though it would be dangerously easy to spot. No machine ever needed a campfire to keep itself warm on a cold night. But then, he wasn't a machine.

He unhinged the mask and breastplate that hid his identity and dropped them to the ground. His plastisteel boots were next and he luxuriated in being able to stretch his bare feet out to the flames. The revealed face and revealed feet were both human, though it was strange that there were only three toes on each foot. Or maybe it wasn't strange. In a world where human bones were the money that could keep a person alive, his toes had been easy to spare.

But that was before, he thought, as he reached into the saddle-bags and drew out the crisp white skull that nestled there. *Yes.* That was before his wife had died and left him a rich man.

FOREVER

At the dawn these soldiers rise
From the fields where bitterness lies
Blue and gray, wide eyed with fear
They gird their loins for battle here
To fight, to kill, for all they hold dear

And so with weapons grim to hand
With throats carved sharp with cries
They strike the music, the martial band
The cannons sing, the grapeshot flies
They loose the fateful battle hound
They charge upon the red, red ground

And death it comes, they fall like sheaves
Of wheat and corn, or like winter leaves
The ragged lines, they bow and bend
The smoke across the land does wend
And the broken only God will mend

But across the way they come on bold
Like the mythic heroes of old
They will not turn, they will not break
Beneath the sun whose rays do rake
They will not, their flag forsake

And from the pall their enemies loom
The bullets whisper, sweep like a broom
The charge it carries to the lines
Through the carnage, through the mines
Hand to hand with foes they grapple
And with gore the fields do dapple

Whisper/screams of doubt and pain
Roil and echo across the plain
The men they fall to move no more
For the queen of war, that faithless whore

Then night descends to cloak the dead
Where these soldiers now are bled
Silence paints the scarlet ways
Till sun and soldiers both arise
Forever through the weary days
Gettysburg, they do reprise

ABOUT THE STORIES

Still Life with Skulls: This was one of my earliest completed stories. Started in the spring of 1986, while in graduate school, and finished in October of 1986, right after I took my first full time teaching job at Xavier University of Louisiana. Although I got my degree in psychology, I've not actually written many pure "psychological" horror stories. This was the first. "Still Life" features a painter who is developing acute schizophrenia. Two things inspired the idea: 1) that catatonic schizophrenics can have racing thoughts while in a frozen state where they don't *physically* move, and 2) Vincent Van Gogh cutting off his ear to send to a prostitute.

Although not the first story I wrote with "the intent of trying to publish it," this was my first story accepted for publication. It was taken by the magazine *Twisted* in 1989, but not printed until 1991. I still remember standing by my mailbox in April '89 while I opened the acceptance letter, and how hard my heart thumped when I read that the story had been accepted. The opening paragraph is still one of my favorites among my own stories.

Chimes: This is a straightforward, non-supernatural horror story. I think I prefer non-supernatural to supernatural horror, though I actually believe the former is harder to write, which perhaps explains why I haven't done it too often.

I think "Chimes" has the most "frightening" opening of any story I've ever done, or at least the best set-up to frighten the reader. The plot is convoluted and involves a woman and her son trapped inside their house with a killer during a hurricane in New Orleans. I actually wrote it well before Hurricane Katrina struck. I think the story has some fairly effective scary scenes in it. It's also a very "psychological" story.

"Chimes" is also one of the few stories I've written with a female protagonist. It was finished in January 1993 and won honorable mention in the 1994 Deep South Contest, which equates to 2nd and/or 3rd place in the category because they only awarded 1st place and two honorable mentions that year. It was published in their contest anthology. "Chimes" was also published as a Kindle ebook in 2010 by Damnation Books, but a lot of changes were required of that story and the version here is closer to the original version, which I personally prefer.

Death Turned Away: This is the first story I wrote that I thought was publishable, and that I wrote with "the intent of trying to publish." A couple of things I wrote earlier than this were eventually published after much rewriting, but this one never had to be substantially revised once in final draft form. "Death" actually *was* the first of my stories to be published, though not the first one accepted, nor the first one to pay me. It was written in grad school, in 1984/85, basically in one late night in the laboratory. When I let my girlfriend at the time read it, she said: "You really are a good writer," a comment that I remember fondly to this day since it was about the first such compliment I ever got.

I have no idea where the idea came from. I was trying to think of a situation that would be about as miserable as possible, and then make it worse. I also learned a lesson from this story, to be very careful when you let family members read your stuff. I let my mom read it and she said to me after: "Is this what you think of me?" There was a "cruel mother" character in the story, but the only similarity with my mom was that the character also had false teeth. But my mom thought it was her and it hurt her feelings. I later gave her signed copies of my books as they were published but I don't know if she ever read any of them. I never pushed her to.

People have told me that the story's title should be changed because it gives away too much, but I just love the title and have kept it intact, even though the story has been reprinted several times. This is still one of my favorites among my own stories. First published in 1989, in *Tales on the Twisted Side*, it was made into an e-book in 1999 and has gotten quite good reviews.

Machine Wash Warm; Tumble Dry: I've always enjoyed "Twilight Zone" types of stories. These are short pieces with a twist ending. This was another of my early attempts at such a tale, and I still think it works. The title comes from the clothing tag instructions, of course. When the story was first accepted for publication the magazine editor asked me to change the title. I'm not sure why, but I changed it to "Dry Spell." That magazine folded before printing the tale, though, so I restored the original title and that's how it was later published.

The idea for this one developed when I lived in an apartment complex and had to wash and dry my clothes in the communal laundry room, often late at night. Written in 1989 and first published in *Crossroads* in 1992.

Roadkill: An interesting thing about twist ending stories is that you can often twist them in a variety of directions without making more than minor changes to the bulk of the tale. In July 2008, I entered a contest at Jason Evans' "The Clarity of Night" webpage to write a story from an image prompt of a motorcycle being ridden at night. I wrote a very gentle piece called "Precious Cargo," which ended up getting the "Reader's Choice" award for the contest. That version was published in 2010 in *The Clarity of Night: Contests: Volume 1*, which you can download for free at: http://clarityofnight.blogspot.com/

In October of 2008, I realized that some minor tweaking to "Precious Cargo's" body and a rewrite of the twist ending could turn the piece into something much darker. So I did it, and here are the results, in print for the first time.

Razor White: When I wrote the first draft of this story in 1986, splatterpunk was popular in horror, and there was beginning to be a pretty graphic erotic/sexual edge on some horror stories. Though this was not what I most liked to read, I wanted to see if I could do that kind of story as a writer. So, I sat down and wrote the nastiest piece of horror I could imagine. I then revised it substantially in 1991/92, and remember being rather gleeful as I figured out what bad stuff was going to happen to my character next.

The first magazine I sent the piece too rejected it because they wanted a psychological rather than a "special effects" ending. I liked the special effects ending and sent it out to an anthology called *Dark Voices IV: The Pan Book of Horror*. I was thrilled when it sold, and it marked the biggest sale of my career up to that time, as well as paying a pretty decent fee. It garnered some very, very good reviews from critics. Unfortunately, this book was published only in England, in 1992. "Razor White" was the first story I ever did with absolutely no sympathetic characters. Everyone in the story was a nasty.

Splatter of Black: This story was written in January 1992 and originally entitled "Turnabout is Fair Play." The editor who took it wanted a title change, however, and I offered him several to pick from. He chose this one, which is from a line in the story, and I'm glad he did. It's much more evocative than the original title and this is how I always think of it.

This story had two incarnations in characters, as well. I originally wrote it as an intense horror story in which all the bad characters were female. By this time I'd written quite a few horror stories and in every single story I'd had the main bad guys be...guys. So I decided to try something different. I finished the story, liked it, and sent it off. It came back with a comment that it couldn't be published because it was sexist. I asked a couple of women I knew to read it and both said it was sexist. This ticked me off because I had only written one other bad female character before in any of the dozens of stories I'd had published up to that time, and she was a vampire.

Nevertheless, I wanted to sell the story and I thought it was pretty good. I went through and changed one thing. I changed the name of one of the bad characters from a female name to a male name and replaced all the appropriate "hers" and "she's" with "his" and "he's." I sent the story back out to the biggest anthology open at the time, *Dark Terrors*, and it sold immediately, for the most money I'd ever been paid for a story up to that time. It was published in hardback in 1995. Sure made me think. Unfortunately, this collection also saw print only in England.

Those of you who have read my horror novel, *Cold in the Light*, may recognize some elements of this story. Parts of this piece appear in a variant form as a dream sequence in that book.

Ruins and Wraiths: Originally written in 1997 as a vignette to entertain some online friends. In 2003, however, when the editor of an SF anthology called *Adventurous* asked me for a tale, I added some plot and turned the vignette into a quazi-SF/horror tale. The editor accepted it, but the anthology was never published. In 2011, a friend starting up a new magazine asked if I'd be interested in submitting a story. I rewrote the piece yet again and shared it with my writing group, who had some helpful comments. I think this will be the last major rewrite, and the story wouldn't be in this collection if the last revision hadn't improved it a lot. I've often thought about using this as an opening for a novel since it leaves many unanswered questions. Who knows if I ever will.

Hell Is for Children: This story was a long time in gestating. I came up with the idea in February of 1986 and wrote the first draft over a two day span. I then left it alone until September 1991, when I revised it. At that time it was called "Let Us Prey." I didn't like the ending and let it sit until January of 2004 when I revised it again to near its current form. That's also when I changed the title. It sold in that form to an online anthology that ultimately never appeared, so I revised it again for its first printing here.

The story could be seen as an indictment of religion, but it's only an indictment of a certain brand of fundamentalism and fanaticism that results in abuse. That's where I was coming from emotionally in 1986. The religious aspects of the story are *not* autobiographical. My parents were very religious but were in no way abusive. We went to church a lot, and prayed a lot, but it was for the most part a positive experience for me. By 1986, however, when I was in graduate school in psychology, I had begun to meet some folks who had been emotionally crippled by a fundamentalist upbringing. That was the genesis of this story.

Haunting Place: I like this story, and so did the first three magazines that accepted it. But all three of those magazines folded and I submitted and submitted it for a number of years after that without a nibble. The story has, I think, some pretty good, surreal writing. It's based upon an actual crime in which a man killed his girlfriend while under the influence of PCP, but had no memory of the murder after—until he suffered a brain injury that caused him to have epileptic seizures.

The piece was written in 1988, then revised extensively in 1992. It was finally published in 2003 in *31 Eyes*. I think the reason it took so long to be published is because the plot is extremely convoluted, involving jumps back and forth through time and a lot of internal monologue. It's not my usual approach to writing, which is much more straightforward, but it was something I wanted to try. I'm glad someone finally saw the worth in it. I hope you will too.

With Eyes Like Fangs: The original 250-word version of this was written in August, 2010 in response to a story prompt from D. Lynn Frazier for a contest on her blog. It actually won the contest and earned me a nice prize. I removed the prompt materials and rewrote it for this book.

Monster Spray: I wrote this story from an idea provided by my first mother-in-law, Ruth Rocker. She told me about putting water in a spray bottle to use as "monster spray" for her kids when they were young so they wouldn't be scared of monsters in their rooms at night. I thought it was a cool idea and put my own twist on it. The story was written in February of 1990 but took forever to sell. I'm not sure why. It first sold in 1999, but that magazine folded. It was finally published in 2002 in *Classic Pulp Fiction Stories*.

Your Nightmare, or Mine: The title of this piece was changed but I no longer remember the original. I remember the story's genesis very well, however, because it was based on a tale I heard growing up in Arkansas. Near our farm stood the Slavely House. Old man Slavely had supposedly hung himself there many years before and had only been found quite a while after he was dead. Older brothers in the area, especially *my* older brothers, loved to scare younger brothers with tales of old man Slavely coming back from the dead. I spent a lot of time thinking about what it must have been like for that man, to hang there in his house, alone, swaying in the hot summer.

I believe I wrote this during my first couple of years in undergraduate school, probably around 1979. It was certainly written long before "Death Turned Away" and is one of only a few stories from that time to ever be submitted. In the original version, the story ended with the old man remembering the anniversary of his death. I later added the twist with the return of the girl. First published in *Classic Pulp Fiction Stories* in 1999, it was reprinted in 2004 in *Bloodletters Ezine*.

Old Bones: I wrote this short horror story pretty early in my writing career, not too long after I had my first story published. The idea evolved from some stuff I'd read by Loren Eiseley about his anthropology work. I created an anthropologist main character (I'd always been very interested in this field and took a number of college courses in it) and gave him a driving ambition to find a very old human ancestral skull. Of course, he did. But it didn't turn out well. This story was written in July of 1989 and published in *After Hours* in 1991.

Anthropologists don't typically use dynamite these days, but they used to and some *still* do. And the fossils and skulls mentioned in the story exist, although some have been at least partially eclipsed in their importance by later finds. I decided not to make changes to these points for the current publication, though, because the piece has a historical feel to me. I did change some elements about the ending so that it's slightly different than in the original published version.

Wall of Love: I personally consider this story to be the sickest and nastiest piece I've ever done, though some might think "Razor White" deserves that dubious distinction. "Wall of Love" involves some rather serious sexual deviations, along with elements of incest, serial killing, and torture. Thus, I kind of like this story. It was written in February of 1997 and sold to a magazine called *Agony in Black* in 1998. Years later, a fellow in Cross Plains, Texas brought a copy up to me to sign. That was just plain cool! You never know who your stories may touch. Or contaminate!

Twenty-Four Mile Bridge: The Causeway Bridge in Greater New Orleans runs 24 miles across Lake Pontchartrain. The first time I ever drove over it I came up with the idea of creating a story that would begin at one end of the bridge and finish at the other. In 1994 I wrote the first draft of *this* story, but the last part was just too...perverted for me and I let it languish on my computer. I've not been able to get the story completely out of my mind, though, and when I decided to put this anthology together I took the piece out again and determined to finish it. The results appear here. I generally like the writing and think the story has some compelling elements, but, frankly, I'm still troubled by the sexual aspects of the tale. I hope you won't hold it against me.

Outsider: In 2008, I ran what I called "Halloween Horror October" on my blog. Every few days I put up another flash fiction horror piece in preparation for Halloween. The original version of this piece, entitled "Isolation," was written as part of that. It's undergone quite a few changes since then and appears here in print for the first time.

Good Night; Sleep Tight: This one was written in July of 2008 and revised in October 2008 for my Halloween Horror blogfest. A revised version was published in 2009 on the webzine *Micro 100*. The present version is slightly longer, with an altered ending. This is my preferred incarnation.

Floater: This may seem an odd story for a horror collection, but I think it's pretty horrific in how it ends and in what it seems to mean. I wrote it in July 1990, and sold it once to a magazine that folded before it was published. I haven't had any luck with it since then, and I think the main reason is that it's just too long for most magazines. It appears here for the first time.

The ideas in this story came from several places. Back in the 1970s I heard a theory about how an intelligent species might have developed among dinosaurs if they hadn't gone extinct. I also read about a proposed twenty-six-million-year pattern in mass extinctions, and the suggestion by some that this pattern was caused by our sun having a dark companion called "Nemesis" whose lethal radiation bombarded the earth every twenty-six million years.

I decided that instead of a dark sun, I'd put a race of savage beings into an orbit that brings them back to earth every twenty-six million years. I decided that the race was native to our solar system but that they'd destroyed their own world, leaving the asteroid belt as its remnant. I know the asteroid belt is considered by many to be a protoplanet. I was also engaging in the perennial SF habit of taking current events, at the time the collapse of the Soviet Union, and following them into the future to see what might result. The religious aspects came from my own upbringing as a Catholic. This is not my favorite story among my own works, but it says something that I think is important and I'm still fond of it.

The Road to Hell: In this story, I wanted to explore the idea that what some people think of as good actions might be bad if considered for their 'long-term' effects. A guy who has lived a "good" life goes to heaven but finds that he has to deal with someone from his past who he wronged. That someone is a person he looked upon as one of his great successes. The original title was "The Road to Hell is Paved with Good Intentions." I wrote the story in January of 1990 and it sold as an ebook to *Fictionwise* in 1994. It was reprinted in *Nox* in 1996.

A Curse the Dead Must Bear: Written in the May/June period of 2003 after reading a lot of Edgar Allan Poe. I always thought it had a Poesque feel to it, and when it sold in 2009 it was to an anthology of Poe inspired tales called *Return of the Raven*. I like it but it is definitely fairly standard fare.

Smoked Meat: I've read a lot of science fiction in my life but I've never been able to write it as well as I'd like to. "Smoked Meat" is the best SF story I've ever done, and the closest I've come to writing it like I want to. I threw in dinosaurs, and Nazis, and time travel. What more could one want? The plot is actually pretty complex but I think it worked out OK. It was written in March 1992 and sold to an early online magazine called Intermix SF/Fantasy Online in 1995. It was even nominated for an award, although it didn't win.

All God's Children Got Guns: I look at this story as one of my first microfictions. I wrote it in June 1992 for a contest that never got off the ground, then basically gave it away to a small magazine in 1999. With only 900 words to play with, any story has to have a simple plot. I was mostly trying for a twisty, *Twilight Zone* kind of ending. I still find the story amusing, though it's not what I consider a high point of my writing career. The idea came from the Super Soaker water guns that my son played with at one stage in his life. The title was borrowed from a western I read as a teenager, which was called *All God's Chillun Got Guns*. That title, of course, was itself a corruption of "All God's Chillun Got Wings."

Crypto: I wanted to write a monster story. A BIG monster story. Sort of like Godzilla. "Crypto" is what came out. Crypto is short for cryptozoology, the study of fantastic creatures (like Bigfoot) that may or may not exist. "Crypto" is also one of the very few stories where I've tried humor. Apparently it worked well enough to sell, and it also appeared in Intermix SF/Fantasy Online in 1995, before "Smoked Meat" actually. It was written in August of 1991. I thought long and hard about including "Crypto" in this collection. Even when it was first published some folks criticized it for having a political agenda. I didn't mean it to. I was just poking fun, and I hope everyone takes it in that spirit.

Do As I Say...: Written in September, 2002, a few days after reading a story by Michael Avallone called "Every Litter Bit Hurts." I just couldn't get that story out of my mind. It was an incredible piece, although horrific in its ending. I think, though, that my story is even more horrific because there are no bad guys in it, just an utterly indifferent universe. I actually think it's the most horrific thing I've ever done, and I hate it in one way while loving it in another. It sold first time out to a British magazine called *Fusing Horizons*, and was published in 2003 to some favorable comments. Someone else said they didn't see the need for it. I'll let you judge.

Once Upon a Time with the Dead: I love horror and westerns, so here we have a "zombie western." Originally written in 2004 as a kind of riff off the "Desperado" movies with Antonio Banderes, it was published in 2008 in a zombie anthology called

Bits of the Dead. I republished it in my Kindle collection called *Killing Trail.* This, however, is a revised and slightly lengthened version. I'm actually quite fond of the writing in this one.

Scritch, Scritch, Scritch: I wrote the first draft of this in July, 2001, then set it aside and didn't get back to it until I decided to put this anthology together. I revised it around Halloween of 2010, dramatically altering the ending, and it appears here for the first time. The genesis of the tale came after reading a bunch of Poe. This is *my* variation on "The Tell-Tale Heart."

Spot: Another of those flash fiction horror pieces written in October 2008 for my Halloween Horror blogfest. It appears here for the first time. I'm not sure where the idea came from. Sometimes when you need them they appear. However, in grad school I did do electrode brain implants. In rats only. I assure you.

The Little Things: I don't kill kids in my stories. I don't even like to make them suffer. But in the real world kids *do* suffer. Some suffer a lot and it breaks my heart. And sometimes you want to tell people a story that will make them scream out that it isn't OK for kids to suffer, that the hurting has to stop.

This story was one of the toughest I ever wrote. I actually completed a draft of it in May of 1989, over a two day span. Then I had to walk away from it. I did a revision in February of 1990 but couldn't bear to send it anywhere. My own son was a little thing at that time, and as a psychologist I was exposed to cases of horrific child abuse. To think about children like my little boy being hurt in that fashion—it just tore me up. But I had to get those emotions out and this story was a way to do that. When I was just about finished putting this anthology together I took "The Little Things" out again and reread it for the first time in almost two decades. I realized I had to make a decision, publish it now or leave it forever hidden away. I decided to include it, and made a few minor changes before I did. I'm not sure I did the right thing. Child abuse is something I don't like to think about, but not thinking about it won't stop it. Here it is.

The Gray Man: I first wrote this in the fall of 2010 as a kind of experiment in memoir. I even submitted it in that form and it was rejected. In June 2011, as I was putting the final touches on this anthology, I sat down intentionally to rewrite it as a horror story. I kind of like the way it turned out, and I hope the end surprised you.

I Can Spend You: This is my favorite among my own stories, and is very much a *Twilight Zone* type tale. This is not to say that the *Twilight Zone* series was a major influence on me. I don't think it was actually, because I never saw more than a few episodes of *Twilight Zone* and *The Outer Limits* while I was growing up. (I've seen most of them as an adult, of course.) But, the concept of a quick hitting story with a macabre twist came to me from somewhere and has been a strong influence on my writing. I just really enjoy these types of stories.

"I Can Spend You" was written in January of 1991 and I owe its genesis to my son, Joshua. At about age four, one of Josh's favorite movies was "All Dogs Go to Heaven." In that movie, the dogs use bones as money. That idea, of bones for money, triggered this story, and it came out fast and furious and sold the first time out to a magazine called *Strange Days*, which published it in 1992. It was reprinted in an SF anthology in 2005, and in another anthology in 2011. I've read this to a few of my classes and always gotten the "gasp" I wanted at the end.

ABOUT THE POEMS

In the Ruins of Memory: I wrote this poem on my birthday in 1994. I was feeling particularly melancholy at the time. It was first published in a writing magazine called *Just Write* in 1995, and was later republished in the HWA Newsletter in 1999. I also used it as a section break header in my first published novel, *Cold in the Light*. Now here it is again. I guess this means that I like it pretty well.

Abraded by Light: Written in October of 2000, first published online in 2004 at GothicRevue.com. I was told once you couldn't write a decent poem that used the concept of poetry within it. So I gave it a try. I kind of like it.

Blind: Written in October of 1997, first published online in 2004 at GothicRevue.com. I'm happily married now, but I've felt the way this poem reads a few times in earlier years as I tried to make relationships work. And failed.

A Choice of Ghosts: Originally entitled "Ghosts of Love," and written in 2000. It was published online in 2003 at the website of "Brutal Dreamer." Revised for this publication.

Branded: Written in the fall of 2007, published in 2009, in *The HWA Newsletter*, Vol. 20, Issue. 104. This is one of what I call my "commuter" poems, which I came up with on my long commute across Lake Pontchartrain. I originally recorded this into the little tape player I take with me on my travels.

Old Dead Woman: Written May 11, 1995. Published in 1996, in *Star*Line*. Just before I wrote this piece I read about the phenomenon known as a "stone fetus," which is a calcified fetus that remains inside the mother's body. It evoked such a powerful emotion inside me that I couldn't resist writing about it.

Altar: Written originally in October of 1997, under the title "Secret Gods." Published for the first time here.

Cold as Love: Written in May of 1999, published in 2002 in *Penny Dreadful*. Revised substantially for this publication.

Forever: Written in May of 2003, published in 2009 in the anthology *Vicious Verses and Reanimated Rhymes*. I don't often write rhyming poems but I wanted to give one a try. This one was stimulated by reading some Edgar Allan Poe. As you can see from the times I've mentioned him, Poe has been a big influence on me.

ABOUT THE AUTHOR

CHARLES ALLEN GRAMLICH grew up on a farm in Arkansas, near the foothills of the Ozark Mountains, then moved to the New Orleans area in 1986. He's since sold several novels and numerous short stories. His tales, while mostly in the genres of horror, science fiction, and fantasy, have also included westerns, children's stories, mainstream fiction, slipstream works, and experimental pieces. He has also published poetry and nonfiction, the latter ranging from reference works to articles on writing.

After Hurricane Katrina smashed up New Orleans, Charles and his wife, Lana, moved to Abita Springs, Louisiana, where they live in the woods with many birds. Charles has an adult son named Joshua.

Charles has a long term association with REHupa (the Robert E. Howard United Press Association), and is a member of HWA (the Horror Writers Association), and the SFPA (the Science Fiction Poetry Association). He produces a regular column on writing for *The Illuminata*, an online magazine. His blog can be found at:

http://charlesgramlich.blogspot.com

www.ingramcontent.com/pod-product-compliance
Lightning Source LLC
Chambersburg PA
CBHW020801250626
47155CB00003B/1170